The flames caught, burst up high. I tried to grab Virgil Sikes, but he pulled back. Then Dad was pulling me off the porch as the boards began to explode into flame.

Virgil took one of the children in his arms and sat down in a red chair, and his wife took the other and sat down beside him in the midst of the flames. As we watched in fascinated horror we saw all four of the Sikeses burst into flame; but their fire-figures were just sitting there in the chairs, as if they were enjoying a nice day at the beach. I saw Virgil's head nod. I saw Evie smile before fire filled up her face. The children became forms of flame—happy fires, bouncing and kicking joyfully in the laps of the parents.

I thought I heard Virgil Sikes laugh like the happiest man in the world.

Greystone Bay

Edited by
Charles L. Grant

The First Chronicles of

Greystone Bay

TOR

A TOM DOHERTY ASSOCIATES BOOK

This is a work of fiction. All the characters and events portrayed in this book are fictional, and any resemblance to real people or incidents is purely coincidental.

GREYSTONE BAY

Copyright © 1985 by Charles L. Grant

First printing: October 1985

A TOR Book

Published by Tom Doherty Associates
49 West 24 Street
New York, N.Y. 10010

ISBN: 0-812-51852-7
CAN. ED.: 0-812-51853-5

Printed in the United States of America

ACKNOWLEDGMENTS

Prologue © 1985 by Charles L. Grant

''Croome House'' © 1985 by Reginald Bretnor. By permission of the author.

''Used Books'' © 1985 by The Cenotaph Corp. By permission.

''Street Life'' © 1985 by Douglas E. Winter. By permission of the author.

''Something in a Song'' © 1985 by Galad Elflandsson. By permission of the author.

''Hiding From the Sun'' © 1985 by Nina Kiriki Hoffman. By permission of the author.

''Memory and Desire'' © 1985 by Alan Ryan. By permission of the author.

''The Red House'' © 1985 by Robert R. McCammon. By permission of the author.

''Night Catch'' © 1985 by Chelsea Quinn Yarbro. By permission of the author.

With very special thanks indeed to Harriet McDougal, whose idea it was, and whose patience with me must deserve a medal, if not a raise.

clg

Contents

Prologue
by
Charles L. Grant

The fog, and the sea, and the tired voice of the ship—
the creak and groan of the slick, battered hull as the waves
slapped against it, lifted it, rolled it, despite the hold of the
anchor; the flutter and snap of furled, mended sails when
the wind sifted through the grey like the touch of a de-
mon's wings; the hollow echo it gave footsteps as they
made their way across the deck, back and forth, steady and
slow.

Below, there were voices. Muffled. Words without meaning though the tone was clear—*after all this time, after all
that has happened . . .*—and Brian Fletcher paused in his
pacing to wonder when the screams would start, when the
weeping would begin, when, in God's name, the damnable
fog would lift and free them.

He stood at the port railing, and had been standing there
since dawn. His black-gloved hands were clasped loosely
behind his back, and he watched the grey wall that waited

1

less than a dozen yards from the thrust of his chin. His face felt covered with webs of damp silk, and his hair was damp and dripped ice beneath his collar. He blinked and wiped his face, ran a palm down the front of his coat, and hooked a thumb under the wide black belt that flared the coat at his hips. His free hand rested on the butt of his pistol.

Nothing, he thought; nothing is out there.

He was effectively blinded by the fog that encased him, and deafened by the endless roar of the surf, out there, just ahead, spume and shattered waves and the brown-black humpbacks of rocks barely seen before the fog had closed in and forced him to anchor. Land, after so many weeks, and unattainable now; land, after storm and pirate and a thriving sickness that fouled the body and reddened the face and turned the strongest man aboard into a whimpering, mewling invalid; land, and he wondered if he would ever live to see it.

A step behind him. He didn't turn. He recognized the tread, the scent of damp wool, and he leaned against the railing and shook his head.

"Bad," he said. "They're talking omens."

Out of the fog a dark figure, from wide-brimmed hat to high-collar cloak, beard and hair black, eyes the same and narrowed. "Will there be trouble, Captain Fletcher?"

"I doubt it," he said wearily. "They've talked before, they'll talk again." He nodded toward the grey, one shoulder high in a shrub. "Still and all, Mr. Greystone, this isn't like any I've seen before."

Winston Greystone sighed, more like a prayer that begged an answer, and knew it would never come. "So close," he whispered. "So close."

There was a moment, as an unseen bird screeched overhead and put a chill to his bones, when Brian felt pity for the man. He and his company had been through Hell and hadn't yet returned, their journey across the Atlantic the final measure of their desperation.

"It will lift," he said at last, forcing confidence to his voice. "You don't have to worry yourself about that."

"Will it? Will it really, Captain Fletcher?"

His hand gestured over the side with more knowledge than he had. "They don't last forever. When the sun warms again and the wind picks up it'll be gone, and you'll never know it was there."

Greystone moved closer, and Brian saw the age he had gained since leaving England in April—cheeks drawn, brow creased, faint streaks of dull white marking his temples. His walk was noticeably slower as well, and his shoulders, once rigid, were now bent under the yoke of the misery his people felt.

And an uncommon lot they were, he thought as he heard a hatch slide forward and the voices below came clear. None of them of means, few of them ever soldiers or sailors, most of them damned by the courts and their villages for being different, for being lettered, for daring to question the nature of things instead of listening to their betters and accepting the life. They were of no particular religion, and shunned politics like the plague, and throughout most of the voyage they had used their time planning the community they would found in spite of the fact they'd never seen the land George's grant had bestowed them.

But they were afraid. As they should have been. For once gone from England they could never return; once out on the waves they were more helpless than children.

And they were more afraid now, because of the fog.

It had come upon them two days before. Land had been sighted, and by the map Greystone carried it was theirs— from the stark cliffs to the north to the rocky bluff on the south; the harbor that seemed too shallow for ships such as this but would be perfect to fish from once trees were felled and shaped; and a thick dark forest that began at the edge of a sweeping narrow beach. The entire company had thronged excitedly on deck, and there were raucous, thankful cheers led by Greystone himself and the usually pompous Harris Croome, songs and hymns over which the baritones of Master Lorcaster and Davey Williams sailed like gulls on the wind. Young Jacob Plummer was already planning his fortune, and Alex Deaken had grabbed his wife and wept on her shoulder.

The celebration lasted most of the morning, but just after noon Fletcher saw the fog. It slipped off the land past the cliffs and the bluff, skating across the water, building to a wall, smothering sight and sound and dimming the sun.

When the stars failed to shine and there was no moon, just the dark, apprehension took hold.

When sunrise was nothing but a lightening of the grey, the company stayed below, and Brian knew what they were thinking: *after all this time, after all that has happened* . . .

Now the fog tightened, and there was nothing but the ship.

"Your men," Greystone said. "What are the omens they speak of?"

Brian laughed and shook his head. "I've not known you long, Mr. Greystone, but I can't believe you'd take stock in such things."

"I listen to everything," the man told him. "There is nothing I dismiss, not even superstition."

Another bird's cry and the sound of its wings. Brian looked up, hoping to see it, hoping to have proof there was really land out there. There was nothing. He couldn't even see the tops of the masts, and when he turned back to Greystone, he was gone.

Bootheels on the deck, heading for the bow.

"Mr. Greystone?"

The hum of taut lines when the wind blew again.

"Mr. Greystone, you'd best be careful, sir. There's—"
He quieted.

The fog reached over and through the railing in ribbons and vines, curling around the masts, slipping around the sails, gathering at his feet in clouds and puffing smoke.

"Mr. Greystone!"

He started forward, skidded one foot on a slick patch of damp, and turned quickly back, climbing the stairs to the quarterdeck, where he stood before the lashed wheel and peered into the fog, watching it fill the ship below him, bury the ship above.

There were no voices.

There were no footsteps.

He could barely hear the breath hissing from his lungs.

Alone; he was alone, as the light drew away and the fog lifted to his knees and passengers and crew were as if they'd never been. He wanted to call out, but held his tongue for fear his voice would sound like a woman's in pain; he wanted to run for his cabin and fetch all the weapons he had, but he thought that down there it would be like closing his own coffin.

Not a praying man, he prayed; not a weak man, he felt his knees begin to buckle; not a family man, he wished there were someone to leave behind, to keep his name and his memory and the way he had been before he vanished in the dark.

He dozed.

He walked.

During the night he felt the fog cloak him and walk his spine.

He lit the lanterns by his station, saw the fog, and blew them out.

He dozed.

He walked.

He waited for the sun.

And when it came, suddenly, flaring at his back like the

torch he couldn't light, he grabbed the railing at his waist and held it until his wrists began to cramp, held it longer for the pain to tell him it was no dream.

The fog was gone.

And they were down there, all of them, standing with their backs to him, heads bare, arms at their sides, clothes stirring in the cool breeze that smelled of leaves and grass, trees and hills, land ripe for planting and flowers for a garden. When he spoke a name—Croome, Williams, Lorcaster, Plummer—they did not turn, did not move; when he called his crew, there was no answer, and no one at the helm.

A gust of wind closed his eyes.

The sound of his name snapped them open.

There, at the bow, standing above them all, Winston Greystone stood with his back to the land, his cloak rippling behind him, his hat in his hand. With the sun full upon him the black that he wore seemed faded, seemed bleached.

"We have arrived," the man said, softly it seemed, but loud enough to hear. "Will you join us, Captain?"

The heads turned one by one; the faces smiled at him one by one.

Brian couldn't answer; he was too busy staring.

The man smiled and beckoned. "Be a good man and join us," he said heartily. "There's nothing back there for you. Be a part of us, Captain Fletcher, and let us be your friends."

And for a moment he was willing. He could stop here, raise a family, start a fleet of his own, and explore the coast of this curious new world. He could, if he were diligent, become a man of means, perhaps even enjoy a few years of power before retiring to a cottage he could build there on the bluff, watch his children grow, and keep an eye on the sea.

It was tempting. Very tempting.

Until the faces turned to him again, and he saw the smiles and the hands, and the eyes filled with spinning smoke.

"This is your new home, Captain Fletcher." The voice soft. "And we know what you're thinking, we know your fears and worry." The voice gentle. "It can be yours if you'll help us." The voice low and pounding. "You'll never go back."

And the leader himself: his eyes and his hair, his clothes and his words—

"Live with us, Brian Fletcher."

—not faded by sunlight, not a blur of his vision—

"Stay here and be with us. Stay here, in Greystone Bay."

—but the color, and the shifting, and the voice of the fog.

Croome House
by
Reginald Bretnor

When I married Gerald Croome I never thought that I would be marrying Croome House. Yet that, I suppose, is what has happened.

Croome House looks out over the town of Greystone Bay, but it is not *of* it. From the beginning it has been an intruder, always with something strange about it, something vaguely felt but beyond the edges of perception. Black Jory used to say that to him it felt as though a dark and ancient presence lurked just around an invisible corner. Cold, cold, menacing.

A *house*? Yes, I suppose that nowadays it's just a house, but it started out to be something of a mansion, built in Queen Anne's reign by Lemuel Croome with the profits of his small ships' midnight sailings to Jamaica and Barbados, to islands even more remote, and to the wild coasts of South America, whence they returned with Negroes to work his fields, and other cargoes for which there was a swift, silent sale.

Lemuel was the first Croome to be born here in America, in the second year after the dreadful crossing, during which the Croomes alone, of all the families aboard, suffered no losses from storm or illness, neither of children nor men nor women, and who were not despoiled by the pirates—if they were pirates—who intercepted them and stole everything of value, leaving nothing but tools, a few beasts for breeding, and the seeds they had hoped to plant. The Croomes lost nothing, and they did not share.

The Croome men were very tall and dark and handsome, one and all, with hard Gypsy eyes that had nothing of the Gypsy fire within them but instead were like black flint. The Croome women—those who were of the blood— were much like them, lovely enough to set men's hearts afire, but their husbands, one and all, were cowed and silent. Yet there was enough of the strange about all those first people who settled Greystone Bay that they understood the Croomes and trod very softly in their presence. At divine service on the quarterdeck before the landing, they took part with all the rest, and this, as Winston Greystone recorded in his log, always seemed the strangest thing of all—except for their joy, their exuberance, their singing when that final cloud descended on the ship and it found itself in Greystone Bay. It was the only time anyone had heard them sing.

But enough of that. Lemuel Croome built his mansion from the dark red brick of Greystone Bay's native clay, a great, grim pile which could never, even in its first glory, have been welcoming. For its site he chose South Hill, in the midst of all those acres, some darkly wooded, many cleared, which the Croomes had taken for their own. Its three stories, pierced by too few small windows and capped by any number of squat chimneys, looked out over the half-mile of hillside that lay between it and the long stretch of land walled with stone and closed by a great iron gate that was the Croome graveyard.

There it stands today, its bricks moist and lichened, staring across that graveyard—or what is left of it.

Croome House looks uninhabited, but it is not. No, no. For I live there. Alone, except for Jory's son John, his widow Beulah, and John's wife Effie, who do for me. So I have lived since three years after Lincoln's murder, the year they pushed the railroad through to Greystone Bay. That was a long time ago, for Mr. Taft is now our President, and Greystone Bay has grown and grown, filled up with new people and new industries.

Beulah and I lived in a very small corner of Croome House, and John and Effie have part of the old servants' quarters. But despite all the changes, when I go downtown to shop or to the library, everyone still avoids me, I suppose instinctively, because after all, even though I am not of the Croome blood, my name still *is* Croome. Even when I go to church I might as well be there alone.

How did I come to marry Gerald Croome? I was twice orphaned, first when my parents were taken by the cholera only months after I was born, then at nineteen when I lost the dear aunt who raised me. She had warned me there wouldn't be much money, that I might have to make my way, and had made sure I'd be prepared to teach in school. A few days after her funeral a friend of hers, a bookseller, told me of a position open in Greystone Bay, in a small day-school run by an offshoot of the Methodist church to which he happened to belong, and gave me the name of the minister. I wrote to him with my references. I was summoned for an interview. Mrs. Galton, his wife, approved of me, and I was duly hired.

I met Gerald on my first Sunday there. He was sitting with his brothers and their families in the Croomes' pew, and from the outset I could feel his eyes on me. Trying not to return his gaze, I could not keep from flushing; and

Mrs. Galton told me later that because of my golden
ringlets and fair skin the color was most becoming to me.
Then, very tactfully, she cautioned me about the Croomes.
No, it wasn't that they weren't faithful members of the
congregation. No, there had been no real scandal regarding
any of them. But—well, they were different somehow,
and many people felt ill at ease with them. Perhaps she
wasn't being fair, *but*—

Gerald had two sisters and five brothers, and he was the
tallest and the handsomest. There were twenty years between him and Tom, the eldest, and everything about him
was vibrantly alive, everything but his eyes—and that I did
not notice until much later. From the outset he courted me,
and from the outset messages seemed to pass between us.
Sometimes I and the Galtons would be invited to have
dinner at Croome House, where I met them all. His father
was now several years dead; his mother was in frail and
failing health, and there was an aunt also, Addie, a poor
old spinster with blackbird eyes, who I was to see much
more of in due course.

There was so much I did not see in those first months of
our courtship and then our marriage. I never noticed the
clotted shadows in the corridors, and paid no heed when
townspeople greeted my mention of the Croomes with
nervous laughter or a quick change of subject. Gerald was
quiet, courteous, kindly, strong with a tightly restrained
strength. To me he was at once father, brother, husband,
and ardent lover. We were married when school closed for
the summer, and I moved into Croome House. As I've told
you, it was a huge place, with ample room for everyone—
men, women, children, servants. It was there we spent our
honeymoon, occupying a bedroom and parlor on the second floor; and it was only after its excitements were all
over that, slowly, I began to understand how much of a
stranger I really was.

One of Gerald's brothers, David, was unmarried; he

commanded the tall tops'l schooner with which they still
traded up and down the coast and to the islands, and was
much at sea. Two of the other four were married to second
and third cousins, Croomes themselves, or of the Croome
blood at least, and lived on farms in the vicinity, as did
one sister with her husband. Those husbands, though they
were good men, simply did not count. To this day I really
do not know how many people lived there at one time, but
there must have been at least thirty or thirty-five, counting
children and servants. The children, all black-haired, black-
eyed, were almost uncannily quiet, never dashing through
the corridors, shouting, quarreling; and often Tom and
Gerald, Tom's tall wife, Lucinda, and perhaps an unobtru-
sive husband sat down to dinner with us in the bleakly
paneled dining room. At Croome House there were no
pictures on the wall; nor, for that matter, were there any
pets—neither dogs nor cats nor even birds in cages.

Tom always sat at the table's head, dour and massive,
never talkative. Always, he turned to his mother at his
right as they sat down, signed to her to say a grace. This
she did silently, cold lips moving unreadably over her
clasped hands, and we sat there with downcast eyes till it
was over. I never did find out what it was she said, and I
suspect now it was just as well.

Perhaps more than anything it was Aunt Addie who
made me realize that I remained an outsider, for I had to
take my turns sitting with her in the afternoon, and she
made no bones about it. To her, the Croomes were the
whole world.

Once, sitting there sewing as she chatted on, I asked her
where the Croomes had come from. Immediately she broke
off whatever she'd been saying, leaned forward with a
rasping of her stiff grey taffeta, seized my hands in hers—it
was like being grasped by some starved bird, her fingers
were so dry, so meatless—and exclaimed, "*Where* did we
come from? *Where?* My dear, we came out of the bogs

and fens and ratholes, the caverns and forgotten ditches,
out of the past!'' And abruptly her mad laughter set the air
a-tremble; it was like the shrieking of tormented sea gulls.
''We Croomes? Why, we're the ones who never have
escaped! The rest of you have left your savage gods behind. They've let you go! But ours—ours have not!''
Again the tortured sea gull screamed. ''So that's where we
came from—the past you've buried and forgotten, which
demands nothing now, no sacrifices, no terrible payments.
Not from *you*.'' She paused. ''B-but you mustn't listen to
old Addie, dear—that's what your Gerald's going to tell
you. Well, you can tell him I said we came by way of
England, think of that!''

With one final shriek of laughter she pulled her hands
away. Her mouth loosened, her eyes, half-closed now,
seemed to turn inward, to stare at some private terror; she
lapsed into an incoherent mumbling.

Of course, Gerald had already told me that I must pay
no heed to anything she said, that she was truly addled;
and yet, while I still believed him, and while I said
nothing to him of the incident, it did alarm me, and at
night I began to listen to the noises of Croome House with
a newfound apprehension, reaching out occasionally to
reassure myself that Gerald was still there beside me.

Justin, our first child, named after his dead Croome
grandfather, was born in the bleak December of 1858;
Thomas, his uncle's namesake, almost two years later.
They were lovely children, the image of their father; and
seeing them, suckling them, caring for them, I found
myself forgetting all my newborn fears. Never before—
and never again—were Gerald and I to feel so close, that
second year of Thomas's birth, the year Gerald's mother
died.

She was not terribly old, but whatever killed her had
wasted her almost to a shadow, feeble and querulous and

antagonistic to everyone who sought to help her. Then one
morning Beulah, Jory's plump wife, as always bringing
her her breakfast tray, found her dead in bed, eyes staring,
mouth sagged open. Beulah had seen the mask of fear that
was her face, and with a scream had dropped the tray, tea,
soft-boiled egg, and all.

Tom and his brothers were already out, but Lucinda,
herself a distant relative and very much a Croome, immediately took charge. Peering through the door, I saw her
close the dead woman's eyes, and do her best to shut that
gaping mouth. Nobody asked me to help at the laying out.
They bustled in and out, those in the house and those who
could leave work, and the only one who, I thought, showed
true grief was Gerald, though I did find Beulah crying
softly in the kitchen.

It was a busy day, and certainly no time was wasted.
One of the sister's husbands, a carpenter, went to work
with Jory's help and, before sundown, had built a pine
coffin, which Tom carried upstairs on his shoulder. They
lined it with an afghan Mrs. Croome had made herself,
and laid her, wearing her best dress, in it.

It was a busy day, a tiring day. Reverend Galton and his
wife came and went, and promised to return at eleven on
the morrow for the burial; and our meals were silent ones,
with no words of regret, no reminiscences.

"Tom and I will sit with her," Gerald told me after
supper. "But there's no need for you to, Alice. There'll be
the boys to put to bed—thank goodness they're small enough
so we won't have to explain about Grandma—and after
that you'd best get a good night's sleep yourself."

I did as I was told, putting the boys to bed in their little
room next to ours, glad enough in all conscience to avoid
sitting silent there with that corpse. Then I undressed and
read a little while, hoping Gerald would come and at least
kiss me good night. And presently he did, carrying a pot
of steaming chocolate on a tray. "Tom's sent all the

servants off," he said, "even Jory and Beulah. Death's a family matter, and they won't be needed." He put the tray down on the nightstand by our bed, poured the fragrant chocolate into a blue-flowered cup, sat down next to me. "There!" he said. "I made it all myself."

I sipped, and it was good. I told him so.

He waited while I drank it, not hurrying me, saying very little. Then, when I finished, he kissed me lightly on the lips and on my forehead, and said, "I love you, dear. Sleep tight."

He left, blowing out the lamp. The chocolate warm within me, I let myself relax.

And slept—a deep and utterly dreamless sleep.

I woke abruptly, alone—and, looking at the bed, I saw that Gerald had not joined me there. The sun, streaming in the window, told me how long I'd slept. Oh, *dear*! I thought. They'll have had breakfast, all of them. It was almost ten o'clock.

Hurriedly I dressed, and almost ran downstairs. Gerald met me in the hall, saw that I was concerned.

"I let you sleep," he said. "You needed it. Beulah's tended to the boys, so that needn't worry you. Come on, you can have a cold snack in the dining room before Galton gets here."

He led me past the door of the great parlor, and I saw Mrs. Croome's coffin there, on trestles, its lid already nailed down, candles guttering at its either end, and Gerald's brothers, their wives, the sisters, sitting still and silent round it. There were no wreaths, no flowers. It was then, I think, that I first noticed the flat stoniness of all their eyes, there by candlelight, in that darkened room.

I ate a little, Gerald sitting with me, and not until years later did I think it strange that I had slept so soundly and so long, deaf even to the crying of my children, had they cried.

The Galtons came, and presently Mrs. Croome's sons

carried her coffin to the buckboard, and we all followed it on foot the half-mile down the hill to the graveyard. The ancient lock had already been opened with a huge fretted key. The barbed iron gate hung wide. The grave, small among so many others, had been dug, and a stone stood there ready. They lowered the coffin gently. Mr. Galton repeated the Service for the Dead, and we stood for a long moment of, I supposed, prayer. Then Gerald and his brothers themselves took spades and softly replaced the excavated earth.

That was the only time until much later, until everything had happened, that I set foot in that graveyard.

Two months went by, and they were happy months for me. The boys were growing, brightly, beautifully. Gerald was with me. The only discords were in my duty-afternoons with Addie, when she seemed to delight in throwing out dire hints about the origins of the Croomes and something vaguely ominous in their overshadowing destiny. I paid little or no attention to her, and I paid even less to what I heard about the Croomes among the people of Greystone Bay. I learned what I already knew: that they were men of substance and of stature, but that none of them ever held any public office, elective or appointive; that they were considered completely honest, but that they never hesitated to take advantage of anyone's misfortune—and that, somehow, in their vicinity there usually seemed to be more than an ordinary number of misfortunes to take advantage of. That last I put down to envy; and when, by the waterfront, I saw one or two of our first few Italians, mostly fishermen, make signs against the evil eye as Gerald and I passed, this I attributed either to stupidity or to their having heard gossip about Aunt Addie's ravings.

Then, when Justin was scarcely more than two and little Thomas was still a babe in arms, in April of '61, the Civil War was upon us.

I learned of it from Jory. He had been in town on an errand, and had whipped his horse into a gallop to come back and tell us, his purchases bouncing in the buckboard as he pulled up into the stable yard.

"They Con-federts done it!" he shouted. "They done shoot dat Foht Sumter! Pres'dent Lincoln done call foh volunteahs!"

Gerald strode out and seized the plunging horse's bridle. Tom, without a word, took the newspaper from Jory's hands. Hearing the hubbub, I ran to a back door, Lucinda at my side. She hadn't heard it all, so I told her what had happened.

She stopped and looked at me. "Well," she said, "that means our lads'll be gone again."

"*Our* lads? You mean my Gerald and his brothers—and Tom, your Tom?"

She was quite unperturbed. "Oh, Tom won't be going, not this time, now he's head of the family. But the rest will, of course. Our Croome men always go to the wars, and"—making an odd little gesture with her fingers, she smiled wryly—"always they come back. *Always,* dear. And they'll come back enriched; they always do. Tom rode back from Mexico with his saddlebags full of gold—hasn't anyone told you?" She laughed, pointing at a great gem on my finger, the one Gerald had given me. "Where do you think that ruby came from?"

Gerald did not leave immediately, not until early in the autumn, when he obtained a commission in a cavalry regiment being raised in the vicinity. One brother had preceded him; one other left shortly after he did. Tom, of course, remained at home, and David continued, despite the war, to sail the sea, probably running risks as great as any soldier's. It was whispered in town that he was running contraband to and from rebel ports, and it was obvious that he was prospering.

I myself had entered what was probably the strangest period of my married life. Without Gerald, I now felt myself far more excluded by others of the family than ever before. We had always been on good, if slightly distant, terms, and that did not change, but there was not one among them in whom I could confide. Constantly worried about Gerald, desperately anxious when weeks went by without a letter, from none of them did I receive sympathy or understanding, and their incessant repetition of phrases like "Don't you worry, hon. Haven't I *told* you our men always come back?" helped not at all. Gradually, I found myself seeking friends outside the family, the Galtons for example, who were very kind to me, often inviting me to the parsonage for supper after services. But my best friends were Black Jory and his wife. He was very capable, a true jack-of-all-trades, and he and Beulah had a way of anticipating my needs. During those hours when the servants were normally permitted in the house, from the lighting of the morning fires until the last of the dinner dishes had been put away, Jory would always take care to let me know when he'd be available to drive me out or run errands for me, and Beulah, who loved my boys, stole time from her many other chores to help me. They, at least, understood my fretting over Gerald.

"Could be it's true these Croome men got some sort of helpin' hand a-lookin' out for 'em, Miz Alice," Jory would say. "I ain't a-sayin' it's so, and I ain't sayin' 'tain't. Lawd-a-mercy! I seen enough queer things round heah you'd not believe—like darknesses where they jest don' belong, an' such. An' I got this feelin' half the time there's a corner we can't see with somethin' waitin', somethin' awful cold, like—well, like a ser-pent out of Scripture."

Jory's mind, I told myself, was full of inherited African superstitions, but even that sort of talk did serve to take my mind off the dangers Gerald might be running. The road to town ran past and around the graveyard, and he always urged the horses into a sharp trot as we passed it in the light carriage. Even Beulah, who often would ride along to help me with the shopping, would laugh at his uneasiness. "You ain't never seen no ghost, Jory Dickens," she'd tell him, "an' you ain't a-goin' to. Jest 'cause they's dead folks lyin' there don' mean they's fixin' to come out an' haunt you."

And Jory would mutter that they were dead Croomes, all of 'em, not jest common folks. "They's some dead folks who's dead right an' proper," he would grumble, "an' they's some as ain't. Why, Beulah, yoh own gran'pappy seen 'em with his own eyes."

I came to understand that, while they could not have been said to love the Croomes, they respected them tremendously, feared them more than a little, and were wholly loyal to them. "That Mr. Justin, Miz Alice," Jory told me, "he bought my pappy right there at the slave mahket down to N'yawleans, an' brung him back up heah an' set him free, an' my mammy too, so we do owe them Croomes a deal, we shore do."

Four or five months passed, and Gerald came home on his first leave. He had traveled by train from somewhere in the Middle West, and had borrowed a horse from an army depot about fifteen miles from Greystone Bay. I shall never forget him riding, straight and jaunty in his saddle, his sabre scabbard and the gold on his new epaulettes—he had just been given command of a company—shining in the sun as his mount pranced and curvetted along the graveyard road. I was not surprised, for he had telegraphed that he was coming, and before he was halfway up the hill I was running down to meet him.

During the next ten days, all my worries and fears fell away. He was delighted with his boys, and he seemed the very same Gerald I had known on our honeymoon. Sometimes, at the oddest times, he would appear abstracted, and

I thought his eyes were assuming some of that hardness I
had noticed in his kin, but all this I attributed to the War.
It was enough that he was home and safe, for a while at
least. But one thing happened which, for a day or so,
cooled my enjoyment of his presence. Three days after his
arrival, a cart came rumbling into the stable yard, and Jory
ran in much excited to report they'd brought a crate for
Captain Croome.

I called to Gerald, and he came downstairs laughing.
"So it's arrived, has it?" he exclaimed. "Have 'em bring
it up, Jory, and see they get paid off. Then you can open it
right in the dining room."

With Jory's help, the crate was carried in. Then Jory
opened it. In it, wrapped in old woolen blankets, was a
perfectly splendid Colonial silver service, salver, tureen,
sauce boats, knives and forks and spoons and salts and
peppers, even branched candelabra, everything.

"The spoils of war!" Gerald laughed, and momentarily,
for no good reason, my heart sank. Neither I nor any of the
others asked how he got it.

The War went on. Occasionally, David would be in port
and would tell us of narrow escapes from rebel raiders; he
too brought home much that was precious, much that was
hard to find in wartime. Homer Beasley, husband of one
of Gerald's sisters, had enlisted, and in 1863 he was killed
in Chancellorsville. Tom remarked simply that he was not
a Croome.

One of the brothers had joined the artillery, the other
was a quartermaster or something of the sort. Both earned
their commissions and neither was so much as wounded. On
several occasions they too came home on leave, and always they too came laden with unexpected treasures, bolts
of silk, furs, a golden chalice. Gerald managed more leaves
than either of them, and on each leave, as the boys grew
taller, stronger, more responsive, he became more and

more wrapped up in them. Toward the War's end, he would walk with them in the garden, just the three of them together, for what he called "man talk," and on each occasion, while he by no means really neglected me, I could sense the concentration of his interest and, again, the subtle hardening of his manner.

Then, at Gettysburg, Lee surrendered. The War was over, and presently, one by one, the three returned. Gerald was the last to come. His regiment had been in Texas.

Of course, they were heroes, and even in Greystone Bay we had our periods of excitements and parades, of lionizing and patriotic speeches. But Mr. Lincoln's assassination put a stop to that, and gradually life returned to normal, a different normality than we had known.

The War had not affected Croome House or the Croome holdings directly, but it had worked great changes in the town. New industries had moved in; the money-making urge to grow was in the air; already there was talk of ending what our politicians called our out-of-date isolation, our dependence on the sea and on the slow speed of horsedrawn vehicles. Our newspaper printed editorials demanding to know why we had no railroad, and presently a company was formed called the Doncaster, Newtown, and Greystone Bay Railway, selling stock, and advertising that it would connect with all major railroads throughout the nation.

None of it seemed to concern me, but my life did change. Justin was now six, his brother almost five, and I could see Gerald's mirror image in each of them; it was as though they had inherited nothing from me, even though I had borne them. It did not trouble me—I loved Gerald too much for that. But now it was quite clear that the central focus of his life had shifted. First I had felt it was myself, then myself and the two boys. Now the boys were primary, and I felt deeply hurt when he first looked at them and boasted, "See that! They're *true* Croomes."

To make things worse, there was a new uneasiness within the family, which at first I did not understand, for the world's news did not concern me much, even that small part of it dealing with Greystone Bay. However, I could feel it, and finally I asked Gerald.

"Tom's worried," he answered, frowning. "They're bound and determined the railroad's coming in—they've already raised the capital—and now it looks as if they'll try to push it through our holdings."

"Do you mean right through this property? Right here?"

"Well, near enough. Their best way would be to avoid the hill completely and come along the flat. That'd give them a straight run into town."

"But—but, Gerald, they can't do *that*. That'd mean going clear through the graveyard!"

"Yes," he said. "Chances are they'd want to move everybody who's buried there. It's been done before, but we're not going to stand for it. If they so much as suggest it, we'll fight."

The cold Croome flint was in his eyes, and in his voice, and suddenly I felt it in my heart.

Within the week the railroad's directors had voted for the route he had described, and a day or so later they came up with an offer for the property—an offer that included the mass transfer of coffins, gravestones, monuments to any site the Croomes might choose. They warned us that, were we to refuse, they would go to the law and seek to exercise the right of eminent domain.

Tom told them coldly to go ahead, and he fought them in the courts for two whole years, but I know now that he did so only to delay what he deemed inevitable. I got my first inkling of it from old Addie, on one of our afternoons together.

"Two hundred years!" she said. "Imagine it! And now we're going to have to push on someplace else, oh yes we are! Tom hasn't told you yet because you're not blood kin, but it's what *they* want."

"*They?*" I asked. "You mean the railroad people?"

Her laughter shrilled. "Not them, silly. No indeed. I mean—" She hesitated, realized she had said something she was not supposed to say. "No, that isn't who *they* are. They're—but it's nothing you need to know. It's something only we Croomes—" She was excited now, and frightened. "Honey, I was just being stupid, truly I was! Just you forget about it. Forget— For—" As always when she was disturbed, her eyes seemed to turn inward; she began to mumble, twisting her hands together, and I left the room to the sound of her keening to herself as she rocked back and forth.

Still, what she'd said remained with me, and as month followed month and the court fight went on, I noticed that, very quietly, Croome families in the area were disposing of their properties, an easy thing to do with Greystone Bay growing and good property at a premium. For the first two years, Tom maintained the pretense of never giving in, but then Gerald's two married brothers started taking long trips out of town and being very close-mouthed about it. A few months more, and they had gone with their families.

Somehow, I knew then that everyone would leave, but I consoled myself with the thought that, wherever we had to go, I would still have Gerald; I would still have my two lovely sons. If the Croomes could not bear to see the desecration of their cemetery and their ancestors' reburial in strange soil, well, that was purely their family affair. Gerald refused to discuss the subject, and I, feeling for him, held my peace.

Tom began selling off the home property, everything but Croome House and the land on which it stood, and the half-mile of sweeping hillside that separated it from the graveyard. In the house itself, room after room was emptied of furniture and closed off; one by one, the servants were discharged.

There was much gossip about it in the town, but almost everybody thought the Croomes were selling out just to get money to prolong their fight, for Tom had sworn he'd carry the case to the Supreme Court.

Gerald had changed; he was cold, remote, detached, his old self only to the boys. More and more often, he and Tom and David would hold long conferences from which even the Croome women were excluded. Never had the two of us drifted so apart and I began to tell myself that it would be a great day when at last we could shake the dust of Croome House from us and start anew.

Then the courts issued their final judgment, giving the railroad all it wanted. In five days they would bring their gangs of workmen and their wagons, and we were warned to have the graveyard ready for them. A bailiff came and served Tom with the notice, and Tom took it without a word, turning his back and striding heavily into his study; and during the next two days it simply wasn't mentioned. The only difference was that now Gerald once again was kind and gentle and considerate to me, very deliberately so, as if he were making up for something lost.

On the third night, immediately after supper, he helped me put the boys to bed, and then he did something he had done only once before. He went down to the kitchen and made me a pot of hot chocolate, just as he had on the day his mother died. He sat with me while I, unthinking, drank it, and just before I slept he kissed me on the lips and on my brow.

Again, my sleep was dreamless and fathoms deep, and when I finally woke I knew instantly that I had slept well into the day—and that something was terribly, terribly wrong.

Croome House was as silent as a tomb.

I could see that Gerald had not come to bed with me. I looked into the boys' room, and found it empty—too empty. No toys, no clothing, nothing spoke of its having been inhabited.

I rushed upstairs. Only silence greeted me. I saw that the door of Tom's study was standing open, and there I learned what had become of me.

On his desk there was a letter, weighted down with the great, fretted graveyard key.

It was from Gerald.

Alice dear, (he had written in his strong, clear hand)

> *What must be, must be. You cannot understand us—not me, not Tom, nor any of us Croomes. No, not even your own sons. Alice, tomorrow you will discover why we have moved on. But I pray you, enquire no further. I do not want you, ever, to share our fear.*
>
> *Croome House and all it now contains are yours for life. You need not concern yourself with what will then become of it. I have arranged for ample funds to be paid to you each month. Jory and Beulah will be staying on to take care of you.*
>
> *Do not try to find us, Alice. Promise me that. Simply remember that we three, Justin and small Tom and myself, leave you now because it is the only thing we can do.*
>
> *Try not to hate me, Alice, for I love you.*

> *Gerald*

I stared at it unbelievingly. With it, there were documents concerning Croome House, concerning money, concerning what would happen to the graveyard. I brushed them all aside.

In the kitchen I found Beulah waiting for me, and I cried my heart out in her enfolding arms. Then, very gently, she and Jory told me how, as soon as I was asleep, everyone had left, telling no one their destination, and how that very morning it had already been reported that the schooner was no longer at her dock.

The afternoon passed like an anguished dream, though the Galtons came and did their best to comfort me, and at my urging stayed for a supper I myself could not eat.

Next morning, when the men came for the graveyard key, I was ready for them, and Mr. Galton too was already there, determined that the exhumed remains should at least be handled reverently. He went off with the railroad's man, and for an hour or so I sat there with Beulah, waiting for word from him.

It came sooner than I had expected. I saw him walking up the hill path very slowly, almost as though he were afraid to, and again the railroad's man was with him.

Beulah let them in and showed them to the study.

Mr. Galton's normally ruddy face was ashen pale; even the other man looked shaken.

"Is something wrong?" I asked.

"Please sit down, Alice." Mr. Galton almost whispered it. "What we have found has shocked me deeply, and mystified us all. I shall tell you about it, but only with reluctance."

I seated myself, and so did he and his companion.

"Alice," he said, "we first entered the tomb of Lemuel and Sarah Croome, using the same key that opens the main gate. Their coffins were lying there, side by side, plain pine coffins, and I cautioned the men with us to lift them with special care because of their great age, and I'm sure they tried." He paused, hesitated. "However, perhaps because of the dim light, one of the men carrying Lemuel's coffin tripped and dropped one end of it, and— well, it burst open."

He stopped, and in my mind's eye I saw a long-dead skull, the shreds of hair and ancient clothing, and moldering bones. I shuddered. "Was the sight so—so terrible?"

"Not in the way you think, my dear." He said it very gently, very fearfully. "Alice, Lemuel Croome's coffin was completely empty. There was *nothing* in it. And there never had been."

"But—but then—?" I stammered. "What on earth does it mean? Surely grave robbers couldn't have—?"

He shook his head. "No, there were no robbers. Alice, we opened Sarah's coffin too, and it was empty. Follard the coroner was there with us, and we started opening others. All were empty—the oldest, the most recent."

"But Mr. Galton!" I cried out. "Gerald's mother was buried there. You yourself conducted the service at her grave. We all *saw* her buried!"

"No, Alice, we saw her coffin buried. There is no one buried in the Croome graveyard. Nobody at all. There never has been."

"Then what became of—?"

"That," he answered somberly, "is a question I would much prefer not even to try to answer."

They left me in a state of shock, after I had given them permission to burn all the empty coffins and to stack the tombstones like cordwood off the railroad's right of way. All the dark hints, the town gossip, the stories told by simple men like Jory flooded again into my mind, and at the last I had to rest ill content with Jory's explanation: that there always had been something behind an unseen corner shadowing over Croome House and the Croomes, something that had powers, something that could protect and could destroy, something unhuman.

Or, as Addie put it, *they.*

Why have I stayed on? Beulah is still with me, but Jory has been dead for years. Now their son, John, and John's wife, Effie, do what must be done. I have no other friends, not even the Galtons, who too are dead. That empty graveyard put fear of the Croomes into Greystone Bay far more effectively, far more permanently, than any number of pitiful dead bodies could. I go to church. I go down to the library. That is all. And the shadows still clot the Croome House corridors.

Why have I stayed? For a time, I suppose I was hoping that Gerald would return to me, bringing my boys. But after that?

I am afraid. I am afraid I'll never learn who or what *they* are, or what happened to all those generations of the Croomes' unburied dead.

But I am more—much more—afraid I will.

I have borne Croome children. But I have not been turned into a Croome.

Have I?

Used Books

by

Robert E. Vardeman

"Boy, I'd love to get into her pants." Tommy Kidd's pale blue eyes followed the girl's trim form as she swayed down Port Boulevard, aware of the male attention she received.

"Michelle?" Tommy's best friend Alan Wolsky snorted derisively. "She's nothing but a prick teaser. Look at the way she flutters those eyelashes at anything wearing pants." He turned and studied Tommy critically. "Hell, if she gives you the hots that bad, go ask her for a date. Bet she'd put out at the drop of a hat."

"Shut up. You don't know what you're talking about."

"Hell I don't. But you wouldn't know about that, would you? You're too chicken to even *talk* to her, much less go all the way. You been going with Patty and haven't even tried to cop a feel."

"That's not true." Tommy flushed hotly at the accusation.

"Patty's a professional virgin. Everybody knows it.

29

That's why you go with her, so you won't have to do anything. You're scared shitless of getting laid, Tommy, aren't you, aren't you? Come on, admit it!''

"Get lost," Tommy shouted, turning down the street and wanting to run. Only through great willpower did he keep his stride short, but he clutched his schoolbooks so tightly his knuckles turned white. As he walked, the fifteen-year-old convinced himself this always happened to the superheroes he read about in the comics. Nobody appreciated them; nobody appreciated him.

He closed his eyes and leaned against a cool stone building, took a deep breath of salt air, and imagined himself walking along the street with Michelle—lovely, tall, sultry Michelle. A gang of Hell's Angels would come riding down on her astride their dangerously roaring chopped hogs, threatening her, yelling obscenities. He would stand up to the greasy bastards and run them off. Yeah. And she'd flutter those long, black artificial eyelashes in his direction and throw herself into his arms and then they'd . . .

He looked around guiltily, moving his books so that he held on to them in front of him with both hands. To cover up his embarrassment so anybody passing by wouldn't see.

Why couldn't it be like he imagined it could be? Why wasn't he less of a coward?

He walked on another block before turning a corner, relieved when his excitement finally passed. Five minutes later he stopped in front of a store window in bad need of washing. Lurid paperbacks proudly marched along a brick and board shelf in the window. He licked dried lips and looked up and down the street. No one he knew was in sight. He'd tried once to buy a copy of *Playboy* down at Krueller's Drugstore and God and everyone had seen him. Alan had told anyone who'd listen, and Tommy had been laughed at for weeks and weeks.

No one saw him now. Maybe he could buy a dirty book.

Maybe the owner didn't care who he sold to. He started in but fear grabbed his heart and squeezed. He wanted to run.

When the door opened and a brass bell tinkled, he jumped a foot.

"Didn't mean to scare you, son. Were you coming in?" The old man in the doorway looked like he was a million years old, all wrinkled and tanned. The odd clothes he wore captured Tommy's attention, though, and kept him from bolting and running.

"Uh, yeah, guess so. What kind of, uh, bookstore is this?"

"If you can't read the sign, you won't get much out of the books." The old man in the billowy-sleeved shirt pointed to the sign. "Cesar's Used Books. Cesar, that's me. Don't get much business down this street. Too far away from the Boulevard."

Tommy nervously looked up and down the street and finally nodded.

"Come in and look around. Tell your friends, for all the good that'll do. No one reads today. Watch the damn telly."

"Telly? You British?" Tommy began wondering about the baggy pants and the calf-high black leather boots that needed polishing. "You look like something out of a Lon Chaney movie. *The Wolf Man.*"

"I should," Cesar said. "I am Romany and I know the secrets of the universe. They are passed down from generation to generation." His voice lowered and he added, "My books contain all the knowledge of the Gypsy. Come in and see."

"Wow," said Tommy, eyes wide. He moved as if drawn by a magnet and began looking over the dusty rows of books. The acrid tang of cheap paper turning yellow and brittle thrilled him, as it always did. Soon enough, he was sitting cross-legged on the floor going through a stack of books written by Sabatini and the Baroness d'Orczy and Fritz Leiber.

He didn't find any Gypsy lore in *Captain Blood* or *The Three Musketeers* or *The Winds of War* but he did find cheap prices on battered paperbacks. He had accumulated a stack marked "fifty cents each"—and would be eating candy bars for lunch for a week because of it—and was working up his courage to ask Mr. Cesar if he had any porno books when a short man dressed in a three-piece suit came swinging into the store, a heavy attaché case in one hand.

"You have it, Cesar?" asked the short man.

"But of course. It will be yours. For one entire week."

Tommy sidled back behind a spinner rack filled with old pulp magazines, imagination running wild. The short guy must be a gangster, Mr. Cesar a dope dealer. Or maybe he was arranging for a mob hit. Tommy's heart beat faster. Mr. Cesar was a contract killer and would snuff the star government witness on the stand just as he started to spill everything.

"Here. Count it," said the short man. He opened the attaché case. Tommy blinked twice. The case was crammed with twenty-dollar bills. Cesar closed it quickly and shook his head sadly.

"I trust you, my friend. If you ever shorted me, there would be no more of these. . . ." Mr. Cesar smiled and drew forth a package the size of a hardcover book. Tommy couldn't see what it was, but the short man snatched it as if it meant his very life. He turned and left the store without another word. Mr. Cesar chuckled and placed the attaché case under the unpainted counter.

Tommy waited another ten minutes, heart ready to explode. Gone was all thought of asking Mr. Cesar about dirty books. He hadn't hallucinated all that money. There wasn't anything in this crappy secondhand bookstore that would bring a price like that. There must have been ten thousand dollars in the case. More.

He approached the counter with his trove of books, trying to keep from straining to look over the far side and see if the black leather case was actually there or if he had only imagined it.

"A good selection, son," said Mr. Cesar. "Four dollars and fifty cents."

"Uh-oh," said Tommy, suddenly realizing he had only three crumpled dollar bills. "I guess I'd better put back a couple."

"No money, eh? Never mind. I am an old man and it cheers me seeing a young man read. The books are yours for three dollars."

"I couldn't."

"Please, humor me. It is a whim on my part. Please."

Tommy eyed the books and guessed at the worlds hidden within them. He nodded, thanked Mr. Cesar, and almost fled the shop.

The street outside was empty. By the time he had walked the eight blocks home he knew he'd only imagined the money, just as he imagined himself taking Michelle in his arms and . . .

After dinner Tommy curled up in a corner chair and started reading. His dad had come by, looked at the cover, and shook his head. The man sat down and unfolded his newspaper.

"Can't understand what you see in junk like that, Tom," he said. "You sit there reading like you were hypnotized or on drugs. You ought to show more interest in current events."

"Like you, Daniel?" said Tommy's mother. "All you read the paper for is the sports page and to see who got killed in the most gruesome way. I swear, you're like some sort of a ghoul."

"It's the times we live in, dear," he said. "Look at this. One of those hotshot million-a-year basketball players was found dead this morning. Cops stopped him wandering the streets like he was some kind of zombie. Brain was burned out, on dope, probably. They're all junkies. Died an hour later.''

"See? Gruesome."

Tommy ignored them and lost himself on the high seas, commanding a pirate ship. He ordered a broadside. Another, and then ordered the captured merchanteer boarded. He swung across the gap between the two heaving ships, his arm circling Michelle's waist. She melted against him, kissing him for rescuing her. . . .

Tommy Kidd awoke just after midnight. He lay on his back, staring at the shadows dancing slowly across his bedroom ceiling.

"I *did* see money," he said. The boy tried to put the picture of all those twenties out of his mind, but he couldn't. The more he fought to go back to sleep the more awake he became.

Finally he rose and silently dressed. He opened his door and listened for a moment, hearing the measured ticking of the grandfather clock in the hallway and the rattling snores of his father from the master bedroom. He swallowed hard and almost chickened out and returned to bed.

No, he thought, I get pushed around enough. This time I'm going to find out what's going on. Maybe get a reward when I turn them all in to the police. He had no clear idea of what crime had been committed or who he was going to call the police on, but that money meant something illegal was going on.

All the way to Mr. Cesar's used bookstore Tommy imagined himself as Dirty Harry kicking in the door, shouting, "Police! Freeze! Unless you want to make my day." Outside the dingy storefront he experienced a rush of confidence. Dirty Harry was never scared.

He peered through the dusty window and saw nothing

but the shelves of books and a yellow sliver of light coming from under the door leading to a back room. He jumped when the squeal of car tires on the pavement echoed down the street. The flashy sports car started braking. Tommy ran to an alleyway and hid.

The elegantly dressed woman climbing from the car made Tommy catch his breath and hold it. "Monique Dupree," he whispered, air leaking from him as if he'd sprung a leak. "She must be about the biggest star in Hollywood."

Monique Dupree didn't even knock on the door; she pushed through into the store, the brass bell tinkling lightly. Tommy started to go back to the front window, then stopped. High over his head was a small window, lit from within. Clambering up the piles of trash in the alley allowed him to peer into the back room of the bookstore.

"Mademoiselle Dupree," Mr. Cesar greeted her, bowing low. "It is so good of you to give your time for charity."

"My agent didn't tell me we'd be working in such a filthy place." Tommy cringed. Monique Dupree's voice grated like a nail file on metal. It wasn't anything like the sexy, seductive voice in her movies. He knew. He'd sneaked into all of them, especially the R-rated ones.

"Just read from this book. I shall record it and do the transcription for the blind later."

"My fucking agent's got balls setting me up with something like this. I got a hot date waiting for me at Luigi's."

"The famous disco?" asked Mr. Cesar. "Please, let us get on with it. Only a few minutes and then you can go and, how do they say, boogie till the cows come home."

"What? I never heard anything like that. But yeah, let's get on with it." Monique Dupree cleared her throat and out came the caressing voice that made Tommy uncomfortable with its immediate intimacy. She read from a romance novel as if it contained the most interesting and revealing words in the world.

Tommy moaned and tried to keep from embarrassing himself. He wiped sweat off his forehead and pressed hard against the wall, hoping it would help. It only made it worse. He craned his neck and got a good look down into the dimly lit room.

Two walls were lined with leather-bound volumes, obviously expensive and not like the cruddy paperbacks in the front room. But he didn't care about the books. His eyes fixed firmly on the blond woman, the way her breasts almost spilled out of the sequined evening gown, the way her fingers slipped up and down the pages of the book. Tommy closed his eyes and imagined Monique running her slender fingers all over him, up and down.

His eyes shot open when the woman stopped reading. She lay with her head on the simple wooden table, asleep. Mr. Cesar turned off the cheap Japanese tape recorder and stood. Tommy heard him chuckle and say, "Well worth fifty thousand to her agent."

Cesar took the book lying open on the table and carefully examined it. He smiled more broadly. He went to a small cabinet and unlocked the door, removing a tiny vial of green liquid. Tommy watched in rapt fascination as the Romany began placing one drop of the fluid on each page of the book. When he had done this for all the pages, he closed the book and shelved it.

The man hoisted the actress into a fireman's carry. Tommy nervously rubbed one dirty hand over his lips, wondering if Mr. Cesar had killed her. The roar of the sports car and the sight of Monique propped up in the passenger seat, Mr. Cesar driving, further confused him.

"Maybe she had too much to drink or something and Mr. Cesar's taking her home." But even as he said it, Tommy knew that wasn't true.

"Come on, don't be chicken," he said, looking back

into the room. He climbed down from the tottering tower of boxes, went to the front of the store, and tried the doorknob. Unlocked. The tinkle of the bell almost gave him a heart attack, but Tommy quickly ducked inside, afraid Mr. Cesar might return at any instant and find him.

The door leading to the back room stood ajar. Tommy advanced slowly, as if this were the gateway into hell. His hand shook as he grabbed the knob and opened the door.

The room was exactly as he had seen it from the high, narrow window. Two walls were lined with books, from floor to ceiling. On the third wall stood the tiny wooden cabinet from which Mr. Cesar had taken the bottle of green ink. And the fourth wall was a mass of peeling grey paint.

"Wow, biographies," he exclaimed, running his fingers over the soft leather bindings. In bright gold along the spines were names both recognized and unknown to him.

Adolf Hitler. Marilyn Monroe. Ambrose Bierce. Françoise Dorléac. Wiley Post.

He took down a volume marked "Jim Morrison."

"Wonder who he is?"

His eyes scanned the first sentence of the book. The very words burned in flame on the expensive parchment. Tommy stiffened as the crowd roared his name.

"Morrison, Morrison! We want the Lizard King!"

He strode out on stage, arrogant, aware of the power he exerted over the thirty-seven thousand screaming fans. Fingers locked in the silver conch belt and he thrust his leather-pants-clad hips far forward, wantonly far, and began a slow gyration as the band behind him swung into a driving, provocatively sensual song.

He held the dumb sonsabitches in the palm of his hand and the power excited him. Sexually excited him.

Tommy stared directly at the floor, and it took a few seconds for him to realize the book had fallen from his nerveless fingers. He bent down and closed the book, returning it to the shelf.

He walked on shaky legs and looked at the other books. Eva Peron. D. W. Griffith. Douglas Fairbanks. Manfred von Richtofen. William Thomas Turner.

Tommy took down this book and read the fiery words. He heaved a deep breath, sucking in a lungful of the salt air as he peered out across the bridge of his 32,000-ton liner. Galley Head lay before the *Lusitania*. The dawn turned deadly when he saw the trotyl-laden torpedo from a U-20 running toward his ship.

Tommy slammed the book shut, eyes stinging and feeling feverish. He replaced the tome and ran his fingers along the spines of the others until he came to the new one.

Monique Dupree.

With hands barely able to grip the leather cover, he pulled it down and opened it. The words leaped from the page and etched with acid intensity into his brain. His lover came to him, one hand on the white satin sheet and the other on his tender, yielding thigh. His legs widened and he reached out to take the handsome, mustached man into his arms. Never had he wanted a man more than he did now.

''Oh, my God,'' Tommy muttered, forcing himself to close the cover. He put it back into its place and sat down at the wood table, shaking all over.

He looked at the shelves in wonder. No other books had been so alive for him. His imagination had been weak, pathetic, in comparison to the emotion, the violence, the lust he had experienced.

He knew he ought to leave. Mr. Cesar wouldn't want anyone even knowing he had all these books. But Tommy couldn't. He wiped more sweat from his forehead and picked up the book on the table, lying to himself that he'd just read this once more and then go.

Tommy Kidd frowned. The pages were almost blank. Only a word here and there appeared and the story made little sense. He leafed through, glancing at the pages, trying to figure out what this one meant, why it didn't have the impact of the other volumes.

As he flipped through the pages, he yawned, and his eyelids grew heavier. Tommy rubbed his eyes and yawned again. Wait till he told Alan about this. And Patty.

No, he'd tell Michelle! That'd impress her. She'd have to go out with him then and he could . . . he could. Tommy forgot what he'd do with her.

"To, uh, to . . ." He tried to remember the name and failed. But it didn't matter. His head tipped forward. He jerked awake. "Got to tell my . . . my friend. His name. What's his name?" Tommy drifted off again. "Home to . . . where?"

He meant to rest for only a moment, to get the sleep from his eyes. Tommy Kidd's head rested on the open volume and he snored as loudly as his father.

"That's all?" the wizened old man asked. "Only fifteen hundred? Why so cheap?"

"This," said Mr. Cesar, "might be looked upon as something of an experiment."

"You mean it's no good."

"Not at all, not at all," Cesar denied. "This book is crammed with youthful courage, adolescent lust." Mr. Cesar lewdly winked at the old man and nudged him with his elbow. "And that commodity we lose as we age—curiosity. It's all here, all as vibrant as any of my special editions. But it is short, very short."

The old man tried to straighten age-hunched shoulders and said, "I'll take it." He reached for his wallet as Mr. Cesar smiled and began wrapping the book.

Street Life
by
Douglas E. Winter

The street has known many names.

Blevyn Campbell's *Bay Historie*, published by The Greystone Foundation in 1848, tells us of "the house by the cemetery at the foot of Plummer Run." But when Jacob Plummer claimed the rockstrewn eastern slopes of South Hill as his own nearly a century before, his hired laborers brought their horsedrawn cart across a dirt track known to them, as to all members of the Greystone Colony, as the Side Cut. Plummer's dream of a tobacco plantation was soon daunted by the unrelenting soil and thick forests inland of Blind Point, but he held fast to his land, fishing and trapping, never once returning to the harborside settlement where he was born.

Plummer was said by some to call the track Katie's Way, for this was the route taken by his strong-willed daughter in 1753, when, at age seventeen, she departed in the arms of an Irish cotter, never to be seen again. No other

Plummer followed her. Jacob buried first an infant son, then a wife, in the small grove behind his cabin where the track ended and the forest began; he joined them in his eighty-third year—the twentieth of the new American nation—leaving two dogs, three horses, and a twisting half-mile of dirt that time had christened with his name.

Jacob Plummer's heirs were the grandsons of his stepbrother Cedric Cushing, whose family had long before foregone fantasies of landed wealth to thrive in maritime brokerage. From their grand, gabled house on North Hill, the Cushing brothers administered to a series of tenant farmers who worked the meager crops in the rocky fields on either side of Plummer Run. By the time of Blevyn Campbell's revisionist history of the Bay settlement, the farms had failed, and the cabins that dotted the slopes of South Hill were the domain of factory laborers; nearly fifty gravestones stood in the quiet grove where once only the Plummer family had made its rest. It was not until 1886, when Colin Greystone's lumber venture began to strip the forests below South Hill, that the dirt track, soon to be widened by the wheels of countless wagons, took another name. By 1899 shells from the beaches of the Bay hardened the surface of South Hill Road, and ironwork gates guarded the two acres of Hillside Cemetery. Although the lumber trade had slackened, the forests stood at a respectful distance from the large-framed house then under construction.

In 1915 Angus Hawkins brought his horseless carriage and his new wife, Dolly, along the cobblestones of Hillside Road to a Victorian manse that peered out to sea from the site once occupied by Jacob Plummer's cabin. Wealth—the new wealth of industrialists and financiers—had come, for a time, to South Hill. It was a brief fashion; the old money clung to North Hill and has never left. When Greystone Atlantic sold the assets of its lumber division to Schaef-Simpson in the weeks before the stock market crash of 1929, the town fathers reserved the small grove fronting Hillside Cemetery for the long-planned memorial to the thirteen sons of Greystone Bay who had died in the distant fields of France. The blacktopped cul-de-sac, home to those whose wealth had vanished as swiftly as it had arrived, was renamed for the late president. Wilson Road became, it would seem, one with the dead.

In 1969 the street that led to the Memorial was again renamed, in honor of First Lieutenant Linwood Greystone, the town's first and only winner of the Congressional Medal of Honor. His remains were brought along freshly paved concrete in a horsedrawn cart not unlike that which had carried the beginnings of Jacob Plummer's homestead to that lonely place more than two hundred years before. He was laid to rest at the foot of the War Memorial, a marble monolith finally erected by the W.P.A. in 1937. It had doubled in size a decade later, and trebled with the conflicts in Korea and Vietnam, towering, like the many years, over the long-forgotten grave of Jacob Plummer.

Although the place of the dead had grown, the houses of the living had shrunk; the once-proud Victorians had fallen into disarray, then ruin, and were buried beneath the blades of postwar bulldozers. Now two-story brick saltboxes stand in perfect rows along Linwood Avenue, with one-car garages and neatly trimmed lawns, white picket fences and quaint shade trees, and red mailboxes every ·ninety feet. There are numbers instead of names.

Only the street knows that there is a difference.

When Bonnie pulled the second time, Kathy's head came off.

Bonnie was smiling as she sat on the curb. Her left leg curled beneath her, green corduroy skirt hiked high above her knees.

Be nice to your friends. That's what Daddy always said. But it was hard sometimes, especially here on Linwood

Avenue, where there were no boys or girls her own age. If Janie Whaley, her very best friend from school, were around, she'd probably know what to do about Kathy's backtalk. But it was Sunday. And anyway, Janie never came to visit; she lived in a big house on North Hill, and even had a lady who made her bed each and every day. So Bonnie had to make Kathy stop in the only way she knew.

"Silly girl," Bonnie said, clutching the headless torso of the doll to her chest. Kathy's lifeless eyes looked up from the gutter. "Silly, silly girl. Let that be a lesson to you. Don't you ever, never, talk back to me again."

She tossed Kathy's head into her Red Ryder wagon, where it landed facedown against the webbed feet of Mister Crow. Then she carefully cradled the body beneath Ken's right arm.

"Just ride like that for a while, silly girl." Bonnie rubbed at her running nose, victim of the chill September air. "And don't say another word, 'cause I'm mad. M-A-D-D, mad!"

She stood, boosting the wagon's back wheels over a deep slash that zigzagged across the concrete pavement. "Step on a crack . . ." she sang, then let go of the wagon with a laugh. The rear end fell, and the passengers shuddered. Tony the Tiger leaped upward, then slumped back against Barbie's shoulder. Mister Crow squeaked in protest, Donny-o began to sing, and Kathy's head caromed between her twisted legs.

Bonnie slapped her hands together, giggling at the antics of her friends. "Okay!" she shouted, then covered her mouth as she laughed again. "Everybody to the front of the wagon. You first, Mister C!" She pushed the dolls into a heap, tilting the Red Ryder onto its front wheels.

"It's a wheelie-barrow!"

And she started down the street, rolling her friends toward number 1438 and hot chocolate and her very favorite television show, *The Brady Bunch*. The sound took her by surprise, and she almost screamed. It was all Kathy's fault; when Bonnie had stopped to teach her a lesson, she had forgotten where she was. But she knew now. She didn't have to look.

The sound told her. It was like those chattering teeth that you wound up and sat on a table for a joke. But this wasn't a joke. This was like teeth that really bit you.

The sound came from the house, the funny house, the one with the windows gone and the big, big weeds instead of a lawn. The house with the dog, and the typing man.

It was the one place she wasn't supposed to be, not ever. If Mommy and Daddy saw her now, it would be badder than bad.

She pushed harder, running from the chat-chat-chattering, but it just grew louder. The wagon rattled over another crack, and Kathy's bodiless head bounced up and away. As Bonnie dared a single look back, she saw Kathy's beaded eyes twinkle in the sun as the doll's head rolled toward the curb, then disappeared into the darkness of an open drain.

Bonnie ran, tears pulling at her bright blue eyes, and the typing chased after her.

He had seen enough. She was just like the rest. A whiny brat, spying on him. A smart-mouth. Hateful. Worthless.

Mutton.

He grabbed the burning cigarette against the typewriter platen, then swept the cascade of ashes from the wrinkled bread wrapper that was his stationery.

He had started another letter.

He had written letters before. Yes he had. But this time it would be different.

This time they would listen. This time they would have to listen. His letter would tell them things. He would tell them about little blond-haired girls and jowl-faced accountants, old Jew hags and blackety-black studs who diddled with white ladies. About the Oath Father.

About this street and about this town.

And most of all, he would tell them about mutton.

He began to read what he had typed.

Bernard Parrott, tousled hair, dark, tired eyes, slipped the tennis sweater over his head and whispered: "Sunday." He shrugged the sweater across his shoulders, lifted the newspaper from the coffee table, and looked out the picture window to take in the sight of a little red wagon bumping its payload of dolls across the street. Too early for stocking caps—a thought barely structured as he watched the tiny Atwood girl tilt the wagon crazily forward. He laughed as she tried to run.

Bernard Parrott flopped on the couch, sliding the sports section expertly from the clutches of Food and Style.

As he read the headline, his thick cheeks flushed, eyebrows dancing in mock alarm. The Cardinals had dropped three full games behind the Pirates. *Summer's almost gone, boys.* He sipped his orange juice, and caught himself looking for a box score with names like Musial and Gibson, Boyer and Flood. He suddenly felt young again—Topps cards clutched like a whirligig tarot in his tiny fists, the slate of chewing gum tucked into his mouth, balled by his tongue, then slammed into his jowl like Nellie Fox's perennial wad of chewing tobacco.

Sunday, unvoiced this time as he curled against the soft pile of the sofa, deep as a grandmother's embrace. The week seemed to slide away, the audits, the tax letters, the balance sheets forgotten.

Sunday . . .

The pages of the newspaper turned with songs of innocence, a newsprint world so far away—a land of Busch Stadiums where the pennant race never ended, an eternal seventh-inning stretch to a world where terrorist bombings were back-page news, where actors played at presidents while mortgages met the definition of usury and the national security was based upon theories of overkill. *Summer's almost gone, boys.* It was the bottom of the ninth, two outs, Groat and Brock perched on second and third. The curve ball hung, chest-high on the outside corner, and he slammed it deep into left field, back, back . . .

The crowd sighed and rose to their feet as one with a cheer that seemed never to end. Rounding third, he tipped his hat.

He was heading home.

But he never reached the plate. He snapped back from his revery as the tapping of a typewriter, carried on the wind, brought him back to Linwood Avenue—to autumn, to middle age, to the house next door.

At 1430 Linwood Avenue the house was dark. There was no electricity. He had eaten the light bulbs long ago, placing the wiry innards along the kitchen sink, robot guardians on station against the cockroaches that nested in the drains.

Here, in the living room, he sat upon a stack of newspapers; the typewriter perched before him on the windowsill. The glass pane was gone; he had needed to breathe fresh air. The light through the empty frame barely colored the linoleum floor, the urine-stained furniture, the crayoned walls. There was this room, then the kitchen, then the bathroom where no water ran. Then there was a door.

A locked door.

Behind the locked door the other one had lived. The one who had come when his daddy went away. The one who had hurt his mommy with his diddling until she died. The one who had worn the grey suits, going away early in the mornings and coming back at night all smelling of garbage.

The one who had told the stories at the state hospital down in Warrenton. The one who had sworn the oaths.

But let the Oath Father swear. Let him carry his garbage. Let him hide and lock doors. Let him move away in the night and leave me here all alone.

He would write the letter. He would write about the Oath Father and his friends, the ones that the Oath Father had brought to live around him on Linwood Avenue.

He would write the letter. He would write the letter. This time he would finish. Then none of them would laugh, because he would tell.

He would tell on them. The words burned in his mind and gave him headaches. He had to type them.

The Oath Father said he had sworn the oaths, and the doctors had taken him away to Warrenton for so long.

But he had come back. He had come back, and he would tell on them. The typing would tell on them. Then they would all have to go to somewhere bad, like Warrenton, only worse, and they would never come back.

Never.

The teapot snorted a cloud of mist, and a laughing whistle crescendoed from its depths.

Wail on, banshee, thought Sarah Berman, on her knees and groping blindly in the broom closet. She was looking for her cat, and she had returned to the tiny closet for the third time in fifteen minutes, each visit venturing deeper into the shadowed rectangle of floorspace beneath the lower shelf. This time, she had braved the sticky cobwebs to find only an empty Drāno can.

The teapot steamed to a shriek, and she winced as she pulled herself up to stand. Arthritis gnawed at her ankles and knees, and the five steps to the stove seemed like the aftermath of a marathon run. Yet she smiled at the fuming teapot, thinking of Rebecca to ease the pain away, thinking of how, even today, she could recall the words of the

lullaby she had sung on those long nights after Rebecca
was born. Twenty-five years ago, but the tune seemed as
familiar as the morning's news. The song had come to her
again last night as she held Rebecca for the final time as
her little girl.

She lifted the teapot from the burner and poured the
foaming water into a coffee mug half-filled with Lipton's
Cup-a-Soup. Sidestepping the bowl of cream at her feet—
futile enticement for the missing Tillie—Sarah limped
through the foyer to the back porch. As she eased open the
screen door, a cool breeze fanned her face. She smiled
tentatively at the fading sunlight; then her footsteps faltered.

"Not again." She had forgotten the aspirin. Returning
to the kitchen was unthinkable now; her legs were at their
limit. She would wait in her rocking chair on the porch.
Rebecca would be home soon; she would retrieve the
aspirin. Tom Moran would walk her, hand in hand, to the
porch steps, smiling that gentle, knowing smile and waving to Sarah with comfortable friendliness. He would do
right by Rebecca; her *sheygets,* as Sarah had teasingly
called him. And in a few years, the children (how many:
two, three?) would sit at Sarah's feet right here on the
porch, listening intently as she told them about Grandpop
. . . about the good lawyer he had been, about that dinner
with Mr. Justice Frankfurter, about the plaque from the
ACLU Fund . . .

She closed her eyes, pulling her memories around her
like a knitted shawl against the early autumn that seemed to
strip away the most colorful leaves of her life. She was not
lonely; there were friends, occasional visitors—though less
and less as the months after the funeral drifted into years.
Of course, Kay Winslow could be trusted to drop by every
January, back from Boca Raton with her basket of or-
anges. And there was Rebecca—and Tillie. But the house
seemed to empty a little more each day. Every Wednesday
she would dust the guest bedroom and the little den, yet

she would not return to those rooms until the next cleaning day. The house was her life—it had been since 1947, when Daniel had used an inherited five hundred dollars and the good office of the G.I. Bill to buy that good place then known as 1448 Wilson Road. But now that life seemed to be shrinking, her sixty-three years collapsing in on her. She saw herself in five years, blanket draped across her aching knees, sipping bland soup and doddering on about the good old days. But that's life, she thought; just like old blue-eyes used to sing.

In time, Sarah Berman fell asleep, but not until she heard the silky purr, the soft thumping, as the chubby calico cat named Tillie pawed up the porch stairs to cuddle at her feet.

She dreamed of a Sunday afternoon unblemished by the sound of a distant typewriter.

the Parrotmen lIves In 1440Linwood Ave this drty FLy inFecKted GREYstonme BAy./To-day so called humans put FoOdbOnE trashoUT uin back of <ME LETTERWRITERS yARD For my pet Hound to FIND Like chicken Bones ect. ect. ect. SO pL:EASE note jhust so theYH Fuck on poor my ANGELA SOUL myPet basset hound. THis oath Reder A SiMple LIGHT as bright as dawn CAN NOT READ THE PRINRT OF oath Law.

THis is about how bright the OPath reder is. HE is afraid AnGwela that basset Hound might HACK it uout in back yARD so NoW ME LETTERWRITER got it dog HACKING tyhe street twuice, sometime three time, as much as JewHAG out of 1448Linwood Ave thisd irty flyinefected GReystone ect. ect.

PLEAsed also NOTE Oath comiss. itslef and freak JEsus here just didDle om ME LETTERWRITERS life, about MRs. Jew Berman, 1448 and THe nmigger-man saw me yeswterday and a day other that HIT

please also NOTE HIT on ME LETTERWRITER,
LItTle girls too, full of **MoRE FroM the NUThoues
all the ShIT oathDFFather was phonyfgut and A hole
like beat ME up ap MY HoUse 1430LiNWOOD this
DirTy ect.

Through the open bathroom window washed the unmistakable rattle of typewriter keys. It reminded Charles Monteith of the office, an alien world just a few blocks distant
from Linwood Avenue. Weekends had become a peculiar
agony, a time of breathless escape that was doomed to end
before it had really begun. Sunday afternoon had grab-
bagged a hundred things to do, but very little had been
accomplished. Rake the leaves, watch a little football on
the tube, run some errands, take a nap—and another day
had slid away, lost and soon to be forgotten.
Time is but a stream I go fishing in. . . . Someone had
written that—Monteith liked to believe that it was Fenimore
Cooper, but he knew just as well that it was that wimp
Thoreau. Well, he thought, let me pop the top on another
Bud and take a few more casts before Monday.
He patted shaving cream onto his face. As he glanced
into the mirror, movement flickered in its depth. Spinning
about, he glimpsed Sheila through the crack of the door.
She stood at the top of the steps to the first floor with
undisguised reluctance; her pregnancy, at eight months,
had given her tiny body an almost comical hugeness. She
had told him last week that descending the stairs gave her
the most frightening feeling of enormity. Her middle seemed
a balloon that kept inflating; she was afraid that she would
miss a step, only to fly upward, buoying against the ceiling.
"Man the mooring cables!" he called from the doorway.
She turned halfway, auburn hair angling across a pale,
freckled face that burned with surprise. "You have better
things to do, sir," she said. "We are running late, you
know."

Monteith turned back to the mirror, speaking to her reflection as he reached for the razor. "Not to worry, kiddo. No one's going to lose any sleep over a few minutes. It's not dark yet, anyway."

She seemed to count the fingers of her left hand, pausing to twist the thin silver band of her wedding ring. "Charlie?"

He passed the razor quickly over the dripping foam.

"Charlie?"

"I can hear you. Let me finish up. . . ."

"I just wanted to tell you something."

He stepped onto the landing. He had left shaving cream along his upper lip, a white mustache that accented the ebony of his face.

"We love you," she said, patting her stomach. "I'll be happy when this is over."

Though she spoke nearly in a whisper, her voice seemed to echo through the house.

His hand reached to take hers.

It was the silence, they realized. The sudden silence.

The typing had stopped.

The hand that laid against the keys was not at rest. It shook abruptly, as if longing to type again. His fingers were long, stained with tobacco, their nails torn with endless biting. Even though he knew that he was finished, still his index finger tapped the letter *i* again and again and again. He paused for a moment, considering the page's final line:

i ii i i I i iI i i i i iI I i IIi I Ii

Then, so that no one would misunderstand, he typed:

ME

He slid the letter from the typewriter, folded it twice, then stuffed it into his shirt pocket. He had no need for an envelope; his letter could not be trusted to the post office. He would deliver it personally to one of the green boxes where the government's mail was sent.

He looked up from the typewriter with reluctance. Outside, the first stars had replaced the afternoon sun, white-hot ashes scattered across a sudden darkness.

The black time meant that he had to walk the dog.

He called for his hound, the sole word he had spoken that day. His throat seemed filled with dry fire.

There was no answer, no gentle growl, no panted breaths, no soft nails clicking across the yellowed linoleum floors.

He called again, backing away from the windowsill, walking slowly into the kitchen. At the base of the refrigerator sat two empty food bowls. Cool air breathed against his face. He saw that the kitchen door was open.

She's gone out, he realized. Gone out without me. I didn't pay her no attention, and she up and went.

That was when he heard the soft whine.

He ran out the kitchen door, down the three short steps, and off the porch. In the sudden dusk he could barely make out the familiar shapes of his backyard and the cemetery beyond. A rusted-out 1963 Chevy convertible sat upon concrete blocks next to the garage; beside it was piled a jumble of tires. But there seemed to be something else.

He squinted, and the shadows seemed to move.

"Hound?" he called, and the shadows *did* move. Then he heard the whine again, softer this time, behind him; in his haste he had gone past her.

He turned; she was curled against the stairs. How could he have missed her? Her head dropped at the corner of the bottom step.

"Hound?"

He bent to grab her collar; then he saw the thick red

stain at her throat. The fur seemed to have been shaved, and a slit several inches in length gaped across her neck. He released the collar with a moan, and the dog's head bounced on the step, then fell away into the shadows below. He staggered backward, shouting unformed words.

From somewhere in the dark he heard metal scrape against metal. Footsteps. A woman's whisper. Hoarse laughter.

A match flickered to life near the useless Chevy; then a small torch erupted into flames.

He saw the black face first—so smooth, so clean-shaven, its lips spread into a leering smile. The black man carried the torch; as he brought it forward, a grinning young white woman stepped beside him, hands clutched protectively around her bloated stomach. Then came another man, this one white and jowl-faced but smiling the same smile. He wore a faded red baseball cap. In his right hand he held a sawed-off baseball bat, snapping it in rhythm as he walked. His left hand curled around the arm of an old woman, helping her forward. Each step she took seemed to scar her face with pain, yet her movements were determined. A straight razor was clutched in her thin, wrinkled hands. She, too, was smiling.

All of them were smiling.

He tried to speak. Then he saw the little girl, hidden by the shadows, only footsteps away. She dragged a tiny red wagon that was packed with tiny creatures. As he watched, the girl stopped and reached down, shunting aside a Barbie doll and a stuffed crow. She grasped the long wooden handle of an ax. And she held the ax upward for the black man to take.

The torch fluttered as the black man tossed it to the ground. The light shifted downward, and the dry grass began to burn.

He could see the little girl clearly now, and she reached

again into the wagon. This time she raised a twisted plastic figure; he saw its naked arms and legs.

As the flames began to dance, mirrored in the blade of the ax, she turned to him, still smiling, and said:

"My dolly needs a new head."

Something in a Song
by
Galad Elflandsson

Sean Michael O'Hara slogged wearily up Port Boulevard, his boots squelching through five inches of snow rapidly disintegrating into slush as the temperature crept above freezing. Around him Greystone Bay swam in a damp drenching of fog that turned street lights into vague nebulas of light, vagrant stars in a tideless sea.

He brushed sodden strands of dark hair from his face with one gloved hand, checked the pocket of his pea coat for the tenth time for the comforting solidity of the small bottle of whiskey, and clutched the handle of his guitar case more tightly. When he turned left to climb Mayfield Street, his stride lengthened perceptibly, and his thoughts turned again to the Waterford Tavern with a cautious jubilation.

"Well . . . you waked Sweeney up and that's a neat trick," the owner had said. "And you're not playin' any o' that damned noise passes for music these days. . . ."

Gerald O'Shaughnassy had winked at him then, his freshly shaven face losing its look of tired indifference as he grinned through the dingy half-light of his establishment.

"Then too, I'm not the one t'turn a deaf ear to a good Irish lad's tunes," he said kindly. "Sure, Mr. Sean Michael O'Hara, I'll take you on for a week or two. I can't pay you much . . . but we'll give you a try, Tuesdays to Saturdays, and see what happens. . . ."

Sean grinned and did an ungainly two-step to the refrain of "The Rocky Road to Dublin." Midway up South Hill he reached the misty void that was his turn onto Dannel Street, and muted clangs and creakings from the wharves below drifted past him; listening harder, he thought he could even catch a faint wash of the tide from the harbor at his back. He plunged into the blank whiteness of Dannel and, halfway down the block, did a fair job of almost breaking his neck on the three steps down to the door of his basement apartment. As he fumbled with his keys, the door swung open and a flood of warmth and golden light rushed out to welcome him.

"Sean, my god, where've you been? I'm half crazy worryin'—"

He stepped blindly through the doorway, set his guitar down, and wrapped his arms around the slender, flame-haired young woman standing there, kissed the dusting of freckles across the bridge of her nose and then sought her lips hungrily.

"Oh Sean, Christ! I've been havin' fits and you've been out drinkin'!"

She squirmed in his embrace and he found himself staring into a wrathful pair of flashing green eyes.

"Just one, Karen," he said, laughing. "I just had one . . . to seal the bargain."

She stepped back from him angrily, hands on her hips, and he drank in the sight of her—legs in dancer's tights and woolen legwarmers, the rest of her soft and glistening in a silvery Danskin.

"What bargain?" she demanded. "Your supper's been two hours in the garbage pail."

He grinned at her shamelessly, took his time closing the door behind him.

"To hell with supper, my dearest darlin'," he said, pulling the bottle of whiskey from his pocket. "Put the kettle on and we'll have ourselves a small celebration with this instead."

Before Karen could approach the foot-stamping stage, he told her the tale of his wanderings and his last, what-the-hell foray into the Waterford on Harbor Road.

". . . So I played some jigs and I played some reels and I played a few Stan Rogers tunes and then Sweeney in the corner woke up and Mr. Gerald O'Shaughnassy decided to take pity on a poor, struggling countryman.

"It's only fifteen dollars a night, Karen," he concluded, "and it's bloody slavery for the five hours, but I can still look for day work, and seventy-five dollars a week, with your wages at the tailor shop, will get us by for now. . . ."

She said nothing as he slipped out of his coat and tugged off his boots, but only stared at him for a moment or two before crossing the one room that served them as living/dining room and kitchen to put the kettle on the stove. From where he sat by the door, he saw her shoulders slump and heard her sobbing.

"Karen . . . ?"

He felt his heart begin a steady pounding in his chest as he followed her, took her in his arms again.

"Karen, what's wrong?"

Her eyes were brimming with tears as she turned to him, clutched at his shirt with an almost desperate ferocity.

"Oh, Sean, I'm sorry. I'm such an ass. It's just . . . it's just that I'm so tired of only gettin' by . . . and fifteen dollars a night, Sean! You're worth more than that—"

"O'Shaughnassy said it could be more if my playin' helped pick his trade up some," Sean said quickly.

"That's not the point, Sean!" she cried. "It's not what I'm goin' on about either," she finished miserably.

She looked up at him and he felt the force of her despondency, saw it with painful clarity in her eyes.

"Your dancing," he sighed.

She nodded, put her head against his chest.

"I'm nineteen, Sean," she whispered. "I've been danc- ing, and practicing, and praying since I was ten years old and I've got nothin' t'show for it, Sean. I can't even afford to pay for a place in a workshop . . . and in a few more years it's going t'be too late, Sean, much too late. I'll spend the rest of my life lettin' out seams and takin' up hems and in the end I'll have sweet fuck all, Sean. . . ."

"Karen . . . I'm sorry, love. . . ." he said hoarsely. "I'm doin' the best I can for us. . . ."

She sensed the hurt in his words and looked up at him suddenly, her eyes wide and bright with new tears.

"No, Sean, I didn't mean it that way. I know you're tryin', I do. I'd've given up a long time ago . . . without you . . . I love you so much, but sometimes it's so hard. . . ."

The kettle started whistling and she turned away to pour the boiling water into a battered tin teapot. When they were snuggled together on the couch, with two whiskey-fragrant mugs of tea between them, he brushed away the last of her tears.

"Things are goin' t'be different real soon, Karen," he said softly. "You'll see . . . things'll change. We'll make 'em change startin' right now."

She sipped her tea slowly, with both hands round the mug, like a child, and nodded.

Sean stepped gratefully into the warmth of the Waterford and collapsed against the door, eyes closed and with a chill certainty in his heart that he had frozen to death; that his body had died and only the sheer intensity of his now-defunct will had brought his corpse in from the cold.

"Good evenin' to ya, Mr. O'Hara," came a voice from behind the bar. "From the look of ya I'd say it was a bit nippy out there."

Sean opened his eyes and found Gerald O'Shaughnassy's grinning face.

"N-n-nippy . . . ?" he managed through chattering teeth. "Mr. O'Shaughnassy, I had t'fight a polar bear t'get through your door."

The Irishman chuckled and reached up to turn off the small black and white television on a shelf above the bar. He turned back to Sean with a serious air.

"Must be the same one I've had t'turn out twice already tonight," he said. "Not allowed t'serve polar bears in a public tavern."

A few snorts and one loud burst of laughter echoed across the taproom, and Sean took his first real look at the Waterford and its patrons—a small wood-floored space occupied by a dozen or so scarred tables, low-beamed ceiling almost black with age, and the thick aroma of years of tobacco smoke and whiskey ingrained in the wood. The bar itself occupied most of the wall to his right, and in the center of the rear wall, framed by two wooden posts, stood the microphone stands and amplifier he had delivered to the tavern that afternoon.

The laughter came from a handful of middle-aged men at two tables in the middle of the room, who nodded and raised their glasses to Sean as he dropped his coat and guitar case beside the amplifier. One of them growled at him good-naturedly.

"You'd better be good, lad," he said, scratching at a day's worth of grey stubble on his face. "The only reason I'm down here t'night's t'see you wake old Sweeney up again."

Another burst of subdued laughter followed, and Sean politely replied that he'd do his best not to disappoint him. O'Shaughnassy beckoned to him and offered a shot glass of amber liquid.

"Here you go, Mr. O'Hara," he said amiably. "Somethin' t'brace you up . . . on the house, of course. I'll not have you disappointin' that rascal MacManus for lack o' warmth in your bones. Drink up, and then we'll let you get on with your business. . . ."

Fifteen minutes later Sean tuned his guitar and swung into a rendition of "The Jolly Beggar" . . . amid shouts of wonder and amazement as old Sweeney in the corner woke up in the middle of the first verse.

". . . It was really strange, Karen. I did a couple o' sets of the lively stuff—jigs and reels and that sort of thing—and by ten o'clock I'd swear there was near twenty old gents in the place havin' a grand time of it. . . .

"Then I slowed things down. Did the best 'Carrickfergus' I've ever done. Followed with 'Carraig Dun' and 'Ae Fond Kiss.'. . .

"And all of a sudden it was as quiet as the grave, and all o' them were starin' at me with the queerest look on their faces and I saw that Polish guy, the one Gerald introduced as Jake, with tears runnin' down his face. I don't think he understood half the words, for all the Scots dialect, but he was cryin' like a baby, Karen!"

She turned to him in the darkness and kissed him sleepily on the lips.

"It sounds wonderful, Sean . . . but I've got t'get up early t'morrow," she said drowsily. "He was probably drunk. . . ."

She rolled over again and Sean stared into the darkness.

"Karen . . . ?"

"Go t'sleep, Sean. You're drunk too. . . ."

*   *   *

. . . What's the use in tryin'
When no matter what you've got
There's nobody buyin'
And layin' down and dyin'
Is all that's left to do . . .

Sean strummed a final chord and let it echo through the
listening silence, looking out over his audience, holding
his breath as he waited for their reaction. Someone near
the door pulled out a handkerchief and blew into it noisily,
and then the rest broke into a respectful sort of applause,
and some laughter at the expense of the handkerchief-
wielder. Sean nodded, set his guitar down, and walked
over to the end of the bar. O'Shaughnassy filled a pair of
shot glasses and joined him.

"Well, Mr. O'Hara," he said, beaming as he placed one
of the glasses before Sean. "It seems that I've made a fine
choice in takin' you on. Scarcely two weeks and you're
playin' to a full house."

He gestured grandly at the taproom, where all but one of
the tables held a full complement of patrons—a ragtag of
dockmen, sailors, factory workers and oldsters—and raised
his glass.

"Here's t'the two of us, Mr. Sean Michael O'Hara"—he
grinned—"and t'the twenty-five dollars a night I'll be
payin' you startin' next week."

Sean choked his whiskey down and sputtered while the
Irishman pounded him on the back.

"Mr. O'Shaughnassy—"

"Gerald, lad, if you please," he said heartily. "And
don't be thinkin' you're takin' advantage of a fellow
Irishman's better nature. I'd not be offerin' the extra money
if I couldn't afford it."

He lowered his voice and leaned across the bar.

"Truth bein', lad, I've not seen this much trade in the

place in years. You've earned the extra silver and you're welcome to it.''

"Thank you, Mist—Gerald," Sean said, smiling. "I'm really happy things have worked out so well.''

"That they have, Sean," he said, nodding. "But I've got a question for you, lad. I didn't recognize a few o' the tunes you did just a while back . . . and that last one, in particular. . . .''

Sean stopped breathing.

"I hope you didn't mind them, Mr. O'Shaughnassy,'' he said slowly. "I didn't think you'd object if I sang one or two o' the things I'd written myself.''

"You wrote them songs yourself?''

Sean nodded. "Were they all right? I mean . . . did I . . . ?''

O'Shaughnassy frowned, peered over the countertop at him.

"Sure they was all right, lad," he said softly. "Not the cheeriest tunes I'd ever heard . . . I'm no judge o' the quality o' such things, mind you . . . it's just that I didn't recognize 'em, that's all. . . .''

"I'll leave off doin' them if you'd rather—''

"Don't be foolish, lad," O'Shaughnassy growled. "You're doin' just fine. They're just a bit different from what I was expectin' and . . .''

The Irishman moved off to serve a customer, muttering the rest of his sentence to no one at all.

". . . And you wouldn't believe what some o' these people have lived through, Karen. There's Jake, the Polish gent . . . his wife and son and his whole family were wiped out during the Second World War. And Sweeney's son went back to Ireland, took up with the IRA and blew himself up with a bomb in Dublin. Then there's Terry O'Leary who lost an arm on an oil tanker . . . and Frank

MacArran's wife with three and a half years dyin' o' cancer . . .''

Karen looked up from the plate of macaroni and cheese before her and put her fork down.

"Sean, I got laid off at the tailor shop today."

"Y'know, you really should come down one night and see it, love. And it's not like you'd be the only woman there now either. A lot o' them are bringin' their wives with 'em these days. Johnny Kirk's wife, Mary, is goin' blind day by day, but you'd never know by lookin' at her. And they're even askin' me t'play the songs I've written . . .''

"Sean, didn't you hear what I just said?"

"Are you sure you won't come down for a night and listen to me, Karen? They're all dyin' t'meet you. . . .''

Sean took a long pull from the bottle of whiskey beside him and grinned at the sea of faces turned to him, all staring with rapt concentration, waiting on his every word, straining to hear every note.

The Waterford was a vast echoing cavern of smoke haze and whiskey fumes, men and women crammed around the tables, standing two and three deep at the bar, lounging against the walls. He tried counting their numbers once or twice, but his tally became muddled between forty and fifty, when all the faces started to look the same—old, grizzled faces, lined and seamed and bristly with grey stubble, eyes with watery, washed-out colors. He shook his head and strummed a few chords.

"See if you can wake Sweeney, lad!" cried a shrill voice from somewhere in the crowd. "We know you can do it. Play somethin' lively-like t'wake old Sweeney . . .''

And Sean played "Rantin' Rovin' Robin" with a vengeance, while the sea of faces swiveled back and forth betwixt him and old Sweeney in the corner . . . and he closed his eyes as he played, his fingers dragging chords from the guitar, and the Waterford rang to his voice and the howl of his audience cheering him on.

"You can do it, lad!"

"Aye! You done it before and you'll do it again!"

"Louder, boy, you'll have t'play louder this time!"

And Sean played louder, pounding at the strings, shouting the chorus as sweat poured from his face with the effort, on and on until it seemed like he had been playing and singing forever and it was the only thing in the world he had ever done in his life, and when a gentle hand fell upon his shoulder he could have screamed with frustration.

"It's no use, Sean," whispered Gerald O'Shaughnassy. "Leave off tryin' t'wake old Sweeney. For God's sakes, it's been almost a week. . . ."

The song ended with an aimless scattering of notes as Sean's hand dropped from the fingerboard and he opened his eyes.

"I could've done it, Gerald," he said hoarsely. "Just a little longer and I could've done it."

The Irishman shook his head wearily, and suddenly Sean noticed how old his employer had become—the glossy cheeks gone grey and sunken, the mop of red-gold hair turned almost white, his sparkling eyes glazed and colorless.

"No, lad, he got too tired and there's naught we can do anymore," O'Shaughnassy said tonelessly. "For a while there he seemed like t'forget, but it came back to him in the end. That song o' yours . . ."

He hummed a few bars of the refrain, stopped abruptly, began again. Sean joined him, and then everyone in the Waterford sang with them . . . softly. . . .

> ". . . What's the use in tryin'
> When no matter what you've got
> There's nobody buyin'
> And layin' down and dyin'
> Is all that's left to do . . ."

The tavern grew still and utterly silent when they were finished. Sean wiped tears from his eyes and looked past O'Shaughnassy, to the uncountable faces that stared at him unwaveringly.

"I didn't mean t'do it," he cried. "It was just somethin' that came . . . one night . . . when Karen was so sad. . . ."

The faces nodded in comprehension, expressionless faces . . . old faces . . . so tired . . . so sad . . .

"Aye, well, it's no hard t'understand, lad," said O'Shaughnassy beside him. "She was in here three . . . no . . . it was four nights ago. You could see it in her face too. She just stood by the door for a few minutes and went away. . . ."

Sean reached for the whiskey bottle and felt the Irishman's hand steadying him on his stool.

"Karen?" he said dazedly. "Karen was here?"

The faces nodded again, making soft rustling noises.

"Aye, that she was. Janey Riley heard her say she was worried on account o' you not bein' home in . . . How many days was it, Janey?"

"Not bein' home?" Sean's hands clawed at O'Shaughnassy's shoulders. "What are you talkin' about, Gerald, me not bein' home?"

"Didn't you know, lad?" he said with a tired smile. "We been here for days . . . weeks . . . I don't know . . . it doesn't matter anymore. . . ."

The old bartender patted him affectionately on the shoulder.

"You just go on playin', Sean, and things will look after themselves. You'll see. You just keep playin' . . . that song . . . the one you wrote yourself. . . ."

He watched O'Shaughnassy shuffle back to the bar, rummage around in one of the drawers beneath it. Then he turned back to the dust and the cobwebs and the nodding faces with dead eyes in bleached white skulls and he began to play again. O'Shaughnassy smiled approvingly as he walked past him, to the washroom at the rear of the tavern.

When the gunshot thundered out of the washroom, Sean closed his eyes and kept on singing.

Hiding From the Sun
by
Nina Kiriki Hoffman

—Home is where the sink is—

I come home from my work at the data center, soap my hands, and wash life down the drain. Take off my shoes—shoes have slapped the surface of life—remove my clothes—clothes have brushed the hems of life—and change into my at-home things. These clothes, ordered from catalogs, arrived in brown wrappings that sheltered them from contact with human hands, coming from warehouses, unpawed by consumers. I wash the clothes thrice before I wear them.

As long as I keep all the curtains closed, life can't get to me at home.

But that boy, that little fat boy keeps rattling the back door knob. He must come from the Land of Good Neighbors, where you can visit any house on the block and not suffer. He comes by every evening. After I pull my car into the garage and press the button that shuts the garage door, I sit in the welcome dark for my five-minute allowance, then open the car door and change my clothes by the car's dome light. The child is always there rattling the knob by the time I come from the garage into the kitchen.

I have seen him. I lifted the curtain a little and peeked out. He is very small, with curly gold hair and rosy cheeks, like a Renaissance cherub. He tugs on the door knob, a meaningless smile in his blue eyes, rattles a few moments in a random pattern I cannot pretend is an appliance, then leaves, still smiling.

He is very small. Even if the Beast is large in him, he is too small to hurt me. Those tiny arms and legs, that tiny torso . . .

I marvel that none of the neighbors have told him I am the witchwoman, the spook of spookhouse, strictly to be left alone. He seems so friendly. Surely he rattles other back door knobs. Surely the others ply him with cookies and gossip. Perhaps he is too young to understand. Perhaps he is too young to play host to the Beast.

But one is never too young to become a victim of the Beast, as I did when I was a little older than he, in my back-door-knob-rattling days.

Perhaps I should warn him.

Surely he can't hurt me.

He is an agent of the Beast.

I let him in yesterday, being careful to keep out of his reach—the Beast can wound with a touch. He smiled and smiled at me. I held my hands ready to cover my ears. The Beast can invade with a word. I blinked, prepared to close my eyes. The Beast can reveal himself by light, and any who have seen him before recognize him much more easily the next time, for they constantly watch for him; they cannot help it; he has spoiled them, polluted them, planted a living terror and disgust in them which cannot be washed away with soap.

"Hello," said the child. "What's your name?"

"Mary," I said. I would not give him my real name, for I know the power of names. The Beast whispered my name, telling me to be still, to never tell, convincing me that to tell would be to end the world. I watched his watch flash with captured light as it swung before me, and listened to his voice possess my name as his body afterward violated my body. Every time he repeated my name, he stole a little piece of my soul.

I have never gotten my name back. It is a word empty of all I once was, badly grafted onto my present self. It is a mask I try to pretend belongs on my face, when all the nerve endings have died. Even so, I never reveal it. Perhaps I still own a sliver of it. I don't want to give anyone else the power to steal it.

"My name's Teddy," said the child.

"Well, Teddy, hasn't anyone ever told you it's dangerous to knock on strangers' doors?"

"No," he said with a beatific smile. He glanced around my gleaming kitchen, where I don't allow even my own fingerprints a moment's rest. He tottered across the linoleum I have scrubbed so often I've worn the patterns off. I watched his wake to see if he left muddy footprints, sand from the beach, but I could not spot any; nevertheless I made a mental chart of his route, reminding myself that his trail would need an extra antiseptic cleansing. Through careful practice, I had almost washed life's spoor off me, but this child, alight with life, would take some cleaning up after.

"There is always someone waiting to kill or harm a little child like you," I told the boy.

"No," he said, smiling at me and shaking his head. Then he pushed the door open and went into my front room.

He had gone too far. It was only another in a series of life's invasions. Even if I had to—to touch him, I resolved to send him out of my house. I followed him into my front room.

He was at one of the windows, pulling at the curtain, not knowing, perhaps, that I had sewed them shut.

"Leave those alone!" I said.

He gave an enormous tug, and the curtains tumbled, rod and all, on top of him, baring my front room to the open eyes of the sky and the street. I stepped aside, into shadow.

"An afternoon's worth of sunshine," he said, fighting his way free of the curtains.

"Get out of my house." I tamed my panic, becoming as much of an automaton as I could. Stimulus. Response. Proper programing eliminates responses to a wide range of stimuli, or categorizes such stimuli in such broad terms that they become intrinsically meaningless.

"Good-bye, Mary. I'll see you tomorrow," he said. He left.

I lost some of my distance after he had gone, letting frenzy and distress come to my aid as I wiped out all his traces and replaced my curtains. But the sun shone on my face while I did it; I could not prevent that; and I could not wait for darkness, because once darkness falls, people can see into an unguarded window more easily than a person inside can see out.

He forced me into the sun. He is the Beast's tool.

I resolved not to let him in again, but his persistent rattling disrupts my concentration. Even when I go upstairs to my workroom, I can hear him at the back door.

In my workroom I am building a dollhouse. I have painted the wallpaper with tiny bunches of flowers; I have framed postage stamps to hang as portraits on the walls; I have crafted tiny, perfect furniture and pieced together little curtains. This work has taken me several years. Just now I am working the floors, carving thin strips of wood to lay down as planking. Every detail is perfect. I have researched my house. It is from Victorian times. From North Hill. I tell myself the Beast did not exist in those days, certainly not in the Bay. I imagine a family living in this house. They are kind and genteel and speak only of picnics and summer, fireworks, homemade ice cream, and church.

But the child has spoiled that. He made me cut myself while I was carving the wood strips. Blood should not invade my house. I had to clean and clean to get it off; then my hands shook too much to continue work. Now I am afraid to go back to my workroom, afraid that I will ruin years of work through carelessness. Instead, I sit in the kitchen and listen to the child rattling the door knob.

He does it for longer periods every day, invading with sound where he cannot in the flesh. Listening to his noise forces me to listen to my self again, to be aware that I am not quite as lifeless as I thought. I notice that my stomach knots with tension as I listen, that my nails hurt my palms when I clench my fists. Feelings travel through me: I am not the thing of crystal, wood, and metal I wish to be. And my house, so carefully fortified, is not impregnable. My safeguards begin to crumble.

Yesterday when I came home I forgot to wash my hands, leaving invisible blemishes everywhere. I was not sure afterward whether I had managed to wipe them all away either: the child's racket distracted me sufficiently, so I could not recall what I had touched. Even as I tried to sleep, I was conscious that I must have missed a few.

I spoke to him today.

I lifted the curtain, chancing the sunlight, knowing it had not touched me since the day I let the child in—it cannot reach into my garage, nor in the parking garage at work, and I tinted all the windows of my car dark grey; sunlight touches me only when I must shop. I can stand a little of it.

"Mary," said the child, "why don't you let me in?"

"What do you want?" I asked.

"I want a cookie."

It was such a little-boy thing to say, a thing only an untouched child would say. The Beast and his brothers are everywhere. One reads of children poisoned, of children who have disappeared, of children who turn up dead or molested. I feared for the child, tiny vessel of the Beast though he might be.

"You must not ask strangers for food," I said. "Never. Never ask strangers for anything you need."

"You're not a stranger. I know your name," he said.

I let the curtain fall, shutting out his cherubic face, but I could not shut out my memories of that blurring, swinging oblong of light, glancing off the watch back, and the Beast's voice, whispering my name. Even a borrowed name could be stolen and used if I became accustomed enough to it.

"Go away, Teddy," I said, wondering if Teddy was really his name, and if it could be used to control him. "Teddy, go away and don't come back."

"I'll see you tomorrow, Mary," he said.

Teddy is probably not his real name.

Those grimy little fingers. I can imagine the oil from their tips eroding away the polished brass of my back door knob, tarnishing it so it no longer catches the sun. I think of his filthy fingerprints on my white back door, eating into the pristine paint. He rattles and rattles the knob, calling the name I have given him. Sometimes he makes it a quick two syllables, and sometimes he stretches the first one out, so I cannot pretend it is just the calling of a bird in the orange tree in my backyard.

I have told him several times to go away. I do not understand his persistence. What does he want from me? Where does he come from?

*   *   *

I let him in again today. It was either that or madness.

This time he did not pause in my kitchen at all, but headed straight for the living room and my curtains. "No!" I said, coming closer to him, wondering what it would feel like to grasp those fat, rosy little arms and pull him away from the window. Would my fingers sink into his flesh? Would his flesh be warm? Would my touch bring blood? A touch always brought blood, in my experience. Touches hurt. But did they hurt the toucher as well as the touched?

He pulled the curtains down before I could reach him, squirmed to the other window, and pulled down the other curtains. Sunlight blazed into the room. I covered my face with my hands.

"What are you hiding from, Mary?" he asked. I heard the Beast uncoil in his voice. "Why are you so pale? Sunlight can't hurt you."

Only in sleep could I be safe. Sleep blinds and deafens me, freeing me from the vulnerable flesh.

"Mary," said the child. "Mary, come into the light."

I lowered my hands and looked at him. He was beautiful, small and tender, as I must have once been. The sunlight seemed to sheath him in innocence.

But it also gleamed from something else in the room. I caught the gleam out of the corner of my eye, and turned. There, in the center of the coffee table it lay. A legacy from a particular vessel of the Beast.

The watch.

I stepped forward, into a light I could not turn off with a switch, knowing at last why it frightened me. It shone through me like an X-ray, revealing the hidden form of the Beast within. My hand reached for the watch chain. Light flashed off the watch as it spun and rose. "Teddy," I murmured. "Teddy. Look at the light, Teddy."

Memory and Desire
by
Alan Ryan

1 / Memory

I can see Greystone Bay from the window of my room in the Atlantic View Hotel.

The surface of the water looks slick, grey-green, strangely glossy. It pulses, undulates as if with a steady but fierce intake of breath. Sometimes it appears to shudder. It is the breeze, or some invisible change of air pressure, I suppose, that does that, but it looks to me as if the waters themselves are alive, like a beast taking up a threatening stance.

Above the Bay, the sky is the same color, roiled with the uncertain shapes of billowing dark clouds, slate grey, pencil-lead grey, trying vainly to be silver. The clouds shift constantly, their shapes twisting as if with slow torture, and re-form into shapes that are darker yet. The daylight itself, thoroughly drained and filtered of life by those shapes, looks grey itself. It has a tangible, if brittle, quality, that daylight. It makes me feel that I could stretch an arm from the window and actually touch it. And it makes me feel that, if I did so, the light itself would shatter and the day would be driven into dark.

The Atlantic View Hotel does not afford a view of the Atlantic Ocean.

At one time the hotel must have been a lovely *grande dame* of a Victorian house. I can imagine it painted peach, for example, with neat black shutters and black trim on the porch and the cornices and cupolas. I can see it blazing with candlelight, gaslight, that special yellow glow of Victorian security that, by itself, could repel the Atlantic winds. I imagine the house felt very secure then to its inhabitants: all these rooms, all of them small and therefore cozy, and all that lovely yellow light. Yes, I'm certain it felt very secure.

It does not feel secure now. Outside, it is painted a uniform white. The painting was not done recently, and the salty winds have left their mark. Walls have been taken out on the first floor and replaced by narrow columns, making room for the Atlantic View Restaurant. Upstairs, the rooms have been furnished with blue-painted nighttables and other motley prizes gleaned at yard sales and barn auctions. There are two bathrooms per floor and the plumbing is noisy. The Jamesons, who own the place, live somewhere at the back. The whole house has a faint odor of fried clams at all hours of the day.

Yet I am one of the lucky ones. My window is at the front of the house, on Harbor Road, and I can see the Bay. I can see the wooden boardwalk across the street—empty of human life now—and the narrow strip of gravelly beach beyond it. If I lean out the window and look to the right, I can see, outlined against the greyness of the sky, the dark, rocky heights of Blind Point. If the weather were nice— which, at the moment, seems unlikely ever to be the case again—I could, presumably, watch nubile young women sunning themselves in red bikinis on the beach.

I think awhile about that, longing for a beach brilliant with sunshine and bathing suits and blond young women, while the day sinks inexorably and before its time into night.

I turn away from the window. What shall I do now? I have books with me but the light in the room is too dim for reading.

But I know I couldn't concentrate on a book anyway. Not yet, at least.

I have crossed a continent to come to Greystone Bay.

I have come here to find the shadow of my father.

And in the hour since my arrival, I have already learned how difficult that will be. Greystone Bay is alive with shadows.

When I come down the stairs from my room, I see Mr. Jameson behind the open half-door that serves as a registration desk. He and his wife do not seem to have first names. THE JAMESONS, PROPRIETORS, says the faded sign outside and the wrinkled folder I was handed earlier. He looks up as I reach the bottom of the steps and his eyes meet mine. There is no expression on his face, neither smile nor frown nor curiosity. He has not shaved for, I would guess, two days. Will he still look like that when I see him again in the morning?

"What time do you serve dinner?" I ask.

"Six to nine," he says. There is still no expression on his face, and his lips barely move when he speaks.

"Do you have a license?"

He looks at me.

"Do you serve drinks? Liquor."

"Yes."

We have reached a dead end and we stand there, looking at each other.

"But you don't have a bar," I say, looking around. "I was looking for a bar." I feel a nasty little pleasure at making this point.

He counters with, "Why did you come here?"

"Saw your sign," I say. I can be laconic too.

"Greystone Bay."

I'll be damned if I'll tell *him*. "Rest," I say. "I wanted someplace quiet. Remote," I add, for good measure.

There is not a flicker of change in his face. He won't allow me to score points.

"Well, then," I say, and start toward the front door. "I'll see you in the morning at breakfast." I have a little triumph in that, but I will have to pay for it by finding some other place to eat and by staying away all evening. No wonder the Jamesons insist on payment in advance. I've already paid for three days.

As I open the front door, he says behind me, his voice still without inflection, "You'll find the girls at the Waterhole. That's where the young ones go."

In fact, I do want to find the girls, but I don't want him telling me that he knows.

I say nothing and close the door behind me.

When I step off the porch, a rainy wind bites me in the face.

The year I was fifteen, my father came to Greystone Bay and was never heard of again.

He was a very pleasant man, always smiling, always ready to listen to me and to take seriously the enthusiasms of a child. We were pals, but we were also father and son, and both of us were conscious of that and both of us enjoyed it.

I remember—or think I remember, because the mind can reconstruct such moments—one thing from the day he left home that last time. "Take care of Mom," he said.

He was a magazine writer and he was going to Greystone

Bay for three days to research an article. He called home that evening to say he'd arrived safely. We never heard from him again.

My mother shielded me from most of what followed. There were days, then weeks, of worry and sleepless nights. I could hear my mother crying in her room—their room—at night, but she never permitted herself to cry in front of me. She made trips to Greystone Bay, three or four, for a few days at a time, but, to my knowledge, she never learned anything at all of what had happened to her husband.

She was a real estate agent, which gave her a fair amount of time and mobility, as well as some money, and I know that she continued to seek information about him long after she and I stopped speaking openly about his disappearance.

Six years later, when I was entering the University of California, my mother and I moved to Santa Monica.

And six years after that, while I was still doing graduate work there, my mother's car was the fifth in a twelve-car wreck on the Pacific Coast Highway. When I reached her bedside at Santa Monica Hospital, she opened her eyes, looked directly at me as if everything were prefectly normal, said, "Greystone Bay," very clearly, closed her eyes, and was pronounced dead ten minutes later.

Now I am the same age as my father at the time he disappeared, and, in the jargon of the day, I am going through a major life crisis.

For the last seven years I have taught English at the University of California, Santa Barbara. My doctorate is completed and I have been duly promoted. I have my own office and must share a secretary with only two other assistant professors. My classroom load is not heavy and I have time for my own research. For the last three years I have been writing a book, a new evaluation of the work of Nathaniel Hawthorne, examining the suppressed sexual tensions in his short stories. My expenses are not great and I have some money in the bank. I rent a pleasantly furnished house with a garden sloping up the hillside behind it. I have a wonderful stereo system designed to let me play Vivaldi or whatever I want in any room of the house. From time to time my bed is warmed by one or another—sometimes more than one—of the attractive female students I teach. I suffer no guilt over this. It's not a bad life and, if I wish, it could continue indefinitely.

But I am now in my thirties and I do not see myself in the same position when I am in my sixties. Will I be the Grand Old Man of the English department? Will I be chucking coeds under the chin instead of getting grass stains on their backs in the garden? Will I be a famed authority on Hawthorne, or will I be a twice-told tale myself?

I am not old, and I do not feel old, but I have grown old enough now to realize that I am mortal. One day I am going to die. I have only so much time. So it is time now to take stock, to make plans, to get serious and purposeful about my life, to shape it and direct it instead of simply allowing it to happen, to construct a solid basis on the past on which to build a livable future.

And if I am to construct a solid basis on the past—and I cannot escape this—then I must find out what became of my father in Greystone Bay.

It is September, the Wednesday after Labor Day. I have the semester off, thanks to a kindly department chairman and a fairly generous grant to complete my book. I am supposedly doing research on Hawthorne in Boston and Salem, and I will, once I am done in Greystone Bay.

I have come here in September for several reasons. For one thing, I had hoped the weather would still be nice. I also wanted to avoid the summer tourists. There will, I imagine, still be visitors here on the weekends for the rest

of the month, and I hope that will brighten my stay a little;
I am determined about this search for information but I have
not been looking forward to it. I want a chance to get to
know the place and to learn what sort of people live here all
year round. Those people, the permanent residents, are the
ones who might tell me about my father.

I do not plan to contact the police. If they were no help
to my mother at the time of his death, they will be no help
now to me.

So I am set to begin. I have enough time and I have
enough money. I have a car I rented at Logan Airport.
And I have one clue.

The evening my father called home to say that he'd
arrived safely at Greystone Bay, I remember my mother
mentioning the name "Vachon." I remember the name
clearly because it sounded so strange and foreign, but I
don't know if it was the name of someone he knew there,
or perhaps of someone he was meeting or had just met. It
might have been the name of a place—a restaurant or
boardinghouse or hotel—or the name of a street. I don't
know. I know only that the name Vachon is the only link I
have—that and the Bay itself—to my father.

I need no photograph of my father to show people in the
hope that they might recognize his face. My own face—I
know from pictures and from my mother—is the living
image of his.

When I leave the Atlantic View Hotel, the evening is
growing rapidly and prematurely dark. It is not really
raining, but a salty stinging spray is blowing in from the
ocean and the Bay. Harbor Road is slick and black, re-
flecting the pale light from streetlamps. The tires of a
passing car hiss through puddles. The neon sign of the
Atlantic View Hotel and Restaurant throws shimmering
streaks of red across the road. Another car passes as I
stand at the curb, and when that is gone, the road is

empty. I cross the street to the boardwalk and lean against the fence above the beach.

There is nothing overtly threatening about the town of Greystone Bay, and yet I feel threatened. Towns like this are stretched in a line up the entire eastern seaboard, especially in New Jersey, Massachusetts, and Maine. Many of them are old and look rundown. None look attractive on a rainy September evening. But none, I am already convinced, feel as hostile to the stranger as this place feels to me.

I take a deep breath and say out loud, trying to sound lighthearted and wishing to hear at least my own voice for company, "Look out, Greystone Bay, here I come."

Beside me, a youthful but slightly smoky female voice says, "Hello, Dan. It's good to see you again." And a gentle hand touches my arm with the casual greeting of an old friend.

I turn around and look into the shadowed face of a beautiful young woman. She is an inch or two shorter than me and her chin is turned up. The light from the nearest streetlamp makes sharp angles of her nose and cheekbones, but I can see that she is beautiful. Her hair is thick and dark, and droplets of spray glitter on its surface like tiny jewels. Her full lips are slightly parted and I can see the tips of very white teeth in her smile. Her eyes are very dark, and her eyebrows are thick. It occurs to me that her pubic hair will be thick and dark too, but I instantly force the thought away.

"Dan?" she says, and cocks her chin slightly. Her smile does not fade and her gaze does not waver.

I stare into her eyes a moment longer. The thought of her pubic hair, thick and soft and musky, rushes in on me again, so vividly that I imagine for a second that I can taste her sex. I take two steps backward.

"Dan?" she says, still smiling, but now perhaps a trifle puzzled, and follows me. "It's Valerie. What's wrong?"

"Valerie?" I say, and my voice sounds both stupid in the situation and tiny in the dark.

She takes a step closer and lightly places the fingertips of her right hand in the center of my chest. She touches me as if she knows my body.

We have moved a short distance and the light is a little brighter here. I can see her better now. She is wearing dark jeans or slacks and a white windbreaker, like my own. Her breasts are large and, even through the jacket, I can see that her nipples are erect. My own body responds at once.

We speak in the same instant.

"Who are you?" I say.

"Who are you?" she says.

We stare at each other.

Her eyebrows draw together in a startled frown. "Oh, no," she says suddenly, and spins away. There is an opening in the wire fence that edges the beach side of the boardwalk. In an instant she has jumped down to the beach and is running in a straight line toward the black waters of the Bay. Little geysers of wet sand are kicked up behind her. In another moment she has disappeared completely from sight. There is nothing left of her except the burning touch of her fingers on my chest and the erection pressing against my stomach.

I grip the fence and lean toward the beach, staring at the darkness that has swallowed her.

My name is Joseph. Dan was my father's name.

The only time I ever heard my parents raise their voices to each other was about a year before my father disappeared. Someone named Valerie was mentioned in that angry conversation. My mother never spoke about the incident to me and never mentioned the name again, but in later years I always assumed that my father had been unfaithful to her with a woman named Valerie.

Now Valerie has just touched me in the dark.

*   *   *

It is morning again, Thursday, my first morning in Greystone Bay.

After Valerie left me—I frame the thought and think her name very casually—I walked for a while on the board-walk, scanning the dark houses and hotels and restaurants of Harbor Road. It must be busy here in the summer but now most places are closed, at least during the week. I walked there for nearly forty-five minutes, and saw only three people hurrying through the dark, none of them near me, and a few cars moving in Harbor Road.

I found a place to eat—not much of a place, but it was open—called the Booth's Bay Inn on Port Boulevard, just around the corner from Harbor Road. The steak sandwich, the most sophisticated item on the menu, was exactly what might be expected. I had a couple of beers and lingered for a while. The place smelled of hamburgers and ketchup. The other people there, about a dozen of them, were obviously locals, mostly oldtimers. It might be a good place for me to become a regular, a place where I might get to know some people and possibly hear something useful.

When I left there, I crossed Port Boulevard and walked up toward what my folder called the North Hill section. There were several handsome old churches, some with small graveyards beside them, and they reminded me that I must check Greystone Bay's cemetery, wherever it is. Then I walked back along Harbor Road to the Atlantic View Hotel. The Jamesons were nowhere in sight when I came in. I could hear a tinny radio at the back of the house. The music sounded like Glenn Miller.

Judging from the silence around me, I must be the only guest in the house this morning. I wonder if there will be more people here on the weekend.

As I pass through the front hall, I see Jameson. He has not shaved, although his beard appears no heavier than it was. We do not greet each other.

The restaurant is empty, so I sit at a table next to the front windows and the porch, facing the beach and the Bay. The sky is still grey but there no longer seem to be faces hiding among the threatening boulders of clouds. Just grey, uniform, lowering grey, pressing down hard on the world, and the slick waters of the Bay a faithful, featureless mirror.

I light a cigarette and the smoke seems to blend with the ashen daylight.

Jameson brings breakfast on a tray, which he sets across from me on the table. There is obviously no choice of what one eats. He goes away without speaking. The tray has a small carafe of coffee, so I will not have to speak a word to get a second cup. There are two fried eggs on the plate, growing cold, as if they have been waiting for me. I feel that I am being rebuked for oversleeping, when in fact, so far as the Jamesons know, I am on vacation. I wish the service were more pleasant here.

I will spend today looking for an apartment I can rent for a month. I saw several faded signs offering apartments in windows along Harbor Road. I'll find a place today, since I don't have to be too particular, and I'll move tomorrow. I'll be better off in my own place. I'm used to being on my own, and I won't have to look at Jameson or his equivalent first thing every morning.

The food cools quickly in the chilly air coming in around the window. I eat what I can and then put the dishes back on the tray. I pour a second cup of coffee and light another cigarette.

Across Harbor Road, on the boardwalk, I see Valerie.

She is walking slowly, with her hands in the pockets of the same white windbreaker she was wearing last night. Her chin is tilted up a little, as if to greet the wind, and her thick auburn hair floats out behind her like a flag, much longer than I thought. The weight of her hands in her pockets pulls the jacket taut across her breasts, which I see in profile. Her lips are full and her hips invitingly wide. She is an island of warmth in the grey chill of day.

I have brought my jacket and scarf with me to breakfast, so I reach the boardwalk in a minute or so. I stand still and watch her, waiting for my heart and my breathing to slow down. She is walking in the direction of Blind Point. Ahead of her, the boardwalk makes a long curve to the left, then, at the edge of vision, seems to end abruptly where the rough ground begins to rise.

She is two or three hundred feet away from me now. I start after her slowly.

Who is she? Why did she call me by my father's name? Why did she run off?

Slowly I draw closer behind her. I am filled with admiration for her hair. It streams behind her as if it would signal me to follow. I want to hold it, bite it, feel its silkiness on my face, my chest, on the insides of my thighs. I feel her sitting over me, face tilted down to my own, that hair a shimmering tent around us.

Her jeans are not fashionably tight, but they are tight enough to reveal her shifting round weight as she walks. If her hair hung straight down her back, it would cloak that movement. Her body invites the way an animal does, at one with ease and grace and nature. I want to press myself against her, joining hard and soft together.

If anyone is watching, it will be obvious that I am following her. It will also be obvious that my interest is sexual, and, in the instant I realize that, I resent anyone thinking that I am merely a man looking lasciviously at a woman and boldly taking advantage of a clear view of her body. It is not like that. She and I are joined somehow— have we not spoken? has she not touched me? has she not called me by my father's name?—and I am drawn along behind her as if by a silken thread.

I am close enough to call out to her but I do not. Her hair continues to stream, beckoning to me.

Ahead, I see the end of the boardwalk. It slopes down to the ground, which is rocky here, no longer sandy. The rocks are a heathenish tumble, with the waters of the Bay slapping and foaming at its precarious base. If the rocks at the bottom shifted only a little, I think, Blind Point would come tumbling down. From the end of the boardwalk a narrow footpath wanders uphill and quickly twists away among the boulders.

Still without looking back, Valerie easily ascends the hill and disappears.

I step off the boardwalk onto a rock, but then I hesitate and stop. With the girl momentarily gone from sight, I feel suddenly freed of a spell. What am I doing? I imagine her screaming, police erupting suddenly from behind the rocks, from among the trees I see higher up the slope, myself trying to explain to cold-eyed strangers that I wasn't . . .

And then that world recedes into silence, the moving spot of heat lures me forward, and I start up the slope of the hill.

The wind is stronger here, and colder. My hands sting in the air but there is dampness on my back beneath my shirt. I keep my eyes fixed upward on the trail. There is no sign of her.

The trail dips and climbs, bends sharply around some boulders and over others, stretching always higher above the Bay and farther out toward the headland at Blind Point. I lose track of how long I have been following her. Perhaps she has turned off the trail somewhere to escape me or to laugh at me. Beneath my flannel shirt sweat is running down my sides.

And there she is.

I come to a stop, breathing heavily, just looking at her. I put my hand against a rock to steady myself and its gritty surface feels warm against my fingers.

There is a kind of shelter here, formed by the rocks, like a grotto. Valerie is lying on the ground there, guarded from the wind, invisible to all except the sky and the ocean and myself. She is on her side, one arm propped on the ground, knees slightly bent. Her jacket is open and pulled back. She is not wearing a shirt. Her heavy breasts glow with warmth and offer ripe full nipples. With her free hand she lifts her hair and holds it out, prepared to make a cloak.

"Dan," she says. "You've come back to me."

Later, when I am able to lift my head and open my eyes, I am alone.

I am lying on the ground, unsheltered, and a salty wind is blowing my hair. I manage to sit up. I am a little dizzy, but it is fading away now that I can see the land and the ocean and feel the solid rocks beneath me. I feel weak but I am all right. Still sitting on the ground, I look slowly all around me. I see the grotto but there is no sign of Valerie.

I look at my watch. I don't know what time I reached this spot but no more than a minute or two can have passed. It was about nine o'clock when I went down to breakfast—I am suddenly pleased by my firm grip on reality—and I ate, drank coffee, smoked, rushed out, crossed the street, followed her, climbed up after her. It is now only a few minutes after ten. Has any time at all passed up here? Have I only just reached this spot?

I am frightened, but I comfort myself with my business-like regard for marking correctly the passage of time. Time, I remind myself, is real.

I climb to my feet and look around, carefully, making a deliberate effort to notice details. The grotto is there. Valerie—if she ever existed—is gone.

Did I invent her out of need? Did I fabricate her out of childish imaginings and garbled memory? Could it be that I resent my father's—possibly imaginary—affair with a girl named Valerie? Could it be that I am jealous of a

passion large enough to take him, even briefly, from the
wife I know he loved?

I am real and sane, I remind myself calmly. And then
my own calmness terrifies me. Madmen are always calm
and utterly self-convincing. I force myself to breathe deeply
to steady my nerves. The air tastes sharp and salty.

I pat my pockets lightly, feel for my wallet, change,
cigarettes, lighter, and also determine that I am not injured. And in the process I confirm to myself that I am still
real and individual, a particular man standing on a particular hilltop by the ocean. I have not been transported into
some other world, or consumed by a phantom. Real. I am
real, like the recognizable and particular world around me.
There is solid ground beneath my feet, sky above my
head, identifiable sounds in the air; my location could be
pinpointed on a map.

I can see whitecaps on the ocean, gulls soaring above it.
Off to my left I can see part of the boardwalk and the town
of Greystone Bay and North Hill rising above it.

I start back down the trail, watching the ground, concentrating on my footing.

When I reach the boardwalk, I put my hands in my
pockets and do my best to stroll casually along.

I cross the road to the Atlantic View Hotel. I open the
door and go in. I see Jameson behind his half-door, but I
ignore him and go upstairs to my room.

My plan is to lie down for a while—after all, I have
been out in the cold, climbing on rocks—and then, in the
afternoon, search for an apartment, which I will move into
immediately after breakfast tomorrow. This is all very
clear to me, these times, places, plans.

I open the door of my room and realize that, all along, I
have been expecting to see her in my bed. My heart
thumps at the thought of her breasts against my face, the
warm musky scent of her damp hair against my lips, the
muscular firmness of her body moving with me. Then the

beating of my heart grows a little slower. I am remembering only something I imagined.

The room is empty.

The bed has not been made. I look around, making an effort to note details. Nothing has been touched.

On the wrinkled sheet where I have slept, there is a small square of paper.

"Darling," it says in a neat female handwriting, "I'll pick you up at nine-thirty A.M. Friday. Be packed and ready to go, okay? Can't wait! How about Italian food? I know a great place called Vivaldi's. Love, Valerie."

I actually manage to sleep for a couple of hours. I am undisturbed because the Jamesons apparently do not trouble themselves about making beds. I do not remember dreaming—about Valerie or anyone else—but when I wake up, I have an erection.

It is nearly two o'clock. I leave the Atlantic View Hotel, turn right, and walk toward Port Boulevard. I go to the Booth's Bay Inn and have another steak sandwich and a beer. There are six old fellows at the bar, three of whom I recognize from the night before. The bartender-waiter does not appear to recognize me.

When I leave there, I walk along Port Boulevard, away from the Bay, looking down the side streets and stopping into a few stores. There are people on the street and in the shops, all of whom look just like ordinary people. It is the place that feels sinister to me. I go as far as the Town Hall, then cross the wide avenue and walk back on the opposite side.

What will happen in the morning?

The thought invades my mind every few minutes. I push it aside each time.

At Harbor Road I turn left. I have not walked here before, only across the street on the boardwalk.

At the next corner, I see the Waterhole.

Jameson said that's where the girls go, the young ones. The place must have been closed last night or I would have seen the sign, which projects out over the sidewalk.

I stop and look in the window. A yellow sign with red plastic letters announces that a band called The Sayings of Sappho is appearing there Thursday, Friday, and Saturday nights. Rock Hard! say smaller letters at the bottom.

I would go in now and have a beer, see what the place looks like, but it is closed.

And I must begin the search for my father.

The folder I have provides an address for the Greystone Bay Historical Society. A little stylized map in the folder locates the points of interest listed. It is a ten-minute walk and I find the place easily.

It is a well-kept house on a large corner lot almost entirely hidden by shrubbery and a tall, wrought-iron fence. On the fence at the entrance a discreet sign identifies the house. I walk up the path and knock with a bronze knocker in the shape of a sailing vessel.

After a lengthy wait, a grey-haired woman in a neat blue suit opens the door and peers out warily.

"Yes?" she says, as if no one had ever come here before.

"I was wondering if you could help me?"

She just looks at me without moving.

"With some information?"

"What sort of information?" She has still not opened the door all the way.

"About Greystone Bay."

"What sort of information?" she says again.

I keep calm. I want to say something like, "I hear the Waterhole has the best young pussy in town, but I wanted to check it out with you first. Is it historically true that the Waterhole has the best young pussy in town?" But instead, I say merely that I am trying to locate someone and that I thought perhaps the Historical Society could be of some assistance. I give her my best faculty-meeting smile.

"Well, come in, then," she says, but she doesn't mind letting me see that I'm far from welcome.

She closes the door firmly behind me and then turns around. Clearly, she will not invite me into any office. The house is old and dignified. The large front entrance where we are standing is handsomely paneled in polished mahogany. There is a faint scent of flowers in the air.

She will say nothing, just waits for me to speak.

"Well," I say. "I'm trying to locate the name Vachon. I'm not certain if it's a person or a place."

She does not react at all to the name. It could be that she has never heard the name before in her life. It could even be that her own name is Vachon.

"Are you familiar with it?"

"Why do you want to know?"

"Are you familiar with it?" I insist. My faculty-meeting smile is gone and I now sound the way I sometimes sound in my office with a lazy student who wants to argue about a grade.

"I am."

"Well?"

"Die here and you'll find out," she says.

I can't believe she has said this. "I beg your pardon?"

"Die here," she says. A little smile touches the corners of her mouth. "You'll find the Vachons quick enough."

At least I've learned something. "The Vachons," I say. "They're a local family?"

"You could say that." She is still terse but appears to be warming up a little now that she's actually talking.

"Have they been in Greystone Bay for a long time?"

"Forever," she says.

"Forever. Would that include about fifteen or twenty years ago?"

Now she actually chuckles, but the sound she makes is

harsh and inhuman, like that of a mechanical fortune-teller in a penny arcade. "Oh my, yes," she says.

"Are they a prominent family?"

"I should say so. Yes, that would be the word."

"They're not in the telephone book. I've looked. Can you tell me where to find them?"

Suddenly her face is closed again. It is almost as if she has turned off, like an arcade machine when the money runs out. She turns away and opens the front door, holding it wide.

"Look, all I need is an address or something."

She does not move, but her stillness seems to gesture me out of the house.

"Okay, okay." I move toward the door. "Thanks for your help," I tell her. I step down to the path.

"Ask Valerie," the woman says. "She'll be able to tell you what you need."

She closes the door firmly behind me.

Greystone Bay is crazy. No rules apply here.

I walk more in the afternoon, still familiarizing myself with the town.

"Ask Valerie," the woman said. "She'll be able to tell you what you need."

What does that mean? How does she know Valerie? How does she know that *I* know Valerie? How does she know I'll see Valerie again? How do *I* know it? Do I? Will I? What is going on here?

I keep walking, walking, all afternoon. That, at least, is real. The sidewalks are real, the roads, the houses, the trees, the lawns. The pavement beneath my feet gives me comfort with its very hardness, its simple, believable, soothing reality. Once, walking on a street where concrete gave way to slabs of slate, I tripped over the edge of a slab. My ankle hurt for the next couple of blocks, and I actually took pleasure in the pain.

Shortly after that I saw my father walking a block or so ahead of me. I recognized his old grey raincoat, a favorite of his, frayed at the cuffs and missing a button, that my mother was always urging him to replace. I instantly thought how nice it would be to have that raincoat for myself, as a remembrance of him, as a token of our continuity, father and son, going down the ages, one after the other. I wondered but could not remember if he'd taken it with him all those years ago when he left for Greystone Bay.

I was hurrying to catch up—after all, I'd come here in the first place to find my father—and stepped into the road at the next corner.

"Dad!" I called. *"Dad!"*

I didn't see the car coming from my left and it struck me hard. I was thrown in the air, high, and I remember the trees and the sky spinning around me. And the noise, the very loud noise. Then I struck the ground.

When I regain consciousness, Leo Carillo, looking the same as he did in his role of Pancho, sidekick to the Cisco Kid, twirls his long mustaches in theatrical fashion, leans his swarthy face close to mine, rolls his eyes, and says, "Wassinabagoose?"

I know what that means and, for a moment, I am so pleased with myself that I forget the pain that fills my body.

When my mother and I first moved to California, a local company called Granny Goose was doing a big television ad campaign for their potato chips. "Granny Goose" was portrayed as a handsome cowboy riding on his horse. Suddenly, in the hills, he is waylaid by a band of Mexican *banditos*. The leader of the *banditos* waves a gun at Granny Goose's saddlebags and snarls, "Wassinabagoose?" Presto, potato chips, and everyone is happy.

"Potato chips," I say, as clearly as I can manage. My mouth is filled with blood and I think some of my teeth are broken, but I think I am speaking clearly enough to be understood.

"Potato chips, goddammit!" I say.

There is some sort of hasty movement around me.

"Shit, he's out of it," I hear someone say.

"C'mon, *c'mon*!" somebody else says.

Another voice is counting, although I can't tell if the numbers are going up or down in sequence because I can't quite recall what the proper order of numbers is supposed to be.

I want to know where Leo Carillo has gone, because I would like to ask him for his autograph. Funny how the mind works. I recognized Leo instantly and remembered his name, but, for the life of me, I can't recall the name of the actor who played the Cisco Kid. Not for the life of me.

There are people around me—I can see their faces—and I wonder if possibly one of them can tell me the actor's name. I open my mouth to ask but all that happens is that a mouthful of blood spills over my chin.

"Oh, shit," someone says. "C'mon, get that fucking thing going!" The voice is extremely tense and, for the first time, I grow afraid.

I must have slept again because I am conscious of waking up once more.

"Well, look who's awake," a pleasant woman's voice says. I can sense her leaning over me. "How are we feeling today?" the voice asks, and I can hear it smiling.

I open my eyes.

The woman from the Historical Society is leaning over me, her face close to mine. Someone else is standing behind her. My head hurts terribly but I am able to roll it on the pillow enough to see past her. The person there moves a little too and comes into my line of sight.

It is Valerie. She is dressed in a terry-cloth robe, and she is wearing a smart little nurse's cap perched on the top of her head. That luxurious hair is pulled straight back on the sides and apparently wound into a bun at the back. She looks very neat and efficient.

"Can you tell me how you're feeling?" the woman from the Historical Society says kindly, eager to convince me that she cares. I can see that her neat blue suit is covered with bloodstains. "You've had a little accident, you know, but everything is going to be all right. Isn't that so, Valerie?"

Valerie comes and stands beside her and I realize that I have to look upward at both of them.

"Absolutely," says Valerie. She is smiling too, but her smile is warmer and more genuine than the older woman's. She is very pretty—not just beautiful, I realize, but extraordinarily *pretty,* which is rarer—and she is smiling tenderly. She nods her head in affirmation. "Absolutely," she says again. "Everything is going to be just as fine as it was the time you held me in your arms. Do you remember that, Joe? The time you held me in your arms?"

I do.

It was after two in the morning and we both had to be up for work by eight. We were on the boardwalk, leaning over the fence, looking down at the beach toward the waters of the Bay. We were teenagers then. There came a moment when we turned toward each other and kissed, I was always convinced of this, by mutual decision. Later, hurrying, watching the time, we walked down on the beach to the water's edge. We stood there and Valerie let me touch her left breast through her shirt. It was thrilling but, curiously, I was more thrilled by the wetness of her mouth and the electric touch of her tongue against mine.

Now Valerie is standing over me and holding a wash-cloth. She lets it touch my stomach, which is naked, and I feel that it is warm. She smiles reassuringly and begins, very gently, to wash my genitals.

I enjoy her hands moving over me although my penis does not stir. I luxuriate in her touch.

When she finishes, I am filled with gratitude for her ministrations, her caring. I feel that, if I had to, I could trust her with my life.

And then suddenly I am shivering with fear because I have just realized—how do I know this?—that I *must* trust her with my life. If I am to live, if all of this is to make sense, it is up to her. I am terrified that she cannot love me enough to keep me alive. She will try her best, yes, in a routine sort of way, but it will not be enough, and then I will die.

Valerie approaches me again. She is looking down at me. Her expression is both affectionate and worried. She smiles, but when she opens her mouth to speak, it is a man's voice, deep and strong, that comes out. Although her face comes very close to mine, close enough for me to feel her breath, even to smell hamburger and ketchup, that deep masculine voice is yelling, as if I am very far away.

"You'll be fine! You'll be okay! Can you hear me? We're taking care of you! You'll be okay!"

I want very much to answer that I understand, but I can't think of the words with which to say it. For some reason I am suddenly too weak even to move my head enough to nod.

2 / Desire

We spent three weeks every summer at Greystone Bay, starting from the summer I was five or six, so the town and its beach and its scenes were always a part of my consciousness over more than a dozen years. Three weeks, regular as clockwork, and the repetition, reliably anticipated every year, became a ritual of my life.

And the ritual, in turn, became a passage. Those three-week periods every summer, myself a full year older each time, became watersheds, stepping stones, tunnels, evolutionary strata in my growth.

I kissed a girl for the first time in Greystone Bay. I touched a girl's breast, tasted a girl's tongue, knew a girl's body there for the first time. I drove a car there for the first time in my life, and had my first job.

The summer I was fifteen, my father died in Greystone Bay. The weather wasn't the nicest we'd had on that vacation—the sky was overcast, I remember, and the air itself seemed grey—but every day of those three weeks was precious to my parents, so they were on the beach although most other visitors had stayed away that afternoon. They had an old Indian blanket that was older than I was, and that stayed all the rest of the year on the top shelf in the hall closet. Every summer that blanket went with us. They had it on the beach that day. My mother left my father dozing there and went to paddle by herself at the water's edge. She came back, glistening with water, after about fifteen minutes. My father was dead, lying there on the Indian blanket on the beach of Greystone Bay.

I had gone to the sandwich shop next to the penny arcade, across the street from the beach, to get a Coke. I arrived back just as my mother discovered that my father was dead. I had to run back to the sandwich shop for help, leaving my mother kneeling on the blanket. By the time the volunteer rescue squad arrived with an ambulance, the sky had grown darker and fat drops of warm rain were making geysers on the sand.

The following summer my mother said we would go to Greystone Bay again as usual. I knew she was doing it partly for me, because those three weeks each year were so special in my life. But I knew too that she was doing it partly for herself. Life is for the living, life goes on, that sort of thing. She would have to walk on the same streets, eat in the same restaurants, lie on the same beach where she and my father had gone together for so many years, but she was determined to do it. And I think that, in the end, we were both relieved to be going back despite the drastic change in our lives.

The summer I was seventeen I got a job in the penny arcade on Harbor Road, opposite the municipal beach, and worked there all summer long, ten full weeks, from two days after the close of school until the day after Labor Day. It was the best summer of my life. It was the best two months of my life.

It was the first summer of my life when I actually felt strong in my knowledge of myself as an individual, that I actually felt myself as independent of my surroundings, with the power to move in a direction of my own choice. It was the first summer in which I began to feel grown-up.

I had gotten better, by that summer, at making friends, and some of the people I knew during those summer months became a permanent part of my consciousness, constant factors, later, in shaping my own awareness of myself.

Mrs. Vachon.

Valerie White.

Leo Holland.

A woman, a girl, a man, roadsigns on my passage through that summer.

The funny thing was, I met the three of them all on the same day.

My mother and I had driven to Greystone Bay on Saturday morning early in May. I had my eye on a job at the arcade near the beach, partly because the location made it seem like a fun place to be, and partly because the only other jobs I could think of meant working in some eatery and washing dishes for two months.

"Are you sure you want to do this?" my mother said as we drove along the long straight stretch of road that leads into the town. "Once you take a job, you know—if you get one—there'll be no backing out. If you agree to do something for somebody, you have to do it."

That was an old familiar song in my mother's bible, and although I sometimes got tired of hearing it, the precept had long since become part of my life.

"I know that, Mom. Listen, we talked about it. I really want to do it. Hey, it'll be good for me."

She glanced sideways at me, a little skeptically, then looked back at the road.

We could see the town itself now. It was strange to be coming here in May, rather than in July or August. It seemed almost like an alien world, although every inch of the road we were on, Port Boulevard, was familiar. In the past we'd always been "summer people," nothing more. Now I was coming here with the purpose of finding a job, making myself a real part of the life of Greystone Bay, and something suddenly made me feel that Greystone Bay might not make me welcome. I was in a period then of feeling private contempt for what I frequently heard referred to as "normal adolescent fears." I forced the fear out of my mind.

"It'll be okay, Mom," I said lightly.

"You'll be alone all summer." She kept her eyes on the road. We were slowing down for the turn onto Harbor Road.

"I'll make friends," I told her. There was no safe thing to say, I realized. If I said I was worried, she'd discourage me. If I said I'd be fine, she'd be hurt that I wasn't going to miss her, that her baby was growing up and beginning to live his own life.

"It'll be okay, Mom, I promise," I said. "And you'll be here for three weeks anyway. That's like a third of the whole summer."

She sighed and said nothing. I knew she was thinking of my father as well as of me, so quickly growing up, and of herself, suddenly so alone. Then we were making the right turn onto Harbor Road, and the water and the empty beach were gleaming beside us.

I was relieved to see that the arcade was open, but I was suddenly filled with sweaty panic when the car stopped at the curb in front of it. I sat very still, not wanting to leave the safety of the car.

"Well?" my mother said, and I could tell from the tone of her voice that she knew exactly what I was thinking and just how scary it was to be growing up.

"Okay," I said.

I took a deep breath and reached for the door handle.

"I'll wait here," she said, very gently and a little sadly. We both knew I was on my own now. I was both glad of it and terrified at the idea.

"Good luck," she added, but I was concentrating so hard on getting out of the car without banging my head that all I did was grunt in reply.

The inside of the arcade was dark as I entered from the bright sunlight outdoors. In the summer there would be plenty of light inside, day and night, but I guessed that the owner was trying to keep his bills down now, since he couldn't be doing much business. I looked around. There were three boys, about twelve or so, at a pinball machine. Otherwise, the place was empty.

There were six Skee-Ball machines against the back wall, looking grey with age. There were a dozen or so pinball machines, all of them familiar to me. There were those machines where you put in a coin and try to grasp a prize from a revolving platform with a dangling mechanical claw. There was a mechanical fortune-teller. A foot-relaxer. Half a dozen electrical football and hockey games. Off to one side there were a couple of little rides for children, a rocking pony, a racing car. Back in one corner

was a dusty glass showcase with some tacky little prizes
you could get by saving up tickets from Skee-Ball. You
needed about ten thousand tickets to get something like a
dangling plastic spider or a little tray with an old-fashioned
Coca-Cola advertisement printed on it. I knew everything
in the place. I'd spent many happy hours in the arcade
every summer for a decade, nearly half my life. I began to
feel a little more comfortable.

I knew the owner was a man named Schiller. ("Hey,
get off the machine, you asshole. Schiller the Killer is
watching us!") Now, as I advanced through the arcade
toward the rear, the only person I could see, besides the
kids playing pinball, was a strange man sitting on a stool
behind the counter at the back. I could see immediately
that he was a dwarf.

I tried not to stare at him, and I slouched a little to look
less tall.

"Is Mr. Schiller here?"

The dwarf looked at me. His eyes looked as if they
never blinked.

"Mr. Schiller?" I said. "He owns the place."

"Mr. Schiller is dead," the dwarf told me. "I own the
place now."

"Oh," I said, and realized with horror that I'd said it
with an elaborate casualness meant to disguise my ner-
vousness. "I mean, that's too bad. I . . . I was hoping I
could talk to him about a job. Here. For the summer."

"You know Greystone Bay?" the dwarf asked me. He
still hadn't moved or blinked. He looked a lot like the
mechanical fortune-teller in the glass case. I thought of
dropping a nickel into his hand to make him move, and the
thought almost made me giggle.

I nodded.

"Tell me," he said. That's all.

I babbled at him. I know I told him about coming to

Greystone Bay every summer but I don't remember what else I said.

"Is that your mother in the car outside?" I heard him ask.

When I said yes, he told me to bring her in.

Most of that conversation is a blur to me now, but apparently the dwarf, Mr. Leo Holland, thought I looked like an honest and reliable sort of kid, and I guess my mother's presence and whatever she said in my behalf were enough to reassure him. I got the job.

By the time we left the arcade, we were also armed with the address of a woman named Mrs. Vachon who ran a boarding house a few blocks away. Leo—it struck me as odd that he insisted on being called just Leo, even by me—said it would be a clean and inexpensive place for me to stay, and also I wouldn't get into trouble there. I wasn't sure what that meant. I wasn't looking for "trouble," but I guess I was secretly hoping that a little "trouble" would find me at some point during the summer.

"Wow, what a weird guy," I said when we were back in the car.

"That's not a nice way to talk about a man who just gave you a job," my mother said, but her tone of voice told me she was pleased with her son's accomplishment in getting the first job he'd ever looked for. "Now I think we should find this boardinghouse and see if we can get that business settled. Then we can look for something to eat."

It took only a minute to drive to Mrs. Vachon's address. It was a nondescript sort of house, three floors, clapboard, painted white but peeling in places, the yard threatening to be overgrown by early summer, the sort of place that looks well-used without actually looking rundown.

We knocked at the door—there was a bell but it didn't seem to work—and Mrs. Vachon quickly appeared. She was a nice-looking lady, in her thirties I guessed, and I sensed right away that her house would be as easy to live

with as her smile. She didn't seem at all concerned that I
was only a teenager and would be staying there on my own
all summer. "I have a houseful every year," she told my
mother. They exchanged that secret look that women do
sometimes, and I knew it was going to be all right.

Mrs. Vachon showed us around the house. The rooms
were small and sparsely furnished. "Of course, they come
here only to sleep," Mrs. Vachon said. I know she and my
mother whispered something while I was looking out a
window, and when I turned around, I could tell from my
mother's expression that everything was settled. Mrs.
Vachon, I assumed, had repeated Leo's assurance that I
wouldn't be getting into any trouble there. After that the
question of money was settled quickly. My mother would
pay now for the first week and then I would pay myself
weekly out of my salary.

All these matters of getting a job, finding a room,
having a salary, paying rent, all made me feel exceedingly
grown-up by the time we were back at the front door.

And then something else happened. As she was opening
the door to show us out, Mrs. Vachon placed her hand on
my back. Not the palm of her hand, but just the fingertips,
very lightly, really just brushing my back through the
shirt. A shiver ran up my back. And at the same time, for
just a second, I felt the pressure of her right breast against
my left arm. It was only for a second, but the touch
shocked me. I was only then—I was already following my
mother through the doorway—aware that her breasts were
remarkably full for a woman so otherwise slender. I felt
my cheeks flush and felt myself stir suddenly down below.

My mother didn't seem to notice my silence after that. I
think she was lost in a silence of her own. Our mission had
gone smoothly, for one thing, and then there was everything it suggested about our changing relationship.

My own silence was for another reason. I could still feel
Mrs. Vachon's breast against my arm. And I could feel,

along with that sensation, the effect her touch had on my own body. And beyond that I was stunned by the glimpse I suddenly had of a world that I had previously hardly known existed. Think of an older woman in a sexual way? I had never done that. It had never occurred to me to do that. There were no specific thoughts in my mind, no luridly detailed images, but I was aware, with a vividness that stunned me, that sex was a part of *all* human life, and not just part—a yearning and painful part, more than anything else—of my own.

After driving around for a while, my mother announced that she thought we should have lunch in someplace decent to celebrate my getting the job. I would have settled gladly for a hamburger or pizza, but I didn't object. In a way I couldn't yet put into words I felt that the occasion called for a celebration too.

My mother decided on a place on Harbor Road, opposite the beach, called the Atlantic View Hotel and Restaurant.

A grey-haired, pleasant-looking woman served us lunch in the dining room, which faced the street and the boardwalk across the way. We sat beside the front windows, and about halfway through the meal a car stopped out front and a girl and woman, mother and daughter, got out and came up the steps. They were seated at the next table and I had a good view of the girl. I figured she was my own age, and she was sort of pretty.

My mother was a real estate agent, with a natural ability to make pleasant smalltalk with strangers, and before long she and the woman were chatting easily. My mother was always doing that with strangers, but this time I didn't mind. The girl and I looked at each other and smiled a little without saying anything. Teenagers can sometimes communicate silently as well as women can. Or men, for that matter. These insights struck me in later years as merely routine, uninspired, but at the time they seemed filled with portent, glimmers of understanding of a new world I was only then preparing to enter.

When we had all finished eating, my mother and the other woman went off together to find the ladies room. Feeling both brave and bold, I took a deep breath and moved over to the other table, carrying my Coke with me.

For all the easy complicity adults sense in teenagers, teenagers themselves have a hard time approaching each other, like territorial animals wary of being challenged. Even so, I was already aware that girls were more sophisticated in social matters, and I was relieved that this conversation opened easily.

Her name was Valerie White, and within less than a minute we discovered we had plenty to talk about. The barrier normal to our age was broken down, and suddenly we were on the same side, with an endless list of common interests that excluded our mothers and all other adults. Primarily, we discovered that Valerie and her mother had just come from seeing both Leo at the penny arcade and Mrs. Vachon at the boardinghouse. They must have been there right after we were. Valerie and I would be working in the same place and living in the same place all summer long. Besides the pleasure of the unexpected discovery, this meant that each of us could face the unknown events of this new experience—Valerie had never been away from home either, or had a job—already armed with a friend, an ally.

It was only a while later, when my mother and I were already heading out of town on Port Boulevard, that I realized I should have gotten Valerie's address. I could have kicked myself. *That* was why she had such a funny expression on her face when our mothers were paying their bills and getting ready to leave. Stupid, I thought. What a drag to be a teenager and so stupid that you don't even think of things like that. And of course Valerie had thought of it but, since she was a girl, she couldn't say anything.

And then I thought of Mrs. Vachon. A woman, grown-up and mature, smart, sure of herself, not troubled by uncertainties like mine. I thought again of her breast touching my arm, and wondered what her breasts looked like when she was undressed. It was the first time I'd ever had a specifically sexual thought about a woman. It scared me and excited me at the same time.

And that led me back to more thoughts about Valerie. Her breasts were smaller than Mrs. Vachon's but she had a good body and she was nice to look at. Even so, because Valerie seemed so easy to be with, I already suspected that she and I were going to become good friends. And if we became good friends, then we could never get into anything physical. I understood enough to know that, puzzling as it seemed. But I didn't know if the knowledge was a disappointment or a relief.

It was terrible being a teenager.

And it was equally terrible to feel myself consciously growing into a man . . . and not knowing the way.

By the middle of July I'd become part of Greystone Bay.

I knew my way around better than I ever had before, and I'd even developed a hearty contempt for other kids who—like myself until this very summer—came here for only a couple of weeks with their parents. I felt myself older than they were, wiser, more mature in the ways of the world.

I worked pretty long hours at the arcade—my job was making change, keeping an eye on the little kids, and unsticking the return mechanism of the Skee-Ball machines, which must have been as old as the Bay itself—but whenever I had a chance I was on the beach and I'd gotten a good tan. I felt great. I'd made some friends too. There was a guy my own age who worked at the hamburger joint next door—the same place where I'd run two years earlier to get help when my father died—and some others who were friends of his. We'd meet at midnight sometimes when the places were closing down and maybe lie out on the beach with a radio. It was a kind of life I'd never known. I called my mother three times a week, but that didn't keep me from feeling I was really on my own at last. I was proud that I was making money and taking care of myself. I even bought a couple of new shirts by myself, something I'd never done before. It was, in so many ways, big and small, a summer of firsts.

Leo Holland. The dwarf.

He was a good man to work for. My first day on the job, he spent about two hours showing me what to do. There was a kind of apron I had to wear with pockets in the front for change. He explained how much I should keep on me, and which kinds of coins. He showed me how to empty the coinboxes of all the different machines. He showed me how to unstick the return mechanism of the Skee-Ball machines with a straightened coathanger. None of it was very difficult but there was a lot to remember. And when he was finished explaining, Leo just said, "Okay, you're on your own." Then he went back and sat in his usual place on the stool behind the counter.

That was it. "You're on your own." It struck me with great force that he *assumed* I would do everything correctly. And that I could be trusted to handle the money. So, naturally, I felt even more responsible about the job than I would have felt if he'd watched me every second.

I quickly learned that Leo had a few quirks. For one thing, he seemed to eat all day long. He always had to have food near him, but he wouldn't keep a supply on hand, so he was always sending me out. Hamburgers, candy bars, popcorn, soda, seven or eight times a day. And every time he sent me out, he'd hand me an extra dollar with the money for the food. "Get one for yourself too," he'd say.

I quickly began to feel guilty about taking so much extra money when he could have sent me out as part of my job. I think it was on the third day that I tried to say something about it, but he wouldn't let me. "Just don't eat too much of that junk," he said. But he handed me the extra dollar anyway.

After a while I began to wonder if that was his way of trying to make me forget that he was a dwarf. If he gave me extra money, I'd like him. But I realized just as quickly that I'd already gotten over any feelings about his appearance. One night, somebody made a remark on the beach about a dwarf and everybody looked at me as if I'd gone loony when I said, "What dwarf?"

So if I was old enough and sensitive enough to see that, then Leo himself must have understood that I'd forget about it naturally after a day or two. And if I'd forget about it naturally, then he wouldn't have to pay me extra to forget, or to act as if I'd forgotten. He would have, must have, understood all that.

In any case, I soon stopped buying soda and candy and peanuts and made six or eight dollars extra, in cash, every day, so I quickly accumulated a good bit of money that no one else even knew about. By the end of the summer I might have four or five hundred dollars in my secret cache, a small fortune in those days, even enough to buy a used car. And that made me feel even more secure than I was feeling already.

But at first I just couldn't get over it. I was even suspicious. One of my friends, during my first week, joked that I better watch out for *that dwarf*! He made it sound very menacing. "What do you mean?" I said. "What do I mean? Man, don't you know about dwarves? They all have dicks like Shetland ponies, man, and they can't get women to go with them, so they're all as horny as hell. And you know what they like? Do you? Pretty little boys, just like you! Yeah! Hey, don't turn your back on that dwarf, man, or you'll be shish-ke-bab!''

But Leo never asked anything of me except that I do my job.

He listened to music all the time, mostly Vivaldi. I think he had every record of Vivaldi's music ever made. He even played it over the loudspeaker in the arcade. Some of the kids who came in grumbled about it but Leo paid no attention. This was the only arcade in Greystone Bay, and they'd be there no matter what he was playing. Sometimes he'd talk to me about Vivaldi. He'd compare, say, the concerti of *The Four Seasons* with those in *L'Estro Armonico*. Or he'd compare different recordings of the same piece and play them one after another on the arcade's sound system so I could hear the differences. I didn't know much about classical music at that time, but after a while I could hear the differences myself.

Always, after that summer, I could never listen to Vivaldi without thinking of Leo Holland.

As my secret fund of extra money began to accumulate, I started going to a record store on Port Boulevard and buying records of Vivaldi myself, even though I wouldn't be able to play them until the summer was over. I bought records of all the different pieces I could find. And when I had them all, I started buying duplicate recordings of pieces I already had.

That fall, when I was back home again, I played all the records and all the different versions by different orchestras and conductors and soloists, and sometimes even different recordings by the same artist made ten or twenty years apart. I could hear the differences in interpretation as plainly as I could hear the differences in one human voice from another.

*   *   *

Valerie. The girl.

We became good friends.

We worked together for at least part of every day, so we had plenty of time to talk and get to know each other. We talked about all sorts of things. There were other times too when we didn't talk at all, maybe all day long, but we could be comfortable with that silence too.

After work we'd sometimes eat together, or we'd walk on the boardwalk in the dark or go down on the beach or hang out with my friends. Whatever we did—or didn't do—it was easy for us to be together. I'd never had a friend like that, boy or girl.

She looked sensational the times I saw her in a bathing suit, and I certainly wasn't indifferent to her body. I know I didn't think of her the way I imagined a guy would think of his sister.

But one day, when a guy I sometimes hung out with looked at her across the street and said, "God, I'd like to get into that," I told him to keep his goddamn hands off her.

"Shit," he said, shaking his head, "she's not *yours*. You act like you don't even know she has tits!"

But I did. Did I ever. I'd even seen them one day.

Valerie and I lived on the same floor at the rooming house and used the same bathroom. Usually, we felt as if we had the house to ourselves, because all the other tenants were older and worked in bars and restaurants and kept different hours, so we hardly ever saw them, even at breakfast. One morning I was heading for the bathroom just as Valerie was coming out. She had a terry-cloth robe on and I could see her nipples sharp against it. Just as I opened my door, she dropped her towel. When she bent to pick it up, her robe fell forward and I had a clear view of her breasts. Neither one of us said anything, but she knew that I'd seen her. I spent a long time in the bathroom after that and I didn't spend all of it in the shower. When I got down to breakfast, late, she was waiting for me at the table. She looked up and I knew instantly that she knew what I'd been doing up there. I felt my face turn hot, but some new boldness I'd never felt before made me look straight back at her. It struck me that each of us now had secret and intimate knowledge of the other. And the knowledge made us partners in a new adventure that neither of us had the words to describe.

But nothing changed in our daily relationship.

Then, a few nights later, she knocked quietly on my door while I was sitting up in bed, reading. I was reading a book of short stories by Nathaniel Hawthorne, and I jumped at the sound. It was about one-thirty but I knew it had to be her.

When she came in, she was wearing the terry-cloth robe. She said she couldn't sleep and she'd seen the light under my door. I told her to sit down and she sat on the edge of the bed. Suddenly I realized I was wearing only my briefs and I had an erection. I yanked up the sheet to conceal it. Valerie pretended she hadn't noticed, but I knew she had.

All of a sudden she said, "Joe, tell me the truth, do you think I'm pretty?"

I stared at her.

"Do you? I mean it. I want to know. I know my hair is kind of nice, but I want to know if you think I'm really pretty."

"Sure I do," I finally managed to say, but I knew my voice sounded a little shaky.

"I need to know," she said. Then she added in a whisper, "I really do."

I desperately wanted to say the right thing but I didn't know the words, although I longed for them, wished I could somehow shape them physically with my hands. I reached for her and, at the same time, she leaned sideways and stretched out against me on the bed. I felt her breasts against my rib cage, her tears running wet against my shoulder. I ached for the right words to say because ordinary words would not reassure her.

"Hold me," she whispered against my neck.

I felt like an oaf—clumsy, thick, and rough in contrast to her. All I could do was put my arms around her shoulders and hold her tight. I had never held a girl—or anyone—in that way before.

After a while, I felt her grow quiet. She shifted, still not saying anything, and settled her body closer against me. I was astonished, and enormously pleased, at how our bodies fit together so easily, like matching halves of the same thing. I could feel her breath softly touching my neck.

And after another while, I heard myself saying, "My father died here in Greystone Bay."

Her arm shifted slightly across my chest.

"Do you want to tell me?" she asked softly.

"My mother and father were lying on the beach," I began, and I told her the whole thing.

When I finished, her hand touched my cheek, but all she said was, "I'll stay with you for a while."

After a few minutes I felt her breathing grow regular as I drifted off to sleep myself.

I have a lover, I thought, a lover I never need to touch.

Mrs. Vachon. The woman.

During my first couple of weeks in Greystone Bay I was conscious of her like something at the edge of my existence, as if I could see her only from the corner of my eye. She was always there, but only just catching my attention, never commanding my thoughts. I had too much else to think about at first: Leo, Valerie, new friends, late nights on the beach, money in my pocket, the life of Greystone Bay itself.

And then there was the Saturday morning. I was the only guest in the house. Valerie was working at the arcade, and all the other residents were out. I had the day off—it was rare to have a Saturday off—and I'd slept so late, I figured I'd have to go out for breakfast. But when I came back to my room from taking a shower, Mrs. Vachon was sitting on the side of my bed and two cups of coffee were steaming on the nighttable.

She was wearing jeans and a red T-shirt and there wasn't even any question about a bra.

I panicked and froze right there in the doorway. Since the house was otherwise empty, I'd come back from my shower with nothing but a towel around my waist.

Mrs. Vachon stretched out a hand, and although she didn't touch me, that hand drew me into the room.

"Here are the rules," she said, in a voice as gentle as a breeze across the beach. "This will happen once, and once only. And after it's happened, it will never be referred to, never at all, by either one of us. It will be a secret we share forever."

I lost track of the sequence after that.

I know I was on my back on the bed, and I know she was naked, kneeling over me, then guiding me inside her. I know we moved together, she by careful and slow design, I by instinct. I know I cried at the end. She cradled my head against her chest, which felt extraordinarily warm to me. I wet her breasts with tears. And I know she disappeared briefly, then returned, and with a warm washcloth, gently wiped my genitals.

Later, when I went downstairs to breakfast, everything was shockingly, stunningly, breathtakingly normal.

After a few weeks in Greystone Bay I discovered Blind Point.

It was south of the town, reached by a rocky path that started upward to the bluff beyond the end of the boardwalk, just past the bathing beach. From the highest, outermost point of the cliffs, you could see the sweep of the

Atlantic Ocean, the jagged circular dish of rocks containing the stiller waters of the bay, and, to the left, the town
of Greystone Bay itself. And beyond the town were the
grey-green masses of hills that separated Greystone Bay on
that side from all the rest of the world.

It was a lonely place, Greystone Bay, and Blind Point
was the loneliest in it.

I went there sometimes by myself when I had a morning
or an afternoon off.

And sometimes I thought of killing myself there by
jumping off the cliff to the rocks below, where the waves
came crashing in.

Greystone Bay. This summer. I was more alive than I
had ever been before, I knew that, and yet the place and
the time had the very feel of death. The air itself was grey
with it.

My father died here. From Blind Point I could see the
beach where he'd been lying. I'd walked many times over
the very spot, sometimes singing with the radio or laughing at some dirty joke, with my arm around Valerie's
shoulder, or the smell of Mrs. Vachon in my mind, or Leo
Holland's music in my thoughts. The very spot, maybe
even stood on the very same grains of sand, while I carried
with me all these things—all this knowledge—that I'd
never had before.

I remember the specific afternoon when I most seriously
considered dying there.

It had rained all day, only easing off late in the afternoon. The sky was dark, town lights just starting to come
on and flicker in the grey, and the bowl of the bay just
starting to fill with fog. The fog swallowed all sound
except the dull roar of breaking waves at the base of the
cliffs. A body there might not be found for days.

Nothing ever stayed the same. Everything passed away.
Could anything be counted on? I wasn't sure. I thought
not.

If I died here, at least there would be a parallel with my father's death.

Death was a physical thing . . . but I was already filled, assailed, with physical things. My own body. Dollar bills, dozens of them, the extras from Leo, valuable not for their monetary worth but for the evidence they bore of my own reality and the slow passage of time. So many dollars, so many days, so many hours. All physical. Leo's Vivaldi, all those brightly dancing notes, each of them physical too. Valerie's tears. Mrs. Vachon's wetness.

Cancel this? Impossible. It would just go on without me. Just close around the hole I left in the world and go right on without me.

And I decided—*decided*—that I wouldn't have that. I wouldn't have it.

I ran all the way back to the arcade, stumbling headlong in places down the rocky path.

I loved myself, Leo, Valerie, Mrs. Vachon, my mother, my dead father, the sand of the beach, I loved Greystone Bay, loved its smell of death and life together that filled my lungs. I'd never come back here, of course, never again as long as I lived, but for now I loved it and Greystone Bay, forever and ever, was mine, mine, mine!

3 / *Memory and Desire*

"You'll be fine! You'll be okay! Can you hear me? We're taking care of you! You'll be okay!"

I wish they'd stop yelling at me. I understand them, and I want to let them know I understand, but they all seem to be very far away and I don't think there's any point in my shouting.

I know it will be a relief to close my eyes because the

sun is shining very brightly on the beach and the water of Greystone Bay.

But now I realize that my eyes are already closed.

I know I hear Vivaldi. I can pick out the two distinct violin melodies and the harpsichord in the background. In just a minute, I know, I'll be able to identify the piece.

I seem to be bouncing a little, but gently, as if steady waves are carrying me in toward the shore.

I suddenly remember and I say, as clearly as I can manage, "I have to meet Valerie."

I know the words come out distinctly because someone immediately replies, "Sure thing, buddy, sure thing."

Something hurts my left arm, but it's not a bad pain—not as bad as dying, I imagine—so I decide simply to ignore it. No big deal.

I'll close my eyes for a while, if they're not already closed, and sort things out. I have a sense that I'm late for something but I can't recall exactly what it might be.

I'll ask Valerie; maybe, she'll know. Or Mrs. Vachon. Or Leo. One of them will know, or all of them. And if I get frightened, I know I can cry in front of them without being embarrassed, because they know so much about me already. Maybe I'll go back to Greystone Bay and look for them. It would be nice to see them again, anyway. That thought makes me feel safe, makes me feel that I can relax a little, and I feel the tension slip away from my body.

"Holy shit, what's this?"

"About twenty cars, it looked like. What a mess. He got caught in the middle of it. Woman we brought back with him is gone."

"Christ."

"We topped eighty on the way back. I think we've still got him."

"Oh, yeah? Well, take another look, friend. Just happened. This one's dead too."

The Red House
by
Robert R. McCammon

I've got a story to tell, like everybody else in the world. Because that's what makes up life, isn't it? Sure. Everybody's got a story—about somebody they met, or something that's happened to them, something they've done, something they want to do, something they'll never do. In the life of everybody on this old spinning ball there's a story about a road not taken, or a love that went bad, or a ghost of some kind. You know what I mean. You've got one too.

Well, I want to tell you a story. Trouble is, there are so *many* things I remember about Greystone Bay. I could tell you about what Joey Hammers and I found in the wreck of an old Chevy, down where the blind man lives amid the junked cars. I could tell you about the time the snakes started coming out of old lady Farrow's faucets, and what she did with them. I could tell you about that Elvis Presley impersonator who came to town and went crazy when he couldn't get his makeup off. Oh yeah, I know a lot about what goes on in the Bay. Some things I wouldn't want to tell you after the sun goes down, but I want to tell you a story about *me*. You decide if it's worth the telling.

My name's Bob Deaken. Once upon a time, I was Bobby Deaken, and I lived with my mom and dad in one of the clapboard houses on Accardo Street, up near South Hill. There are a lot of clapboard houses up there, all the same shape and size and color—kind of a slate grey. A tombstone color. All of them have identical windows, front porches, and concrete steps leading up from the street. I swear to God, I think all of them have the same cracks in those steps too! I mean, it's like they built one of those houses and took a black and white picture of it and said, "This is the ideal house for Accardo Street," and they put every one together just the same right down to the warped doors that stick in the summer and hang when it's cold. I guess Mr. Lindquist figured those houses were good enough for the Greeks and Portuguese, Italians and Poles who live in them and work at his factory. Of course, a lot of plain old Americans live on Accardo Street too, and they work for Mr. Lindquist like my dad does.

Everybody up on Accardo pays rent to Mr. Lindquist, see. He owns all those houses. He's one of the richest men in Greystone Bay, and his factory churns out cogs, gears, and wheels for heavy machinery. I worked as a "quality controller" there during summer break from high school. Dad got me the job, and I stood at a conveyor belt with a few other teenage guys and all we did day after day was make sure a certain size of gear fit into a perfect mold. If it was one hair off, we flipped it into a box and all the rejects were sent back to be melted down and stamped all over again. Sounds simple, I guess, but the conveyor belt pushed thousands of gears past us every hour and our supervisor, Mr. Gallagher, was a real bastard with an eagle eye for bad gears that slipped past. Whenever I had a complaint about the factory, Dad said I ought to be thankful I could get a job there at all, times being so bad and all; and Mom just shrugged her shoulders and said that Mr. Lindquist probably started out counting and checking gears somewhere too.

But you ask my dad what kind of machines all those gears, cogs, and wheels went into, and he couldn't tell you. He'd worked there since he was nineteen years old, but he still didn't know. He wasn't interested in what they did, or where they went when the crates left the loading docks; all he did was make them, and that's the only thing that mattered to him—millions and millions of gears, bound for unknown machines in faraway cities, a long way off from Greystone Bay.

South Hill's okay. I mean, it's not the greatest place, but it's not a slum either. I guess the worst thing about living on Accardo Street is that there are so many houses, and all of them the same. A lot of people are born in the houses on Accardo Street, maybe move two or three doors away when they get married, and they have kids who go to work at Mr. Lindquist's factory, and then their kids move two or three doors away and it just goes on and on. Even Mr. Lindquist used to be Mr. Lindquist, Junior, and he lives in the same big white house that his grandfather built.

But sometimes, when my dad started drinking and yelling and Mom locked herself in the bathroom to get away from him, I used to go up to the end the street. The hulk of what used to be a Catholic church stands up there; it caught on fire in the late seventies, right in the middle of one of the worst snowstorms the Bay ever saw. It was a hell of a mess, but the church wasn't completely destroyed. The firemen never found Father Marion's body. I don't know the whole story, but I've heard things I shouldn't repeat. Anyway, I found a way to climb up to what was left of the old bell tower and the thing creaked and moaned like it was about to topple off but the risk was worth it. Up there you could see the whole of Greystone Bay, the way the land curved to touch the sea, and you got a sense of where you were in the world. And out there on the ocean you could see yachts, workboats, and ships of all kinds passing by, heading for different harbors. At night their lights were especially pretty, and sometimes you could hear a distant whistle blow, like a voice that whispered, *Follow me*.

And sometimes I wanted to. Oh yeah, I did. But Dad said the world beyond Greystone Bay wasn't worth a shit, and a bull should roam his own pasture. That was his favorite saying, and why everybody called him "Bull." Mom said I was too young to know my own mind; she was always on my case to go out with "that nice Donna Raphaelli," because the Raphaellis lived at the end of the block and Mr. Raphaelli was Dad's immediate supervisor in the factory. Nobody listens to a kid until he screams, and by then it's too late.

Don't let anybody tell you the summers aren't hot in Greystone Bay. Come mid-July, the streets start to sizzle and the air is a stagnant haze. I swear I've seen sea gulls have heat strokes and fall right out of the sky. Well, it was on one of those hot, steamy July mornings—a Saturday, because Dad and I didn't have to work—when the painters pulled up in a white truck.

The house right across the street from ours had been vacant for about three weeks. Old Mr. Pappados had a heart attack in the middle of the night, and at his funeral Mr. Lindquist gave a little speech because the old man had worked at the factory for almost forty years. Mrs. Pappados went west to live with a relative. I wished her luck on the day she left, but Mom just closed the curtains and Dad turned the TV up louder.

But on this particular morning in July, all of us were on the front porch trying to catch a breeze. We were sweltering and sweating, and Dad was telling me how this was the year the Yankees were going to the World Series—and then the painters pulled up. They started setting up their ladders and getting ready to work.

"Going to have a new neighbor," Mom said, fanning herself with a handkerchief. She turned her chair as if to accept a breeze, but actually it was to watch the house across the street.

"I hope they're *American*," Dad said, putting aside the newspaper. "God knows we've got enough foreigners living up here already."

"I wonder what job Mr. Lindquist has given our new neighbor." Mom's glance flickered toward Dad and then away as fast as a fly can escape a swatter.

"The line. Mr. Lindquist always starts out new people on the line. I just hope to God whoever it is knows something about baseball, because your son sure don't!"

"Come on, Dad," I said weakly. It seems like my voice was always weak around him. I had graduated from high school in May, was working full-time at the factory, but Dad had a way of making me feel twelve years old and stupid as a stone.

"Well, you don't!" he shot back. "Thinkin' the *Cubs* are gonna take the Series? Crap! The Cubs ain't never gonna get to the—"

"I wonder if they have a daughter," Mom said.

"Hey, don't you talk when I'm talkin'. What do you think I am, a wall?"

The painters were prying their paint cans open. One of them dipped his brush in.

"Oh, my God," Mom whispered, her eyes widening. "Would you *look* at that?"

We did, and we were stunned speechless.

The paint was not the bland grey of all the other clapboard houses on Accardo Street. Oh, no—that paint was as scarlet as a robin's breast. Redder than that: as red as the neon signs down where the bars stand on Harbor Road,

crimson as the warning lights out on the Bay where the
breakers crash and boom on jagged rocks. Red as the party
dress of a girl I saw at a dance but didn't have enough
nerve to meet.

Red as a cape swirled before the eyes of a bull.

As the painters began to cover the door of that house
with screaming-scarlet, Dad came up out of his chair with
a grunt as if he'd been kicked in the rear. If there was
anything he hated in the world, it was the color red. It was
a Communist color, he'd always said. *Red* China. The
Reds. *Red* Square. The *Red* Army. He thought the Cincin-
nati Reds was the lousiest team in baseball, and even the
sight of a red shirt drove him to ranting fits. I don't know
what it was, maybe something in his mind or his chemis-
try, maybe. He just went into a screaming rage when he
saw the color red.

"Hey!" he yelled across the street. The painters stopped
working and looked up, because his shout had been loud
enough to rattle the windows in their frames. "What do
you think you're doin' over there?"

"Ice skatin'," came the reply. "What does it look like
we're doin'?"

"Get it off!" Dad roared, his eyes about to explode
from his head. "Get that shit off right *now!*" He started
down the concrete steps with Mom yelling at him not to
lose his temper, and I knew somebody was going to get
hurt if he got his hands on those painters. But he stopped
at the edge of the street, and by this time people were
coming out of their houses all around, to see what the
noise was all about. It was no big deal though; there was
always some kind of yelling and commotion on the street,
especially when the weather turned hot and the walls of
those clapboard houses closed in like cages. Dad hollered,
"Mr. Lindquist owns these houses, you idiots! Look around!
You see any of the others painted Commie red?"

"Nope," one of them replied while the other kept on painting.

"Then what the hell are you doin'?"

"Followin' Mr. Lindquist's direct orders," the painter said. "He told us to come up here to 311 Accardo Street and paint the whole place firehouse red." He tapped one of the cans with his foot. "This is firehouse red, and that's 311 Accardo." He pointed to the little metal numbers up above the front door. "Any more questions, Einstein?"

"These houses are *grey!*" Dad shouted, his face blotching with color. "They've been grey for a hundred years! You gonna paint every house on this street Commie red?"

"Nope. Firehouse red. And we're just painting this place right here. Inside and outside. But that's the only house we're supposed to touch."

"It's right in front of my *door!* I'll have to look at it! My God, a color like that *screams* to be looked at! I can't stand that color!"

"Tough. Take it up with Mr. Lindquist." And then he joined the other painter in the work, and when Dad returned to the house he started throwing around furniture and cursing like a madman. Mom locked herself in the bathroom with a magazine, and I went up to the church to watch the boats go by.

As it turned out, on Monday Dad gathered his courage to go see Mr. Lindquist on his lunch break. He got only as far as Mr. Lindquist's secretary, who said she'd been the one to call Greystone Painters and convey the orders. That was all she knew about it. On the drive home Dad was so mad he almost wrecked the car. And there was the red house, right across the street from our own grey, dismal-looking clapboard house, the paint still so fresh that it smelled up the whole block. "He's trying to get to me," Dad said in a nervous voice at dinner. "Yeah. Sure. Mr. Lindquist wants to get rid of me, but he don't have the guts of his father. He's afraid of me, so he paints a house

Commie red and sticks it in my face. Sure. That's what it's got to be!'' He called Mr. Raphaelli up the street to find out what was going on, but learned only that a new man had been hired and would be reporting to work in a week.

I tell you, that was a crazy week. Like I say, I don't know why the color red bothered my dad so much; maybe there's a story in that too, but all I know is that he started climbing the walls. It took everything he had to open the front door in the morning and go to work, because the morning sunlight would lie on the walls of that red house and make it look like a four-alarm fire. And in the evening the setting sun set it aflame from another direction. People started driving along Accardo Street—*tourists,* yet!—just to take a look at the gaudy thing! Dad double-locked the doors and pulled the shades as if he thought the red house might rip itself off its foundations at night and come rattling across the street after him. Dad said he couldn't breathe when he looked at that house, the awful red color stole the breath right out of his lungs, and he started going to bed early at night with the radio tuned to a baseball game and blaring right beside his head.

But in the dark, when there was no more noise from the room where Mom and Dad slept in their separate beds, I sometimes unlocked the front door and went out on the porch to stand in the steamy night. I wouldn't dare tell them, but I *liked* the red house. I mean, it looked like an island of life in a grey sea. For a hundred years there had been only grey houses here, all of them exactly the same, not a nail or a joint different. And now *this*. I didn't know why, but I was about to find out in a big way.

Our new neighbors came to the red house exactly one week after the house had been painted. They made enough noise to wake the rich folks in their mansions up on North Hill, hollering and laughing on an ordinarily silent Saturday morning, and when I went out on the porch to see, my folks were already out there. Dad's face was almost purple, and there was a mixture of rage and terror in his eyes. Mom was stunned, and she kept rubbing his arm and holding him to keep him from flinging himself down the steps.

The man had crew-cut hair the color of fire. He wore a red checked shirt and trousers the shade of Italian wine. On his feet were red cowboy boots, and he was unloading a U-Haul trailer hooked to the back of a beat-up old red station wagon. The woman wore a pink blouse and crimson jeans, and her shoulder-length hair glinted strawberry-blond in the strong morning light. A little boy and little girl, about six and seven, were scampering around underfoot, and both of them had hair that was almost the same color of the house they'd come to inhabit.

Well, suddenly the man in red looked up, saw us on the porch, and waved. "Howdy!" he called in a twanging voice that sounded like a cat being kicked. He put aside the crimson box he'd been carrying, strode across the street in his red cowboy boots and right up the steps onto our porch, and he stood there grinning. His complexion looked as if he'd been weaned on ketchup.

"Hello," Mom said breathlessly, her hand digging into Dad's arm. He was about to snort steam.

"Name's Virgil Sikes," the man announced. He had thick red eyebrows, an open, friendly face, and light brown eyes that were almost orange. He held a hand out toward Dad. "Pleased to meet you, I'm sure."

Dad was trembling; he looked at Virgil Sikes's hand like it was a cowflop in a bull's pasture.

I don't know why. I guess I was nervous. I didn't think. I just reached out and shook the man's hand. It was hot, like he was running a high fever. "Hi," I said. "I'm Bobby Deaken."

"Howdy, Bobby!" He looked over his shoulder at the woman and two kids. "Evie, bring Rory and Garnett up here and meet the Deakenses!'' His accent sounded foreign, slurred and drawled, and then I realized it was Deep South. He grinned wide and proud as the woman and two children came up the steps. ''This is my wife and kids,'' Virgil said. ''We're from Alabama. Long ways from here. I reckon we're gonna be neighbors.''

All that red had just about paralyzed my dad. He made a croaking sound, and then he got the words out, ''Get off my porch.''

''Pardon?'' Virgil asked, still smiling.

''Get off,'' Dad repeated. His voice was rising. ''Get off my porch, you damned redneck hick!''

Virgil kept his smile, but his eyes narrowed just a fraction. I could see the hurt in them. He looked at me again. ''Good to meet you, Bobby,'' he said in a quieter voice. ''Come on over and visit sometime, hear?''

''He will *not!*'' Dad told him.

''Ya'll have a good day,'' Virgil said, and he put his arm around Evie. They walked down the steps together, the kids right at their heels.

Dad pulled free from my mother. ''Nobody around here lives in a red house!'' he shouted at their backs. They didn't stop. ''Nobody with any sense *wants* to! Who do you think you are, comin' around here dressed like that? You a Commie or somethin'? You hick! Why don't you go back where you belong, you damned—'' And then he stopped suddenly, because I think he could feel me staring at him. He turned his head, and we stared at each other in silence.

I love my dad. When I was a kid, I used to think he hung the moon. I remember him letting me ride on his shoulders. He was a good man, and he tried to be a good father—but at that moment, on that hot July Saturday morning, I saw that there were things in him that he couldn't help, things that had been stamped in the gears of his soul by the hands of ancestors he never even knew.

Everybody has those things in them—little quirks, mean-
nesses, and petty things that don't get much light; that's
part of being human. But when you love somebody and
you catch a glimpse of those things you've never seen
before, it kind of makes your heart pound a little harder. I
saw also, as if for the first time, that my dad had exactly
the same shade of blue eyes as my own.

"What're *you* lookin' at?" Dad asked, his face all
screwed up and painful.

He looked so old. There was grey in his hair, and deep
lines on his face. So old, and tired, and very much afraid.

I dropped my gaze like a dog about to be kicked,
because Dad always made me feel weak. I shook my head
and got back inside the house quick.

I heard Mom and Dad talking out there. His voice was
loud, but I couldn't make out what he was saying; then,
gradually, his voice settled down. I lay on my bed and
stared at a crack in the ceiling that I'd seen a million
times. And I wondered why I'd never tried to patch it up
in all those years. I wasn't a kid anymore; I was right on
the edge of being a man. No, I hadn't patched that crack
because I was waiting for somebody else to do it, and it
was never going to get done that way.

He knocked on the door after a while, but he didn't wait
for me to invite him in. That wasn't his way. He stood in
the doorway, and finally he shrugged his big heavy shoulders and said, "Sorry. I blew my top, huh? Well, do you
blame me? It's that damned red house, Bobby! It's makin'
me crazy! I can't even think about nothin' else! You
understand that, don't you?"

"It's just a red house," I said. "That's all it is. Just a
house with red paint."

"It's *different!*" he replied sharply, and I flinched.
"Accardo Street has been just fine for a hundred years the
way it used to be! Why the hell does it have to change?"

"I don't know," I said.

"Damned right you don't know! 'Cause you don't know about *life*! You get ahead in this world by puttin' your nose to the wheel and sayin' yes sir and no sir and toein' the line!"

"Whose line?"

"The line of anybody who pays you money! Now, don't you get smart with me either! You're not man enough yet that I can't tear you up if I want to!"

I looked at him, and something in my face made him wince. "I love you, Dad," I said. "I'm not your enemy."

He put a hand to his forehead for a minute, and leaned against the door frame. "You don't see it, do you?" he asked quietly. "One red house is all it takes. Then everything starts to change. They paint the houses, and the rent goes up. Then somebody thinks Accardo Street would be a nice place to put condos that overlook the Bay. They bring machines in to do the work of the men at the factory—and don't you think they don't have machines like that! One red house and everything starts to change. God knows I don't understand why Mr. Lindquist painted it. He's not like his old man was, not by a long shot."

"Maybe things need to change," I said. "Maybe they *should* change."

"Yeah. Right. And where would *I* be? Where else am I going to find work at my age? Want me to start collectin' garbage the tourists leave down at the beach? And where would *you* be? The factory's your future too, y'know."

I took a step then, over the line into forbidden territory. "I'd still like to go to college, Dad. My grades are good enough. The school counsellor said—"

"I've told you we'll talk about that later," Dad said firmly. "Right now we need the extra money. Times are tough, Bobby! You've got to pull your weight and toe the line! Remember, a bull should roam his own pasture. Right?"

I guess I agreed. I don't remember. Anyway, he left my

room and I lay there for a long time, just thinking. I think
I remember hearing a boat's whistle blow, way off in the
distance, and then I fell asleep.

On Monday morning we found out where Virgil Sikes
was assigned. Not the line. Not the loading dock. He came
right into the big room where my dad worked on one of
the machines that smoothed and polished the gears until
they were all exactly the same, and he started working on
a machine about twenty feet away. I didn't see him,
because I worked on the loading dock that summer, but
my dad was a nervous wreck at the end of the day. Seems
Virgil Sikes was wearing all red again; and, as we were to
learn, that's the only color he *would* wear, crimson right
down to his socks.

It began to drive Dad crazy. But I know one thing: The
first week Virgil Sikes worked at the factory, I carted
about twenty more crates than usual off that loading dock.
The second week, the factory's quota was up by at least
thirty crates. I know, because my sore muscles took count.

The story finally came from Mr. Raphaelli: Virgil Sikes
had hands as fast as fire, and he worked like no man Mr.
Raphaelli had ever seen before. Rumor was circulating
around the factory that Sikes had labored in a lot of
different factories along the coast, and in every one of
them he'd boosted production by from twenty to thirty
percent. The man was never still, never slowed down or
even took a water break. And somehow Mr. Lindquist had
found out about him and hired him away from a factory
down South; but to come to Greystone Bay Virgil Sikes
had asked one thing: that the house he live in be painted as
bright a red—inside and out—as the painters could find.

"That redneck's a lot younger than me," Dad said at
dinner. "I could do that much work when I was his age!"
But all of us knew that wasn't true, all of us knew nobody
at the factory could work like that. "He keeps on like this,

he's gonna blow up his damn machine! Then we'll see what Lindquist thinks about him!''

But about a week after that word came down to assign Virgil Sikes to *two* polishers at the same time. He handled them both with ease, his own speed gearing up to match the machines.

The red house began to haunt Dad's dreams. Some nights he woke up in a cold sweat, yelling and thrashing around. When he got drunk, he ranted about painting our house bright blue or yellow—but all of us knew Mr. Lindquist wouldn't let him do that. No, Virgil Sikes was special. He was different, and that's why Mr. Lindquist let him live in a red house amid the grey ones.

And one night when Dad was drunk he said something that I knew had been on his mind for a long time. ''Bobby boy,'' he said, placing his hand on my shoulder and squeezing, ''what if somethin' *bad* was to happen to that damn Commie red house over there? What if somebody was to light a little bitty fire, and that red house was to go up like a—''

''Are you *crazy?*'' Mom interrupted. ''You don't know what you're saying!''

''Shut up!'' he bellowed. ''We're talkin' man to man!'' And that started another yelling match. I got out of the house pretty quick, and went up the church to be alone.

I didn't go back home until one or two in the morning. It was quiet on Accardo, and all the houses were dark.

But I saw a flicker of light on the red house's porch. A match. Somebody was sitting on the porch, lighting a cigarette.

''Howdy, Bobby,'' Virgil Sikes's voice said quietly in its thick southern drawl.

I stopped, wondering how he could see it was me. ''Hi,'' I said, and then I started to go up the steps to my own house, because I wasn't supposed to be talking to him and he was kind of spooky anyway.

"Hold on," he said. I stopped again. "Why don't you come on over and sit a spell?"

"I can't. It's way too late."

He laughed softly. "Oh, it's *never* too late. Come on up. Let's have a talk."

I hesitated, thought of my room with the cracked ceiling. In that grey house Dad would be snoring, and Mom might be muttering in her sleep. I turned around, walked across the street and up to the red house's porch.

"Have a seat, Bobby," Virgil offered, and I sat down in a chair next to him. I couldn't see very much in the dark, but I knew the chair was painted red. The tip of his cigarette glowed bright orange, and Virgil's eyes seemed to shine like circles of flame.

We talked for a while about the factory. He asked me how I liked it, and I said it was okay. Oh, he asked me all sorts of questions about myself—what I liked, what I didn't like, how I felt about Greystone Bay. Before long, I guess I was telling him everything about myself—things I suppose I'd never even told my folks. I don't know why; but while I was talking to him, I felt as comfortable as if I were sitting in front of a warm, reassuring fireplace on a cold, uncertain night.

"Look at those stars!" Virgil said suddenly. "Did you ever see the like?"

Well, I hadn't noticed them before, but now I looked. The sky was full of glittering dots, thousands and thousands of them strewn over Greystone Bay like diamonds on black velvet.

"Know what most of those are?" he asked me. "Worlds of fire. Oh, yes! They're created out of fire, and they burn so bright before they go out—so very bright. You know, fire creates and it destroys too, and sometimes it can do both at the same time." He looked at me, his orange eyes catching the light from his cigarette. "Your father doesn't think too highly of me, does he?"

"No, I guess not. But part of it's the house. He can't stand the color red."

"And I can't stand to live *without* it," he answered. "It's the color of fire. I like that color. It's the color of newness, and energy . . . and change. To me it's the color of life itself."

"So that's why you wanted the house changed from grey to red?"

"That's right. I couldn't live in a grey house. Neither could Evie or the kids. See, I figure houses are a lot like the people who live in them. You look around here at all these grey houses, and you know the people who live there have got grey souls. Maybe it's not their choice, maybe it is. But what I'm sayin' is that *everybody* can choose if he has the courage."

"Mr. Lindquist wouldn't let anybody else paint their house a different color. You're different because you work so good."

"I work so good because I live in a red house," Virgil said. "I won't go to any town where I can't live in one. I spell that out good and proper before I take a man's money. See, I've made my choice. Oh, maybe I won't ever be a millionaire and I won't live in a mansion—but in my own way, I'm rich. What more does a man need than to be able to make his own choices?"

"Easy for you to say."

"Bobby," Virgil said quietly, "everybody can choose what color to paint their own house. It don't matter who you are, or how rich or poor—*you're* the one who lives inside the walls. Some folks long to be red houses amid the grey, but they let somebody else do the paintin'." He stared at me in the dark. His cigarette had gone out, and he lit another with a thin red flame. "Greystone Bay's got a lot of grey houses in it," he said. "Lots of old ones, and ones yet to be."

He was talking in riddles. Like I say, he was kind of

spooky. We sat for a while in silence, and then I stood up and said I'd better be getting to bed because work came early the next morning. He said good night, and I started across the street.

It wasn't until I was in my room that I realized I hadn't seen any matches or a lighter when Virgil had lit that second cigarette.

Lots of old ones, Virgil had said. *And ones yet to be*.

I went to sleep with that on my mind.

And it seemed like I'd just closed my eyes when I heard my dad say, "Up and at 'em, Bobby! Factory whistle's about to blow!"

The next week the loading dock moved at least thirty-five more crates over quota. We could hardly keep up with them as they came out of the packing room. Dad couldn't believe how fast Virgil Sikes worked; he said that the man moved so fast between those two machines that the air got hot and Virgil's red clothes seemed to smoke.

One evening we came home and Mom was all shook up. It seems she got a telephone call from Mrs. Avery from two houses up. Mrs. Avery had gone nosing around the red house, and had looked into the kitchen window to see Evie Sikes standing over the range. Evie Sikes had turned all the burners on, and was holding her face above them like an ordinary person would accept a breeze from a fan. And Mrs. Avery swore she'd seen the other woman bend down and press her forehead to one of the burners as if it were a block of ice.

"My God," Dad whispered. "They're not *human*. I knew something was wrong with them the first time I saw them! Somebody ought to run them out! Somebody ought to burn that damned red house to the ground!"

And this time Mom didn't say anything.

God forgive me, I didn't say anything either.

Lots of old ones. And ones yet to be.

Rumor got around the factory: Virgil Sikes was going to

be in charge of three polishing machines. And somebody in that department was going to get a pink slip.

You know how rumors are. Sometimes they hold a kernel of truth, most times they're just nervous air. Whatever the case, Dad started making a detour to the liquor store on the way home from work three nights a week. He broke out in a sweat when we turned onto Accardo and had to approach the red house. He could hardly sleep at night, and sometimes he sat in the front room with his head in his hands, and if either Mom or I spoke a word he blew up like a firecracker.

And finally, on a hot August night, his face covered with sweat, he said quietly, "I can't breathe anymore. It's that red house. It's stealin' the life right out of me. God almighty, I can't *take* it anymore!" He rose from his chair, looked at me, and said, "Come on, Bobby."

"Where are we going?" I asked him as we walked down the steps to the car. Across the street the lights of the red house were blazing.

"You don't ask questions. You just do as I say. Get in, now. We've got places to go."

I did as he said. And as we pulled away from the curb I looked over at the red house and thought I saw a figure standing at the window, peering out.

Dad drove out into the sticks and found a hardware store still open. He bought two three-gallon gasoline cans. He already had a third in the back. Then he drove to a gas station where nobody knew us and he filled up all three cans at the pumps. On the way home the smell of the gasoline almost made me sick. "It has to be done, Bobby," Dad said, his eyes glittering and his face blotched with color. "You and me have to do it. Us men have to stick together, right? It's for the good of both of us, Bobby. Those Sikes people aren't *human*."

"They're different, you mean," I said. My heart was hammering, and I couldn't think straight.

"Yes. Different. They don't belong here. We don't need any red houses on our street. Things have been fine for a hundred years, and we're going to make them fine again, aren't we?"

"You're . . . going to kill them," I whispered.

"No. Hell, no! I wouldn't kill anybody! I'm gonna set the fire and then start yellin'. They'll wake up and run out the back door! Nobody'll get hurt!"

"They'll know it was you."

"You'll say we were watchin' a movie on TV. So will your mom. We'll figure out what to say. Damn it, Bobby— are you with me or against me?"

I didn't answer, because I didn't know what to say. What's wrong and what's right when you love somebody?

Dad waited until all the lights had gone out on Accardo Street. Mom sat with us in the front room; she didn't say anything, and she wouldn't look at either of us. We waited until the Johnny Carson show was over. Then Dad put his lighter into his pocket, picked up two of the gas cans, and told me to get the third. He had to tell me twice, but I did it. With all the lights off but the glow of the TV, I followed my father out of the room, across the street, and quietly up to the red house's porch. Everything was silent and dark. My palms were sweating, and I almost dropped my gas can going up the steps.

Dad started pouring gas over the red-painted boards, just sloshing it everywhere. He poured all the gas out from two cans, and then he looked at me standing there. "Pour yours out!" he whispered. "Go on, Bobby!"

"Dad," I said weakly. "Please . . . don't do this."

"Christ almighty!" He jerked the can from my hand and sloshed it over the porch too.

"Dad . . . please. They don't mean any harm. Just because they're different . . . just because they live in a house that's a different *color*—"

"They shouldn't be different!" Dad told me. His voice

was strained, and I knew he was right at the end of his rope. "We don't like different people here! We don't *need* different people!" He started fumbling for his lighter, took from his pocket a rag he'd brought from the kitchen.

"Please . . . don't. They haven't hurt us. Let's just forget it, okay. We can just walk away—"

His lighter flared. He started to touch the flame to the rag.

Lots of old ones, I thought. *And ones yet to be.*

Me. Virgil Sikes had been talking about *me*.

I thought about gears at that instant. Millions and millions of gears going down a conveyor belt, and all of them exactly the same. I thought about the concrete walls of the factory. I thought about the machines and their constant, pounding, damning rhythm. I thought about a cage of grey clapboard, and I looked at my dad's scared face in the orange light and realized he was terrified of what lay outside the grey clapboards—opportunity, choices, chance, *life.* He was scared to death, and I knew right then that I could not be my father's son.

I reached out and grabbed his wrist. He looked at me like he'd never seen me before.

And I heard my voice—stronger now, the voice of a stranger—say, *"No."*

Before Dad could react, the red-painted front door opened.

And there was Virgil Sikes, his orange eyes glittering. He was smoking a cigarette. Behind him stood his wife and two kids—three more pairs of orange, glowing eyes like campfires in the night.

"Howdy," Virgil said in his soft southern drawl. "Ya'll havin' fun?"

My dad started sputtering. I still had hold of his wrist.

Virgil smiled in the dark. "One less grey house in Greystone Bay, Bobby."

And then he dropped the cigarette onto the gas-soaked boards at his feet.

The flames caught, burst up high. I tried to grab Virgil, but he pulled back. Then Dad was pulling me off the porch as the boards began to explode into flame. We ran down into the street, and both of us were yelling for the Sikeses to get out the back door before the whole house caught.

But they didn't. Oh, no. Virgil took one of the children in his arms and sat down in a red chair, and his wife took the other and sat down beside him in the midst of the flames. The porch caught, hot and bright, and as we watched in fascinated horror we saw all four of the Sikeses burst into flame; but their fire-figures were just sitting there in the chairs, as if they were enjoying a nice day at the beach. I saw Virgil's head nod. I saw Evie smile before fire filled up her face. The children became forms of flame—happy fires, bouncing and kicking joyfully in the laps of the parents.

I thought something then. Something that I shouldn't think about too much.

I thought, *They were always made of fire. And now they're going back to what they were.*

Cinders spun into the air, flew up and glittered like stars, worlds on fire. The four figures began to disintegrate. There were no screams, no cries of pain—but I thought I heard Virgil Sikes laugh like the happiest man in the world.

Or something that had *appeared* to be a man.

Lights were coming on all up and down the block. The flames were shooting up high, and the red house was almost engulfed. I watched the sparks of what had been the Sikes family fly up high, so very high—and then they drifted off together over Greystone Bay, and whether they winked out or just kept going I don't know. I heard the siren of a firetruck coming. I looked at my dad, looked long and hard, because I wanted to remember his face. He looked so small. So small.

And then I turned and started walking along Accardo

Street, away from the burning house. Dad grabbed at my arm, but I pulled free as easily as if I were being held by a shadow. I kept walking right to the end of Accardo—and then I just kept walking.

I love my mom and dad. I called them when the workboat I signed onto got to a port up the coast about thirty miles. They were okay. The red house was gone, but of course the firemen never found any bodies. All that was left was the red station wagon. I figured they'd haul that off to where the junked cars are, and the blind old man who lives there would have a new place to sleep.

Dad got into some trouble, but he pleaded temporary insanity. Everybody on Accardo knew Bull was half-crazy, that he'd been under a lot of pressure and drank a lot. Mr. Lindquist, I heard later, was puzzled by the whole thing, like everybody else, but the clapboard houses were cheap and he decided to build a white brick house across from my folks. Mr. Lindquist had wanted to get rid of those clapboard things and put up stronger houses for the factory workers anyway. This just started the ball rolling.

My folks asked me to come back, of course. Promised me everything. Said I could go to college whenever I wanted. All that stuff.

But their voices sounded weak. I heard the terror in those voices, and I felt so sorry for them, because they knew the walls of their cage were painted grey. Oh, I'll go back to Greystone Bay sometime—but not until later. Not until I've found out who I am, and what I am. I'm Bob Deaken now.

I still can't figure it out. Was it planned? Was it happenstance? Did those creatures that loved fire just fit me into their lives by accident or on purpose? You know, they say the devil craves fire. But whatever the Sikeses were, they unlocked me from a cage. They weren't evil. Like Virgil Sikes said, fire creates as well as it destroys.

They're not dead. Oh, no. They're just . . . somewhere

else. Maybe I'll meet them again sometime. Anything's possible.

I may not be a red house. I may be a blue one, or a green one, or some other color I haven't even seen yet. But I know I'm not a grey house. I know that for sure.

Night Catch
by
Chelsea Quinn Yarbro

A following sea made the rudder treacherous, and the *Cinzenta Filha* wallowed in the darkness. Juliao Peixe struggled at the helm, trying to find the two-mile buoy that marked the approach to the harbor of Greystone Bay. If he could reach it, he could lay over for the night, and worry only about fending his fishing boat off the buoy instead of battling the ocean that pursued him so relentlessly.

He had left one trawling line out, not in the hope of making a catch, but because the line had snagged some- where high up the pole and he dared not try to free it until he had gained himself some measure of safety in the blowing night. As the *Cinzenta Filha* pitched through the waves, he could hear the heavy line snap and tug at the pole, for all the world as if he had something enormous moving on the three-pronged hook that trailed in the water.

"Bom Mãe," Juliao muttered, hurriedly crossing him-

140

self as the fishing boat shuddered the length of her keel. His hands were raw from cold and salt.

The boat lurched and swung to starboard; the swell toyed with her, almost pressing her far enough so that she shipped water abeam. She groaned the length of her decks as Juliao strove to hold her against the enormous drag of the ocean.

"I was a fool," he muttered through his clenched teeth. He had let his brother Manoel goad him into braving the sea when they both knew the storm was coming. It was a stupid, childish rivalry and they were both old enough to put it behind them forever. Yet they did not, and every time there was an opportunity to revive the contest, they did.

The wind howled, a sound like fingernails on taut cloth. The one trawling line cracked, then went taut, thrumming.

Juliao stared at it, too fascinated and terrified to move. *Something was on the hook*. He laughed unconvincingly. Nothing could possibly be caught on a night like this. There had to be another explanation, one that accounted for the tight line without requiring that there be a fish on it. Perhaps some driftwood. Juliao opened his mouth to try to laugh. If it were driftwood, it would have to be the entire trunk of a tree to hold the line like that.

There was a sound over the wind and the hungry roar of the sea, and Juliao wanted desperately to believe that it was the two-mile buoy with its ancient, unmelodic bell. But this was not metallic or penetrating—it was soft, insinuating, like a latch being lifted in the night.

Why, in God's Holy Name, had he consented to this madness? Manoel's prodding wasn't reason enough, and MacPherson's promise of double pay if he could bring back sea bass and scrod for his restaurant on the bluff south of Greystone Bay could not account for Juliao's bravado. He ranted at himself for what he had done even as he gripped the wheel with hands so cold they burned.

The line played out, then was taut once more.

He watched it, and felt the drag on his boat as the line held. "Something's . . . *got* . . ." He could not bring himself to finish the thought; he strove to hold the *Cinzenta Filha* with the sea at his back.

The boat moved, sliding as if something has passed under it, brushing it. He had felt that sensation before, but never at night, never during a storm. He muttered the names of all the saints he could think of and peered through the blowing wetness at the face of the ocean in the hope that he would be able to see what it was. "The line's got tangled," he said in an effort to reassure himself. "It's the line grabbing on the bottom of the boat, that's all."

It grew rougher and it took all of Juliao's failing strength to keep his boat with her back to the sea. All it would take was a little nudge to send him into a trough with the waves hitting broadside and he and his boat would be under the water before he could cross himself and pray. He had to find the buoy, and quickly, or his arms would fail him. He had an absurd, panic-filled impulse to call out to the thing on the line to give him a tow, to help him as far as the buoy, and if it would, he'd promise to cut it loose. There were only two sea bass in his locker, in any case. The whole venture had been irresponsible from the start. He chided himself as he flexed his hands on the wheel in the vain attempt to keep them from becoming numb.

After another long, wallowing ride through the waves, Juliao permitted himself the luxury of throttling back enough to listen for the sound of the bell once more. He knew he should have reached it before now, but with the weather so foul and his trawling line dragging that unknown weight, he knew he could not trust his estimations. The wind howled around him, raising spume so that it frothed over the deck.

Then, miraculously, he heard—just barely—that unmelodious clank that identified the buoy.

Juliao muttered a prayer and steered toward the place he thought the sound had come from, his shoulders shaking with the effort to keep the wheel under control. Cold, fatigue, fear—all numbed him to anything but the irregular sound of the bell.

Whatever was on the trawling line turned against the boat, as if trying to drag it farther out to sea, away from the haven of the buoy and Greystone Bay. The *Cinzenta Filha* shuddered, her frame groaning under the onslaught.

"You can't have her," Juliao promised the thing down there. "If I could cut you loose, you'd be gone to the devil!" His face ached with cold and the words came out badly, but that did not trouble him as much as the ferocity of the will that pulled at the end of the line. "You can't have my boat!" In his mind he cursed Manoel and Mac-Pherson along with the intruder, refusing to let his dread overwhelm him. "The buoy is near," he informed the wind. "And I'll tie up there. I'll put out sea anchors, and then we'll tend to you."

This time the bell was much nearer, and he had to restrain his fear that he had overshot the mark and was now passing the cliffs and would drift onto the salt marshes north of Greystone Bay. He set his jaw and forced his attention to listening as he clung to the wheel. He had never known what tenacity he had within him until this hellish night. Desperately he reached out with one hand and flipped on his searchlight in the hope that he would find the buoy not far away. The boat dipped through a wave and he nearly lost his one-handed grip on the wheel. Keening in panic, he flailed his arm in an attempt to regain his hold on the wheel. On the second try his fingers touched the wood. He strained every sinew of his body to keep that hold.

The bell rang like an ax on steel.

Juliao bit back a scream of relief. It would not do to let himself relax yet, for he had not got a line on the marker,

he had not set the sea anchors, and he still had to fend his
boat off the unforgiving steel sides of the buoy for the rest
of the night. He reduced the throttle and peered along the
faltering beam of light that raked the waves.

At last an angular structure wobbled out of the storm, its
bell clanking erratically as the sea buffetted it. Juliao
lowered his speed to little more than a crawl, hoping that
he would be able to secure to the buoy with no more than
one or two passes at it.

The *Cinzenta Filha* shivered under his feet, and the
trawling line ragged out to the side of the boat. The prow
began to swing away.

"No!" he yelled, and opened the throttle for greater
speed as he dragged the wheel over with all his strength.

It was several eternally long minutes before he felt his
boat respond, and in that time he overshot the buoy; the
sound of the bell mocked him from astern.

"You can't have this!" he shrieked at the trawling line.
"I'm not going to let you have my boat!"

As if in response to his vows, the line slacked, and
Juliao watched as the thin cable started to whip in the wind
again. It soared and danced with the storm, but the hooked
end remained ominously under the boat; whatever was on
it had not been released. Or had not let go.

Juliao shuddered as he looked away, his determination
to reach the buoy giving him strength to hold the wheel
and to ignore the line's unnatural behavior. He opened the
throttle more, nudging the lever with his knee so that he
would not have to relinquish his grip. He could feel the
resistance of the rudder as he leaned into the wheel and his
shoulders bunched and knotted as he strove to keep his
boat on course.

His light swept the water, and in the middle distance he
saw the buoy once more. Juliao muttered a scrap of a
prayer, thanking São Pedro and São Anselmo for their

protection and ordering them to stay with him a little longer.

The trawling line snapped tight.

The *Cinzenta Filha* bucked like a half-broken horse. Juliao cursed, upbraiding the saints for their caprice. His shoulder hurt so intensely that his eyes burned and his stomach turned queasy with it.

Ahead, the buoy rose on the waves, the clapper sliding around the inside of the bell, making a sound of a blade being honed.

This time Juliao was taking no chances. He throttled back and reached swiftly for the nearest coil. With agonizing effort he swung the heavy rope and flung it out toward the marker as he brought the boat as close as he dared to it. Why, in the name of all that was holy and good, had he insisted on coming out alone? If there had been just one more person with him, all he would have had to do was hold on course while the other person secured them to the buoy. But no. Manoel had challenged him, and that had put him on his mettle. Juliao's father was famous for his luck at sea and his skill at seamanship. No matter what the weather, Juliao's father had ridden it out and come back to port with a catch and his boat intact. Diniz Peixe had been famous in Greystone Bay, even among the Protestant fishermen who excused his success on the grounds of Catholic sorcery. Juliao had never been quite the same temper as his father—more cautious, more successful in the long run—and had earned a reputation for good sense, but never for bravado, never for *greatness*. Juliao knew that when he retired from the sea, he would be forgotten by most of the others who went out after the lobsters and fish. His father had been dead more than a decade and still they talked about him, often in that jocular way that said more of respect than hushed voices ever could.

A jerk on the line brought him back to himself, and to the danger around him. He tightened the rope he had thrown, and was amazed to find that it grew taut in his hands. He let out a sigh that was more like a sob. He would have crossed himself if either of his hands were free.

He cut the throttle so that the *Cinzenta Filha* was as close to motionless as he could trust her to be, and he went to pull the rope in, preparing to secure his boat to the buoy.

The aft swung ominously, pulled by whatever was on the end of the trawling line.

Juliao refused to pay this any attention. He busied himself with his work, and as soon as the knots were in place, he prepared a second line to be cast. He glared out at the buoy, thinking suddenly that the ugly black structure looked more like a trap than like his salvation. He hesitated, and then, chiding himself for his reluctance, he swung the second line and peered toward the buoy, hoping to see the weighted rope land.

Now the aft had swung farther and the waves were hitting the boat abeam. The line securing her to the buoy sobbed with the pull exerted by the drift, and the prow cracked hard against the metal body of the buoy. The second line hung slack, dipping beneath the churning froth of the water.

Juliao panted with exertion and fear. His face ached from the cold sting of the spray and the rictus of dread that marked his features. His hands were clumsy as paddles. He forced himself to think calmly, to assume a steadiness that he knew he lacked. "You must get the fenders," he muttered to himself. "For the moment that is what you need the most. Bring the fenders. Then secure the second line. Do that." His face could hardly move and so the words came out strangely muffled, as if he were more than half drunk. "The fenders first," he told himself, ignoring the rising grate of his voice and listening only to the intent of his words.

The *Cinzenta Filha* swung through the water, the deck canting dangerously, and for a moment she stood almost on her beam ends before easing back into the trough of the waves as if she had no strength left.

"Your boat must have strength," Juliao's father had said many times. "It is not your strength alone, but the strength of your boat that will save you when the ocean is hunting you. If you have no faith in your boat, in her strength, then the fishes will have you for dinner."

With an oath Juliao lurched toward the nearest fender, trying to shut out the memory of his father while battling against the sea. His boat was fine—*fine*. He would trust the *Cinzenta Filha* at any time in any sea. It was not the boat that filled him with the terror that swam in his veins, but that thing that hung on the trawling line, a thing with strength enough to pull his boat against the whole of the storm-driven ocean. His thoughts froze and he stared into the streaming night, hypnotized by the fall of the sleety rain. It was not possible to imagine such things. There were no such creatures in the ocean, and surely if there were, they would not want so little a thing as his boat. It would be nothing to them—hardly a morsel, hardly a toy. . . .

The buoy clanged ominously as the lines of the *Cinzenta Filha* pulled and whipped around it.

Juliao raised his head, trying to gather his thoughts again. He was too tired, he decided. It was the cold and the fatigue that distorted his mind, that drove him to such desperate reverie when he had far better use for his time. He hurried toward the side, reaching for the cord that held the fender in place.

The weight of the truck tire was more than he had anticipated. His shoulders knotted in protest as he attempted to drag it toward the bow of the little fishing boat.

Above him, the trawling line slackened.

With more strength than he had dreamed he possessed,

Juliao seized the heavy rope and dragged the fender forward, cursing as loudly as possible as he went. His eyes
blurred with the effort and he moved strangely, as if his
body were an unfamiliar machine. At last he was able to
drop the huge tire into place near the bow. His hands
trembled and burned as he strove to secure it. Knots that
he had learned as a child were now too difficult and
complex and the results were clumsy, unsafe.

"I will tie it again later," Juliao said, speaking to his
boat. "You will be safe, my girl."

The boat wallowed, drifting more dangerously toward a
position where a sudden wave might swamp her. The
planking moaned and the wheel swung sluggishly in response to the movement of the water across the rudder.
The trawling line remained slack.

"Go away," Juliao breathed as he watched the line.
"Go away and leave us here."

The slack line moved closer, the high end slapping
against the brace that held it out from the boat, making a
cracking sound like mirthless laughter.

"Go away!" Juliao shouted, and started to make his
way down the starboard side of the boat to the second
fender. Once he had set it in place, he would be able to
lash the wheel more tightly and have to worry only about
fending the boat off from the buoy.

Slowly the trawling line drew away from the boat.

Manoel would mock him for his fear, Juliao decided as
he felt his legs tremble. His brother had always thought
him a coward, and this would confirm his opinion, he
knew it. Manoel would tell everyone in the town, everyone who drank at the Waterford Tavern, that Juliao had let a
dragging trawling line frighten him, that Juliao had been
foolish enough to be frightened into tying up to a buoy in
the middle of a storm simply because the trawling line was
pulled about by the water and the storm. "He believes in
the tales," Juliao could almost hear Manoel say. "He

heard about the creatures of the night that prey on fishing boats, and he believed them. Juliao thinks that he will be taken down to the caves under the sea and that monsters will pick their teeth with his bones.'' The laughter rang in his ears as if his brother stood beside him, his smile growing broader as Juliao tried to hold himself straight.

The trawling line straightened to aft, tightening across the wind.

Juliao forced himself not to look. He continued down the canting deck toward the second fender.

A sudden shiver ran down the planks and the two lines to the buoy straightened and strained as the trawling line ran out toward the open sea.

"Bom Mãe!" Juliao shrieked as he slipped and fell heavily. He could feel the wood quiver, and his heart slammed in his chest. "No, my girl,'' he crooned in panic. "No, do not surrender, not yet. Hold on, girl.''

The boat whined and the trawling line keened in the wind.

Carefully Juliao began to crawl, his knees sliding on the wet surface. He kept his eye on the devil plank and refused to watch the trawling line as it began to swing around to port. The boat moaned with every jarring blow of the waves; the relentless tension from the trawling line did not lessen as the stern began to swing.

He reached the fender line and used it to drag himself to his feet. He clung to the rail, his vision ruined by the rush of water from the storm. He could hear the low throb of the engine begin to falter as he started to drag the fender line toward him.

Now the trawling line had pulled the *Cinzenta Filha* so that the waves struck the bow hard enough to drive the boat back toward the buoy. The first impact with the metal was cushioned by the tire already in place, but the second took the full brunt of the buoy's swing on her exposed side, just aft of the prow.

"You cannot do this!" Juliao yelled, lurching along the rail, hands locked on the fender line. His knuckles were bleeding but he could not feel it, nor the sting of the salt in the cuts. "Stop!"

The next blow was a glancing one, but it was sufficient to throw him off his feet. *"Pare! Pare!"*

The boat continued to slide through the water, moving against the thrust of the waves at an angle to the wind.

"You cannot do this!" He clawed himself back to his feet and went a few steps farther before the *Cinzenta Filha* struck the buoy again, and this time with a sound like the sob of a wounded animal. Juliao clung to the side of the boat, and felt the change in her as she shifted away from the buoy.

There was damage, of this he was sure. He knew his boat too well not to recognize the slightest alterations, and now that sense warned him that she had been harmed by the last impact. He propelled himself to the bow, dragging the fender line after him, cursing as he went. As he worked to secure the heavy rope, he tried to listen to the boat, to hear her movement with the water. He did not dare to go below, for fear that he would not be able to reach the deck again. What did it matter if he found her taking on water? He would have no opportunity to fix the damage, or even the time to shore her up in lieu of repair. "Hold on, girl," he said, touching the wood as if it were the arm of a friend. "Hold on."

The trawling line was moving once more, and the *Cinzenta Filha* shifted sluggishly to the drag.

Abelardo Chave had told a story once, late at night when he was more than half drunk, of a night many years ago when he and his uncle had been caught by a storm. They had almost lost their boat, Abelardo had said, and then had retreated into silence, cursing Greystone Bay for the things that clung to its harbor. "They were mad, those English who came here. They thought the horns would protect them, but they were fools. Everyone who fishes from here is a fool.'' After that he had retreated into silence and had insisted later that it was only drink that had made him say such things. ''Don't you know enough to ignore what a man tells you in his cups?'' he had asked with uneasy humor. ''All fishermen tell tales.'' Diniz Peixe had not laughed with the others, but had given Abelardo a hard, searching look. ''Did you make a night catch?'' he had asked Abelardo, and plainly did not expect an answer.

The grumble of the engine faltered and coughed.

''No!'' Juliao screamed. ''You must hang on, girl!'' He had named her properly, he reminded himself. He had named her for her home, for her harbor, the Grey Daughter, and she had been blessed by the priest on the Feast of São Anselmo. She had been sailing out of Greystone Bay for years, and it pleased Juliao to know that she had been one of the most steadily successful fishing boats on this part of the coast. Now she was failing him, and worse—he was failing her.

What was on the trawling line? He watched it play out and pull again, his mind trying to picture the thing on the end of the line. Why did it bother with him? What had he got?

The *Cinzenta Filha* rode up a wave, wobbled over the crest, and settled lower in the water as the wave passed on. Her body shook as if she were ill with fever.

Leaving the bow, Juliao stumbled back to the wheel and unlashed it, determined to keep the boat from further damage. He put his hand on the throttle and tested it. To his horror, the engine sputtered and failed.

In the howl of the storm the world was strangely silent. The *Cinzenta Filha* slid nearer the buoy as the trawling line tugged her nearer the looming metal structure.

What had his father told him so many years ago? What was it that he had warned him of? At the time Juliao had

thought the whole conversation a joke, one of the strange
jests that Diniz sometimes made with those he knew.
"There are things in the sea," he had told his son, and had
not elaborated on this for some little time. Finally he had
leaned back in his chair and stared up at the ceiling. "The
ocean is there for daring. But there are other things that no
man can dare." Looking at the trawling line, Juliao prayed
that his father had meant something other than the sinister
presence that bedeviled his crippled boat.

Abruptly the line changed direction and there was a soft,
terrible shriek in the water as it approached the boat. As
the rope hit the rail, the *Cinzenta Filha* jerked as if stung
by a lash.

"What do you want?" Juliao railed at the unseen presence. "It is not enough that I have the wind and the sea?
Must you come against us too?" He lifted his bleeding
hand in protest, then lowered it as the boat dipped low in
the wave, shipping water along the deck, riding a little
lower when she righted herself.

Abelardo had not gone out at night after that episode, or
so he claimed, and Juliao's father had not questioned his
wisdom. "It is one thing for me to do so, for I have made
arrangements. But it is another thing for Abelardo. He has
not negotiated with . . ." Diniz had never finished his
sentence, and when Juliao had tried to question him further, he had insisted that there was nothing more for him
to say. Looking down into the sea, Juliao wondered how
his father could have negotiated with anything like the
monstrous—for surely, unseen though it was, it was
monstrous—*thing* at the far end of his trawling line.

Juliao felt the boat quiver as it rubbed against the buoy,
and the hull groaned at the pressure as it was dragged
along the metal. He reached the rail, hoping to fend off the
worst of the impact, his thoughts scattering as he reached
out over the frothing water.

"Everyone makes pacts with fate, *meu filho*. Some are

paid in strange coin, but everyone makes pacts and all the pacts are honored.'' Diniz had been standing on the prow of his fishing boat, the *Noite Vinho*, his eyes fixed on the grey flanks of the ocean. "We are here on tolerance, only that." Juliao was used to his father's philosophizing in this way, for he often talked of fate and fortune after an especially good catch. "If we acknowledge our fate, then we are . . .'' He had chuckled. "Never mind; you'll find out, Juliao. When you're an old man like your father, you'll find out."

The trawling line had pulled his boat around and was now dragging the port side across the metal body of the buoy. The *Cinzenta Filha* shuddered, her planks whimpering at the abuse.

"Let us go!" Juliao demanded, his voice now only a croak. "Let us go!"

Once more the line shifted, the water making a low, ominous snort as the bow crossed the front of the storm. Something slid along the underside, rubbing against the keel as a cat rubs a leg. The very *familiarity* of the movement made it a vile caress, more frightening than the might of the storm.

Juliao felt determination return. He shook his head, then made his way back to the wheel. He lashed this down methodically, going through the motions automatically while he tried to think of some way to keep his boat from sinking until the storm was passed and he could cut the line free. It would take more than the knife in his belt, he knew, for the trawling line was made of nylon-clad wire cable and nothing less than the massive-jawed cutters in the pilot house would be capable of severing it. He made certain that the lashing on the wheel was secure, then began to make his way aft, where his long grappling poles with their long steel hooks lay. With one or two of these he was fairly certain he could keep the *Cinzenta Filha* from being dashed to bits against the buoy.

"I will save you," he promised as he scrabbled up the deck. "I will not let that . . . *thing* have you." As he said this, he patted the wet, cold planking in reassurance.

As he neared the prow, he reached for line, knowing that he would have to lash himself to the rail. He was afraid that exhaustion would claim him before the storm was over, before he could be rid of the thing on the trawling line. "I have to stay awake," he ordered himself. "I must not fall asleep."

The rope in his hands was stiff with salt; the long poles clattered and rattled as he held them. He looped the line over the rail, and had one instant of doubt. If he tied himself too securely, he might not be able to get free if the boat went down. . . . "Do not think this," he growled. "We will survive."

Once the line was fixed around his waist and over his shoulders, he let himself relax into the bonds, saving his waning strength for holding the pole out where he could use it to press the marker back from the boat and the fenders. Looking down, he saw that the old tire on this side of the boat was coming apart. In two or three more scrapes, it would be almost useless.

Without warning the trawling line tightened and the bow of the *Cinzenta Filha* was raked over the steel side of the buoy. Juliao stretched, hoping to keep the buoy at some distance. He watched in despair as the pole he held shattered and fell away into the ocean. In the next instant the boat slammed against the buoy and Juliao was flung against the rail with such force that he gasped for air, his body leaning helplessly in its restraints.

He was dazed: He stared at the buoy and could not recall what it was, or why he was here, or how he had come to be so wet. He waved one hand and felt a deep stabbing pain in his side. Moaning, he shifted his weight to ease the pain and discovered that his bindings would not permit the movement.

"You have to understand, *meu filho*, that it was not
what I wished to do. A man makes compromises in his
life, and many of them are not pleasant. But what could I
do, after all?" The voice was as clear as anything Juliao
had ever heard, but it was too much of an effort for him to
turn to face his father. Besides, his father had been dead
for years, and he could not now be on the *Cinzenta Filha*,
during the storm. *"Meu pai?"* he whispered.

The trawling line swung toward him, cutting his cheek
as it moved.

Juliao cried out, and tried to staunch the blood that
welled, and ran down his face as he resisted the sharp hurt
that came with the movement.

"It is this place, *meu filho*. Greystone Bay is marked,
and those who sail out between the horns are marked as
well."

He made no sense of the words; his sight clouded and he
wondered if it was fog or something worse.

"Juliao, do not blame your brother. By rights it should
be Manoel who came here—he knew the bargain, for he
was with me when I made it. But he is a weak man, and
he does not love the sea, he does not know his boat. I
should have willed you the *Noite Vinho*, not Manoel. I
realize that, *meu filho*."

Manoel. Yes. He could picture his brother sitting in the
Waterford Tavern, a cigarette in his hand, his head wreathed
in tendrils of smoke while he chided those around him for
their lack of spirit, their lack of ovos. No one had been
willing to take his challenge but Juliao, his brother. He
had said that it was Diniz who had been the only true
fisherman in the family, that neither he nor Juliao had any
claim to that name. He had reminded Juliao of the offer
from MacPherson and of the night that their father had
been caught in weather far heavier than what was expected
this night. He even offered to loan Juliao the *Noite Vinho*.
How odd it all seemed to Juliao as he tried uselessly to

work the knots holding him captive to the rail. It might have happened years ago, in another country, for all the sense it made to him now. Manoel had said that he was a coward and Juliao had proved only that Manoel was wrong—Juliao was not a coward, he was a reckless idiot. He coughed and the pain sharpened.

The buoy bell made a sound like breaking rock, and it snapped his attention back from the odd, dreamlike remembrances.

It took all his will to ignore the agony that went through him as he reached for the second pole. He could not see where the trawling line had got to, but he felt the steady drag on his boat as the stern was dragged around to the east, once again bringing the waves abeam. It was dangerous to remain in this position, and the risk of sinking was suddenly more of a certainty than it had ever been. The buoy rocked, leaning toward the prow, and for one mad instant he wondered if he dared to cut himself free of the buoy, to drift on the ocean until the storm wrecked the fragile craft. If the engine had still been working, he might have taken the chance, but without power the danger was too overwhelming. Juliao set his jaw and once again reached out over the seething ocean, the pole grasped in his numb hands. He squinted at the water, seeing patterns form in it, hoping that one might reveal what was on his trawling line.

The *Cinzenta Filha* was dragged against the buoy, her entire hull protesting.

Juliao prodded and poked, unable to reach the buoy at first. When the pole at last was within range, the boat capriciously lurched closer, and the collision went through him like a turn on the rack. He clung to the pole, desperately praying he would not drop it. The far end of the pole flailed at the marker, and made one ineffective swipe at the upper struts, where the hook tangled in the cross-bracing.

Horrified, numb, Juliao gripped the pole and wiggled

it, wishing that he could break free. Instead of a much-needed aid, the pole had now become more dangerous than he could have imagined. He dared not let go now, for it might then swing back, bringing more damage than had already been caused.

"No!" he protested to the streaming sky. "No."

The trawling line slapped at his face again and a new runnel of blood appeared just above his eyes.

The *Cinzenta Filha* pitched heavily; the pole was yanked from his hands.

"Let it go, *meu filho*," his father's voice said, very near at hand. "It need not take long."

He blocked out the gentle seductiveness he heard in those words. "I will not let us fail," he vowed to his boat. "You are my girl, my boat, and I will not fail you. But you must stay afloat, at least until the storm lets up." He heard something else on the wind, and in the next moment the end of the pole slammed into the side of his head.

The Waterford Tavern was darker than usual, and there were many men that Juliao did not recognize seated around the hatch-cover tables. Most of them were fishermen—they had the look of it: weathered faces creased and hardened by salt and wind and sun; hands huge and tough as leather; movement that seemed, even on land, to be controlled by the constant shifting of a deck underfoot. Many wore outmoded clothing and carried pipes of a design that Juliao had seen only his grandfather smoke.

Diniz sat with another man, his pewter-colored hair shining in the dim light of the lamp. He nodded to his companion, saying, "I didn't want to make the bargain."

"Nor I," the other agreed in a Protestant New England accent. "I promised my da that I would not fish at night, that I would never have any truck to the Master of the Horns. How was I to guess that a so'wester would keep me out long into the night? I didn't want to bring in my nets, but . . . ."

Diniz nodded. "It was that or be sunk. I couldn't cut my nets away. I tried."

The other man nodded. "I heard that it was old Jared Holmes made the first pact, some said it was 1694 when he did." He glanced across the room toward a distant, shadow-filled corner. "Never had the guts to ask him."

"What good would it do?" Diniz lifted his tankard but could not drink from it. "I heard it was 1704 when he did."

"Probably some Algonquin brave was the first, or one of the old Vikings who come here in the old days," the fisherman said. "Hawkins said that his gre'granda was the first of his family to do it. You recall how they lose their sons in that family."

Neither man wanted to talk, and neither could keep from speaking. At each of the tables the same hushed, unwelcome conversations were taking place.

"The Master of the Horns," Diniz muttered, awe and repugnance in his tone. "Who thought of that, do you think?"

"A waggish lad," the other man said. "Someone with no one to lose but himself."

"Or another son, perhaps," Diniz said, his voice hollow with grief.

"It can't be helped," the other sighed. "What are we to do?"

"If you'd known, would you have done it?"

"I don't reckon I would have gone down when there was another way, if that's your meaning." He shook his head slowly. "Why that bargain, of all bargains? Why trade the sons for ourselves?"

"Because it wouldn't save them if we'd refused," Diniz responded after a silence. "It would come to them as easily as it came to us. If we did not bargain, if we went down, it would not spare our sons or their sons."

"You did well for yourself, and for them, Diniz. You

made the most of the bargain. Better nor some of the others. Think of Black and Williams. What difference did it make to either of them?" He leaned back. "I told my Jake about it, warned him that he'd have to find another life for himself, but what good did that do? His own Danny ended up going down while out with the Boy Scouts. The Master won't be denied." He lowered his head. "I ask myself, sometimes, why I didn't leave here, go to another town, take up another work entirely, but then I'd think of my nephews and their sons, and I knew there'd be a time the Master would come for one of them, and there'd be no warning, and it might not stop with one. They said that Trampe went to Wisconsin after it got him at night, and four of his nephews and a cousin went down for him. Trampe got killed in a train wreck, they say."

"Trampe was a coward," Diniz said in a neutral tone. "He wasn't a very good fisherman either."

"But . . ." The other man sighed, and looked around the room. "If there were a way to warn them."

"Can't," Diniz snapped. "The Master takes us *and* them if we do."

"Why? What does it gain?" This time the fisherman shook his head with vehemence. "If we warned them, they could be prepared. That would help."

"Would it? Or would it make it worse? Manoel only guessed, and he sent his brother out. Juliao took the challenge because Manoel was too frightened to risk the night. He's a careful man, but only of himself. Juliao thinks of honor and his reputation, and Manoel knows it. So Juliao will pay and Manoel will leave the sea."

Under the building the waves sucked and worried the pilings, and the sound penetrated to the tavern itself, as if some huge creature in the next room was enjoying a succulent meal.

"The storm will blow itself out before long," the other fisherman said to Diniz.

"And fog's on the way." Diniz looked up, his features ragged with despair. "And what then?"

"You know what then," the other man told him sadly.

The lick and murmur of the waves was louder and it drowned the soft susurrus of conversation, making everything indistinct, and a low howl, the sound of distant wind, rose over the waves.

And Juliao blinked his eyes against the stinging spray and felt his broken ribs shove deeper into his chest.

The buoy had rocked far toward the *Cinzenta Filha* and had struck a glancing blow at the bow of the boat. Now there was a deep gouge in the rail and some of the side beneath had buckled. Juliao stared at it, and felt through his body that the boat was starting to list to starboard.

"We told you not to fish at night," Diniz's voice came, a thready whisper on the screaming wind.

"São Pedro!" Juliao called, hoping that he had been dreaming. His body trembled with pain and cold. "Save me."

The good saint who was made a fisher of men did not heed this cry. The storm continued and the trawling line cut across the air and cut into Juliao's shoulder. He arched away from the line, but could not escape.

"I must get out," Juliao said to himself as he stared at the knots holding him to the rail. "Then I can do something, if only I am free."

The fender on this side of the boat was in shreds, providing no protection to the hull. Looking down, he could see that there were many places where the buoy had banged and scraped the wood. He assumed that the other side was as bad. Grimly he set about the task of untying the knots that held him. His battered, bleeding fingers worked slowly, with difficulty, and the hurt was greater than he had anticipated, since he had assumed his hands were numb. Movement wakened feeling once more, and each time he forced the sodden rope to give, he could feel the agony build up in his arms.

More rain sprayed over him, and with it stinging sleet. His foul-weather gear deflected some of it, but with the shoulder cut, his clothing was quickly soaked.

"The Master of the Horns fishes at night," Diniz's voice said, filled with grief and reproach. "The Master demands his due, and he will have it."

"I . . . I have to save my boat," Juliao said weakly as he watched the trawling line start to bring the *Cinzenta Filha* up to the buoy once more. His hands were raw from working the ropes, and still he was not free of them.

"We who sail from Greystone Bay make pacts with the Master," Diniz's voice went on. "We are very successful fishermen—even when others find no fish, we come back with full nets. The pact promises this to us. But it promises for a price. You must not forget the price, for the Master never does."

"Be quiet, father," Juliao mumbled. He was so cold and so wet, and his thoughts came sluggishly. He had no idea how long he had been trapped here, but it seemed so much longer than one night. His head throbbed from fatigue and he wanted nothing more than to close his eyes and sleep.

"The pact must be honored. It should have been Manoel who took the obligation. He should have brought the *Noite Vinho,* for that is the boat that was promised to the Master. He will not be excused through sending you."

Although he heard the words, they made no sense. Juliao turned his head away from the buoy, no longer willing to watch its ruthless course of damage that it brought to the boat. He continued to work at the ropes, and gave all his concentration to the little progress he was able to make as the tough fibers inched through their complicated knots. He was aware that the boat was riding lower and that she rolled more heavily with every wave that washed over her. He shivered, hoping that he would soon see the distant promise of dawn in the clouds.

The trawling line pulled harder and the boat rolled toward its pull.

With a scream of metal on wood the buoy raked the length of the *Cinzenta Filha*, throwing splinters through the air. Another deep bite was taken out of the rail, and for the next several seconds the bell of the buoy clanged overhead in triumph.

One of the knots was undone, but the rest remained firm, resisting Juliao's efforts to get free of them.

"There are reasons to fish from Greystone Bay," said Juliao's father in the howling wind. "The fishermen always prosper. But they always pay for their prosperity. Never forget that."

Juliao shook his head. He was alone on his boat. His father had been dead for years. He had not come out on this wailing night to honor a pact made with some *thing* called the Master; he had come to catch fish at a premium price because MacPherson had offered and his brother Manoel had goaded him into taking the chance. That he was now caught in this dire predicament was not the result of his father's dealing with supernatural forces, but his own arrogance and stupidity. He recalled all the times that the priest had spoken against the legends that were so much a part of Greystone Bay. "They are nothing more than dangerous illusions, invented to beguile the hours after supper in a little, isolated community. It is wrong for those who believe in God and worship him to put credence in the legends of impious souls who have nothing better to do than make up tales to frighten children." Juliao nodded several times, muttering a prayer as he did: "God protect me; São Pedro, São Anselmo, protect me. Guide my boat back to the harbor." He crossed himself slowly, his whole body alive with pain.

The trawling line swung around, and this time the

Cinzenta Filha took the blow against the buoy directly on her prow. The hull screamed as seams buckled and the sea got into her.

"God! *God!*" Juliao cried to the storm-driven clouds. "No!"

The trawling line came sliding through the water, moving against the wind, and a large, dark, scaly flank rolled just the other side of the buoy.

Juliao blinked and tried to wipe the saltwater from his eyes. He had seen sharks and dolphins and whales, even a huge squid once, but nothing he had ever known before was like the hide he had glimpsed. He fell to his knees as the boat began to settle toward her starboard side. From the sound belowdecks, she would go down fast. He looked around, wishing he could reach the hatchet that could cut him free before his boat was pulled to the bottom. There was a scaling knife tucked in the outside strap of his boot, and he fumbled for it, hoping it would keep enough of an edge to sever the lines that held him. He wished he had reached for it earlier, when his thoughts had been so confused, for he had lost precious time. At last he gripped the handle of the knife and tugged it out of its sheath.

The buoy slapped the side of the boat, almost playful now that the worst had been done.

Something passed under the boat, rubbing the length of the keel, drawing the trawling line after it.

"You cannot do this," Juliao vowed, but this time his voice was high with dread, and in his unsteady hands the knife cut his thumb instead of the rope.

"It does not take long, *meu filho*," Diniz's voice crooned. "The Master is severe, but he isn't cruel. Your nephews will fish without harm because of you."

"You're dead!" Juliao yelled. "You died years ago!"

"But the pact goes on," was the unperturbed response. "Whether I am alive or dead, the pact goes on."

"There is no pact." He watched in horror as the first

wave came over the side and did not fall away. The
sucking, chuckling of water was very loud.

"As fishermen catch fish, they are caught. That is the
pact. The Master is fair."

Desperately, Juliao tried to cut the ropes and was able to
saw two of the strands when the *Cinzenta Filha* slipped
toward her beam ends, slamming him against the deck,
pinning him there with the force of the slide. Water sprayed
over him.

The trawling line stood still, waiting.

Seawater rushed over him, and he held his breath, his
eyes tightly closed, hoping for the wet to be gone so that
he could gasp for air again.

Seconds went by, stretching toward a minute. There was
something in the water ahead of him, huge and monstrous,
coming toward the boat at a leisurely rate. He opened his
eyes and closed them, but the presence did not change. His
lungs burned, his throat spasmed, he tugged ineffectually
on the ropes holding him, and there was darkness surrounding him. As if from another country, he heard the
buoy bang out the mourning note.

"It's almost over," Diniz said. "The pact is fulfilled."

Outraged, Juliao opened his mouth to protest, and water
invaded him.

The *Cinzenta Filha*, falling through the water, broke
first one and then the other line holding her to the buoy as
she carried her offering toward the Master of the Horns in
the cold, silent depths.

Nocturne
by
Robert Bloch

Listen to me, darling.

You don't mind if I talk now, do you? I'm not sleepy yet, and there's so much I want to tell you. I couldn't before, because I was always afraid.

If that sounds funny to you, I can understand why. When you're young and beautiful there's nothing to be afraid of, is there?

I'm the one who was always getting put down, laughed at, rejected. And because of that I guess I came to the point where I rejected myself. Looking back I can see how that would make me afraid, make me a loner.

But you changed all that. I'm not afraid anymore, and with you beside me the loneliness is gone too.

That's another thing you never had to worry about, darling. People like you are never lonely, because they always have love. You get it from your folks when you're a kid, you get it from friends along the way, and then

165

when you grow up you've got it made. Don't think I haven't noticed—all those jocks, the Big Men On Campus, coming on to you, making their moves. And you smiling, taking it all for granted.

Don't get me wrong, I'm not blaming you. Why shouldn't you take it for granted when that's how it's always been?

The reason I'm telling you this is to try and make you understand how different it was for me. Ever since I can remember, I was running scared. And the worst time was at night when everything came together—being afraid because I was all alone in the dark and nobody cared, not even my folks.

I used to lay awake here in bed, crying because of the things Mom said, the things Dad did to hurt me. Looking back now I don't think they tried to make me feel bad on purpose; it's just that they didn't know how sensitive I was. To them, telling me I had a zit on my nose was just a joke. When they called me a klutz it was only their way of reminding me to be more careful. Saying that wearing glasses would keep me from making the team didn't mean they blamed me for it. But at the time it really got to me.

That's what made me afraid the most—when I realized I hated them for what they said, how they laughed. If my very own father and mother didn't care about hurting my feelings, how could I expect better from anyone else? To the other kids, the teachers, I must be ten times worse, so I hated them too. But I didn't want to hate them, I was afraid of hating everybody, so—like the shrink said—I projected my fear on the darkness instead.

Oh yes, I went to a shrink. You didn't know that, did you, darling? My folks never told anyone they sent me; it was a kind of guilty secret, something they were ashamed to admit. Their son going to a head doctor because he cried at night. And wet the bed. What's the matter, a big boy like you, acting like a baby? Grow up, be a man, they told me.

The shrink never said that, of course. He tried to help, I know he did, and after a while I got over the enuresis. That's the word he used, I've always remembered it. I remember a lot of things he told me, the things he taught me. But the main thing he taught me was something he didn't realize. He taught me not to show my feelings.

He thought he cured me of being afraid of the dark, and that's why I could stop seeing him. What really happened was I just stopped talking about the things that scared me. I wanted to please him, please my folks, get a taste of what it was like to be praised instead of blamed.

But all I could taste was the fear.

I'd lie awake in the dark night after night, fighting to keep from trembling. Now, instead of being afraid of hating others, I was afraid of *things*. Things like shadows, the shadows that crawled out of the corners, things like the wind howling outside the window. I'd hide my head under the pillow to shut out the shapes and the sounds, but it never worked.

Because then I'd fall asleep and the dreams came. That's when the wind-sounds changed into voices laughing at me, and the shadows turned into faces, all staring eyes and mouths that grinned. Every night they came, and every night I'd wake up screaming.

Please, darling, try to remember I'm not telling you this to frighten you, only to make you understand what it was like for me all these years.

The worst part was that I couldn't say anything to anyone. Now I was adult and everyone thought I'd outgrown my "little problem."

That's what my folks used to call it, my "little problem." At least they didn't talk to me that way when I got older. Instead, it was, "I don't see what a humanities major is going to do for you when you get out of school. Time you started thinking about something practical, a

career. Here you are, going on twenty-one already, and
you still have no idea what you want to do with your life."

Not true, of course. I knew what I wanted to do. I
wanted to crawl into a hole somewhere and die. And if I
couldn't manage that, maybe I'd have to do something
else. Like committing suicide.

Don't think it hadn't crossed my mind. Nights like this,
lying alone in bed here, I even planned the ways. But it
was no use; I knew I didn't have the guts to go through
with it.

Afraid to live, afraid to die. So I read a lot, listened to
music, went to the movies, watched TV. It filled time, but
it couldn't fill up my life. For that you need friends,
people who care.

Please don't get the wrong impression, darling. It isn't
like I just turned my back on everybody. I got to know a
lot of people on campus and in my classes, and I tried to
make friends with them, but it never seemed to work that
way. Nobody wanted to hang out with me, invite me to
their parties. I guess I know why. Who cares about a
skinny little runt with glasses, somebody who's afraid to
look anyone in the eye, and stutters when he tries to talk?

You never had that problem, did you? I know, because I
was watching. Ever since the day you enrolled in English lit
class I used to watch. Only it was more than just watching—I
memorized you. The way you looked and walked and
smiled and laughed, even little things like brushing the
hair back from your forehead before you stood up to
answer a question.

I don't suppose you noticed me at all. And I never got
up enough nerve to talk to you or even say hello, not with
that gang always around you—all those grinning guys with
Burt Reynolds mustaches doing their macho numbers. Oh,
I can't blame you for liking that attention. It's just that I
didn't have a chance, and I knew it.

But I needed someone to care, and for a while I thought

my folks might still be the answer. Seeing me graduate *magna cum laude* and all that, maybe they'd change their minds about me.

I remember how excited I was when they phoned and said they were cutting their vacation trip short and coming back in time for graduation ceremonies, and how good it felt driving out to the airport to pick them up.

You know what happened, of course. It was on the news, all over the papers. That damned freak crash, taking off from the stopover in Denver. They never got to see me graduate and I never saw them again, just the closed coffins. Then the funeral, and the lawyer, and settling the estate—but I don't want to talk about it. I'm not looking for sympathy, darling, just trying to make you understand.

At first it looked like things would get better for me, because I inherited enough to live on without worrying about a regular job. And there was nobody to put me down now or boss me around.

But that's what made it so bad. I was all alone, rattling around in this big house with no one to see or talk to. I got a feeling like I was in solitary confinement, and maybe I went a little stir-crazy.

That's the only way I can explain what I did. Up to now I've been ashamed to tell anyone, but I can tell you. Maybe you've already guessed the reason I had.

It's because I'd never been with a woman.

Hard to believe in this day and age, isn't it? Twenty-three years old and still a virgin.

So I went to this hooker.

It happened because I couldn't stand being alone anymore, so one night I drove over to this bar. That's another thing—I never did dope and all I'd ever had to drink up until then was a beer or two once in a while. But this time I thought to hell with it, I'm going to find out what it's like, and of course the straight shots hit me right away.

I didn't even know I was drunk, just felt relaxed, almost

like I am with you now. I was all alone in the place and I got to talking to the bartender. I don't remember exactly what I said or how it came up, but he told me about this hooker and gave me the address. He even phoned to let her know I was coming—I suppose they had some kind of an arrangement.

If it wasn't that I was drunk, I'd never have gone through with it, but I went up to her apartment and she was waiting for me. She was a lot younger and prettier than I expected, more like a high-class call-girl. Looking back now I can see she must have known what the situation was and did her best to make things easy, even helping me get my clothes off, and then—

And then, nothing. I won't go into the gory details, I don't want to think about it even now, but everything went wrong, and I couldn't, and she started to laugh and called me a name. I didn't care; all I wanted was out of there.

It wasn't until later that I thought about the name she called me. Then I got mad, but I was really angry at myself for being such a fool.

The only thing I got out of it was learning how the drinks could help. I bought some whiskey to keep in the house and did my drinking at home. Don't worry, I'm not an alcoholic or anything like that. I can quit whenever I want, and I know how to handle the stuff. But a few shots make me sleep better, without the dreams. The trouble is, when I'm awake I still get uptight and I have to take a couple of drinks just to calm down.

But I won't have to depend on whiskey anymore. Now I have you. I don't know how you feel, but to me it's like a miracle. A dream come true.

Because sometimes even the drinks don't help. Like tonight, when I got so worked up remembering all the bad things and wondering if there was any sense in trying to go on. Sitting here in the house when the storm started, listening to the wind rattling the shutters, looking at the empty bottle on the table, I knew I just had to get out.

I hadn't eaten anything since breakfast, so I figured some food might help. The rain was really coming down heavy when I left. It was hard to see ahead and the car kept skidding, so I decided to turn off Harbor Road and take the long way into town.

That's when it really hit me—driving inland with no lights anywhere, no traffic, nothing but the woods all around. I guess the drinks were hitting me too because when the fog started rolling in from the Bay I got this terrible empty feeling inside, as if I was all alone and lost in the middle of nowhere. And I knew that even if the storm stopped and the fog lifted, I would still be alone, and nothing would ever happen to save me.

Then you happened, darling. You saved me.

The moment I saw you standing there next to that silly little red convertible and waving your flashlight, it was as though everything changed. Just recognizing you, knowing that you were really there and calling to me turned a nightmare into a dream come true.

Maybe you think it was just chance that made me take the side road so that I'd find you stranded there after your tire blew. But it wasn't chance, darling—it was fate. Looking back now I can see that it was meant to be.

Driving you to the service station, finding it closed, bringing you here to the house to use the phone, all this was fate too.

And the way you looked at me, the way you smiled, did something I can't explain. For the first time in my life I felt like a real man. And for the first time in my life I could act like a man.

Let me confess something. I lied when I told you the phone was out. It really worked, but I didn't want you to know. What I wanted was to have you here with me, have you and hold you the way a real man holds the woman he loves.

That's what I did and I hope you understand now. I hope you realize what this has meant to me, and that it means something to you too. I knew I loved you too much to force you, so I'm glad it worked out the way it did. Everything just seemed to happen, because it was fate.

You were so wonderful, darling—not like that hooker, not like the girls who always laughed. I can forget them now, forget the shame and the tears, because I have you. From now on we'll always be together.

Thank you, darling. Thank you for making me happy with the gift of your love.

I only wish now that I hadn't killed you first.

A Heritage Upheld
by
Joseph Payne Brennan

I wasn't sure where we were heading until, at Leffing's signal, I turned off the main north-south interstate into Port Boulevard.

"We must be bound for Greystone Bay!" I exclaimed. "Why all the secrecy?"

Three days before, Leffing had telephoned to tell me that he had accepted "a case which might be of some interest." He mentioned "a small city, some two hours by car, north from New Haven." Beyond that, almost nothing. His frequent reticence often irritated me, but I had come to accept it.

This time he appeared to sense my annoyance. "I was sworn to the strictest secrecy, Brennan. I promised not to mention even our destination."

I was not mollified; I had worked with Leffing for years. I had thought I was to be trusted. But I bit my tongue—almost literally—and said nothing.

The town, partially visible as we drove over the western hills from the highway, lay about four miles away. Beyond glittered the natural harbor that had given the city part of its name.

Some years before, while on vacation, I had driven along Harbor Road, which skirts the town proper. But fog had been blowing in from the Bay, limiting visibility. I remembered a wide boardwalk on my right and the sound of heavy waves pounding a rocky shoreline below.

I did know a little about the town's history. It had been founded before the Revolution by a somewhat motley shipload of emigrants: dissenters, free-thinkers, even downright undesirables, at least in the eyes of their European neighbors. In spite of, or because of, their origins and reputations, they had worked diligently to establish an ordered and ultimately prosperous community, naming it after their leader, Winston Greystone. Over more than two centuries the town had absorbed persons of widely varying ethnic and economic backgrounds, but many of the old families remained prestigious, powerful, and affluent.

After driving through a relatively recent residential development, encompassing a somewhat incongruous assortment of house styles and sizes, we passed a pleasant rural section of carefully tended truck farms, wood lots, and boulder-strewn pastures. Very shortly these were succeeded by a group of box and shoe factories, along with warehouses and acres of parking lots. Beyond lay a few marshy meadows and then we were in the bustling heart of Greystone Bay.

Leffing looked ahead, frowning. "Our destination is the police station. It stands next to City Hall, which we should see shortly."

City Hall, an oversize and rather ugly edifice of weathered grey-white granite, was the centerpiece of a large and not particularly attractive city plaza. The much smaller granite police station stood only yards away, separated from municipal headquarters by a driveway flanked with rows of white birch trees which looked oddly out of place alongside the massive piles of granite.

Cruising along, looking for a parking spot, I saw a large sign: MUNICIPAL PARKING. TAKE TICKET AS GATE OPENS. The lot was nearly full but I found a space at the far end.

As we walked toward the street, Leffing glanced at his watch. "I have an appointment with Chief Honderman at eleven. It is now just eight minutes of the hour. Excellent timing!"

Pushing open the heavy wrought iron and glass doors of the station, we encountered a middle-aged policewoman sitting at a desk in the entrance hall. She eyed us with evident disapproval.

When Leffing identified himself, her manner changed. "Yes, sir. Just a minute." She hurried down the hall.

Within minutes we were shown through a ground-glass door into a private office.

A large, rather ornate desk plaque left no doubt of the identity of the big man sitting before us: VERGIL HONDERMAN. CHIEF OF POLICE. GREYSTONE BAY.

He got up slowly, extending his hand. "Mr. Leffing."

After they shook hands, Leffing introduced me. Honderman hesitated before he reached across the desk again. His handshake was less than hearty. He shot my friend a questioning look.

Leffing was quick to reassure him. "Brennan has been aide and confidant in most of my major cases. He can be trusted without question."

Honderman nodded. "I see." He waved us to chairs, sat down himself, rearranged some papers on his desk, and leaned back.

"You may think I'm a bit overboard on this secrecy business. But it's necessary. Greystone Bay is a quiet town, a sort of self-contained town, seclusive even, you might say. Oh, we have the summer people, and a few of the natives tend to be rowdy at times, but mostly it's just traffic violations, petty theft, perhaps a family spat finishing up with fists. . . ." He paused, inspecting us with blue eyes that looked faded but alert, skeptical and, I thought, faintly hostile.

He resumed. "We have a sort of aristocracy here. Families going back two hundred years or more. They want order, peace, privacy. You can easily imagine what the splashy tabloids would do with these—recent events."

There was a hint of impatience in Leffing's voice. "We sympathize with your desire for secrecy," he replied crisply. "We shall be discreet as possible."

Honderman did not look entirely satisfied but he nodded. "Good. Well, to get down to cases."

For more than a minute he sat silently, drumming on the desk with his fingers, a large, slow-moving man with an air of careful deliberation, accustomed to both the responsibilities and privileges of authority. Now he looked uncomfortable and more than a little out of his depth.

He ran a hand through his white hair. "We've had three murders in the past five weeks. Before that, the last was over twenty years ago. Worse, there's something peculiar—weird, I guess you'd say—about these killings."

Leffing leaned forward. "And what is that?"

The office door was tightly closed but Honderman lowered his voice. "The victims weren't just killed. They were, well, slashed, torn, mangled. Mutilated. Mostly about the face, neck, and throat."

He sighed and shook his head. "You can readily imagine what the newspapers would do with that! We've managed to cover up these details pretty well so far, but if the attacks continue . . ." He spread his hands in a gesture of hopelessness.

"In most instances I do not approve of withholding information from the press," Leffing said.

Honderman sat back. "In this instance, Mr. Leffing, it

is vital that you approve. As you will recall, I indicated previously the need of discretion in this case—at the very least until the killer is found. I was authorized to hire you only on condition that you observe strict silence."

Leffing nodded. "I recall your admonition, Chief Honderman. By the way, may I inquire who authorized you to hire me?"

"The board of police commissioners," Honderman replied stiffly.

"Fair enough then. We will impart no information to the media. And now may I see your file on the victims?"

Unlocking a side desk drawer, Honderman withdrew a folder, which he passed to Leffing.

"Fortunately," he said, "all three victims were, ah, from the lower orders, nobodies, down-and-out drifters. One a common town drunk, another an aging prostitute, and the third a failed fisherman who had descended to panhandling. All loners. Nobody claimed the bodies."

"Fortunate indeed," Leffing commented. "In other words, the—mutilations—are known only to the police, morgue attendants, and the doctor certifying death?"

Honderman hesitated. "Well, just about that. Two were found by my own men. One by an early morning jogger. He stumbled on Jules Ramonez—the fisherman—at the bottom of a flight of steps along Harbor Road. We convinced him that Ramonez had been severely injured in the fall. Luckily, he wasn't much interested."

He looked aside with a casual air that was far from convincing. "As soon as possible we put all three bodies six feet down in the potter's field section of our local cemetery."

"Chief Honderman," Leffing exclaimed angrily, "you know perfectly well that since I was being called in to investigate, those bodies should have been preserved in the morgue until I had an opportunity to examine them!"

Honderman looked flustered. "Well—yes—the burials

were a trifle hasty. But—the fact is—the decision to bring you in wasn't made until after the interments. In any case, you'll find pretty detailed photographs of the bodies and the, ah, lacerations, right there in the file folder.''

Leffing shook his head ruefully. ''Photographs may be helpful but they can scarcely be expected to yield up the evidence that might be extracted from a victim's corpse.''

He stood up. ''We will study the file and report to you if we have any suggestions—once we settle in suitable rooms somewhere.''

Honderman arose. ''I gather you haven't arranged for accommodations yet. I might mention The Ocean Arms. Right on the Bay along Harbor Road. Up toward North Hill. Just a suggestion. You're free to go where you like. Let me know of course.''

''The Ocean Arms sounds fine. We will look into it at once.''

We shook hands and departed.

As we left the building, I sensed that Leffing had lapsed into one of his not infrequent states of moody silence. He said not a word until we were turning off Port Boulevard into Harbor Road.

''Imbeciles!'' he exploded. ''I've half a mind to insist they disinter all three victims!''

''Small towns—cities—aren't accustomed to handling these things,'' I said in conciliatory tones.

''They had better get accustomed. Small-town crimes, though less in number perhaps, can equal in savagery any committed in major metropolitan centers.''

We drove north along Harbor Road, passing on the left a succession of small shops, restaurants, bars, and old private homes, the majority restored or at least well maintained. Just beyond a spacious boardwalk on the right we could hear surf stroking the shore. Two fishing boats rocked at anchor out in the Bay.

The Ocean Arms is located at the far northern end of the

city's business section. Beyond, on slopes to the left of
Harbor Road, lies North Hill, Greystone Bay's prime residential area, an exclusive section occupied by many of the
town's oldest and wealthiest families. Some of the houses
date back to the Revolution; others are opulent Victorian
mansions. Nearly all are situated on several acres of ground.

Leffing glanced along one of the winding roads leading
upward on the left from Harbor Road. "We must find time
to explore North Hill, Brennan. I have been told that a
number are absolute showplaces!"

As we drove into The Ocean Arms's parking lot, I was
gratified to notice that it was only half full. That indicated
summer people were already starting to leave. We should
have no difficulty getting rooms.

The Ocean Arms, a three-story brickfaced building, is a
relatively small hotel, apparently established to cater to
more affluent summer visitors. We were assigned a recently vacated suite of two rooms, connected but with
separate shower facilities.

As soon as we had unpacked and showered, Leffing sat
down with Honderman's file folder. Feeling cramped after
the long drive, I told my friend I was going for a walk,
unless he objected.

Already engrossed in the file contents, he waved me
away.

I walked partway down Harbor Road, along one side
and back up the other. By the time I returned, I had
developed an urgent desire for lunch.

Leffing looked up as I entered.

"Any luck?" I inquired.

"No immediate leads. We have our work cut out for
us."

Briefly, he summarized the facts contained in the folder.
The first victim, Jason Deming, 63, the town drunk, was
found on the beach just beyond the boardwalk. Severe
lacerations to neck and throat. Apparently bled to death.

Killed sometime after midnight, Tuesday, August 27. The second victim, Janet Satengo, 41, prostitute, found in an alley off Harbor Road. Face and throat ripped. Virtually unrecognizable. Immediate cause of death, rupture of carotid artery. Time of death estimated between 2 and 6 A.M., Tuesday, September 3. Third victim, Jules Ramonez, ex-fisherman, panhandler. Found sprawled at the bottom of a flight of stairs leading to a vacant house on the left side of Harbor Road. Throat mangled. Neck broken (probably in fall down flight of stairs). Cause of death: loss of blood and/or broken neck. Time of death estimated between 1 and 5 A.M., Wednesday, September 11.

The photographs were graphic. I dropped them back into the folder with a shudder. "It looks like the work of a maniac—or a wild animal!"

"A maniac perhaps," Leffing replied, "but I can think of no wild animal that would kill in this fashion—unless rabid perhaps."

"We are looking for a lunatic then?"

"A question of semantics, Brennan. We may be searching for someone, otherwise normal, who has nurtured a long-term obsession, a psychosis, that has finally grown to monstrous and overpowering proportions."

"Sounds too much like a textbook to me," I commented. "Couldn't it be just another drifter with a forty IQ who goes berserk with too many drinks?"

Leffing smiled ruefully. "Dear me, Brennan, you would drive the textbook people out of business!"

I laughed. "Too many of them compiling books anyway. I have only one final question. Nowhere in the reports is there any mention of a weapon. A knife?" I lifted the photographs out of the folder and shuddered again. "All that—ragged mangling and tearing. What kind of knife would do that?"

"No kind that I know of."

"What then?"

"Teeth."

I stared at him. *"Teeth?"*

"What else can you suggest?" Leffing asked. "Some sort of meat hook? A jagged shard of metal?"

"Probably not—but you ruled out animals. What else—?"

A new thought struck me. *"Human* teeth? It's too melodramatic, Leffing! Then we're looking for—a *werewolf?* In Greystone Bay! It's just too inconceivable!"

He got up and strolled to the window. Clouds had come up and a few patches of fog were forming along the beach. The harbor, sparkling in the sunlight a short time before, was beginning to look grey and cold.

Leffing stood silently for a few moments. Presently he spoke. "Greystone Bay is an old city, Brennan—old for this country at least. Who can say what the past may have thrust into the present?"

After telephoning Chief Honderman that we were settled in at The Ocean Arms, we walked down Harbor Road and stopped for lunch at a small restaurant, Best on the Bay.

Leffing chatted lightheartedly about the food, as if we were on vacation, without a care in the world.

When we arrived back at The Ocean Arms, we were informed that Chief Honderman had telephoned, asking that Leffing return the call.

I looked up, questioningly, as he hung up.

"Chief Honderman reports that a Mr. Miles Lorcaster wishes to see us."

"And who is Miles Lorcaster?"

"Lorcaster is a North Hills descendant of one of the oldest families in Greystone Bay—and also president of the board of police commissioners."

About a half mile beyond The Ocean Arms, Sea Cove Drive leads left from Harbor Road up North Hill. We drove slowly along the winding road, admiring the park-like precision of surrounding shrubbery and a profusion of carefully tended flower beds.

As the ground began to level off, we passed a succession of imposing Victorian mansions with characteristic round towers, deep porches, and projecting balconies. Several preserved original carriage drives complete with porte cocheres. Many boasted manicured garden pavilions with eye-catching gazebos.

Leffing exclaimed in delight, "High Victorian Gothic, Brennan! Some of the best examples I've seen!"

Miles Lorcaster's home, a huge shingle-sheathed Colonial-type house with gambrel roof and mullion windows, was located at the extreme northern edge of North Hill. We rang the bell and waited.

Minutes passed before a stoop-shouldered and very elderly servant dressed in a black suit opened the door. His white face, which was about the same hue as his white hair, bore an expression of settled melancholy.

"Mr. Lorcaster is expecting you. Please follow me."

We trailed after him down a long, poorly illuminated reception hall. On one side, a long row of family ancestors peered down at us. Attired in Colonial or early-English costumes, most of them appeared properly severe.

The centenarian servant knocked on a door at the far end of the shadowy corridor.

"Come in."

As the door was closed softly behind us, Miles Lorcaster got up from behind an oak desk at the other end of the study and walked toward us. After shaking hands, he waved us toward armchairs in front of the desk and resumed his seat behind it.

I judged him to be in his early fifties. For his age he looked lean and rangy, like a worthy competitor on the tennis court. With his neatly groomed greying hair, bright eyes, and chiseled features, he was almost handsome. An aura of power, with a suggestion of aggression, seemed to emanate from the man.

He wasted no time on preliminaries. "I'm not sure

Chief Honderman made your mission here entirely clear. Let me do so. Your *primary* and ever-present mission is to—frankly—suppress at all times any type of widespread or sensational publicity that may arise from the unfortunate incidents Honderman has told you about. Greystone Bay is a highly conservative town with an abiding dislike of outside intrusion—particularly the meddlesome kind. We don't want an influx of seedy curiosity-seekers on the heels of raucous newspaper reporters from Boston or New York. We value privacy and we intend to maintain it.''

He paused, obviously waiting for Leffing's reply—which was not immediately forthcoming—and went on.

''Don't misunderstand. Of course we want the crimes solved. But unless this can be done quickly and without vulgar fanfare, we would actually prefer that the whole business be dropped.''

He lifted a crystal paperweight from his desk, inspected it, and set it back down. ''After all, gentlemen, the victims were of no social consequence whatever. At the risk of sounding callous, I might say that they are of no great loss. All three of them, I am advised, were engaged in unlawful activities.''

When he spoke, Leffing's voice was level and controlled, but I knew from long observation that he was exerting great effort to keep it that way.

''It was my understanding, Mr. Lorcaster, that I was summoned here to solve three brutal—savage—murders, not to act as a sort of censorship shield between Greystone Bay and inquisitive reporters. If that understanding is incorrect, I shall return to New Haven within the hour. I might add that I have never been concerned with the social standing of murder victims—unless their status, or the lack of it, indicated a possible *motive* for murder.''

Lorcaster listened impassively. Although his expression did not change, I sensed that he sat surveying my friend with growing, though grudging, respect.

He picked up the paperweight again. "No need for hasty decisions, Mr. Leffing. Perhaps I have been a trifle overemphatic for the sake of making my point. Let us agree, then, that you will be as discreet—in regard to publicity—as conditions allow. Your known discretion, in fact, was one of the reasons we went to you in the first place."

Leffing hesitated. He told me afterward that he very nearly "chucked the whole business" then and there.

"I will exercise the degree of discretion which is routine—and expected—in all my cases," he said finally. "However, I shall not make strenuous or extreme efforts to conceal any facts from the public—once those facts have been fully established."

Lorcaster weighed this statement with obvious care. When, at length, he nodded, I gained the impression that he did so with reluctance.

"All right. That seems acceptable."

He stood up. "You will keep me advised of any new developments?"

"Chief Honderman will be kept updated at all times."

This reply did not appear to entirely satisfy Lorcaster, but he extended his hand. "Well, good luck. Kemble will show you out."

As we proceeded along Sea Cove Drive toward Harbor Road, I turned to my friend.

"What was your impression of Lorcaster?"

"An arrogant and unprincipled tyrant, accustomed by inheritance to power and authority. A familiar type, Brennan."

By the time we arrived back at The Ocean Arms, fog, drifting in from the beach, was beginning to swirl across the highway. The Bay was completely obscured.

The rest of the afternoon passed swiftly. Leffing, employing a powerful magnifying glass, inspected the victims' photographs again. I wrote an overdue letter and skimmed through a magazine.

Although The Ocean Arms did not serve lunch, they did provide breakfast and dinner. I looked forward to a leisurely meal in the hotel's dining room.

I glanced up from my magazine to see a ragged scarecrow emerge from the adjoining room.

After a speechless moment I found my voice. "Good grief, Leffing, you can't enter the dining room looking like that!"

"I do not intend to enter the dining room. I have no doubt we can obtain a bite in one of the waterfront bars."

A familiar crooked smile crossed his face as he inspected me. "You had better go through your luggage, Brennan. The clothes you are wearing will not do."

From long experience I had learned to include some worn knockabout clothes in my bag. Shaking my head, I got up and began digging them out.

Leffing watched with amusement. "The chances of obtaining any information at The Ocean Arms are not promising. On the other hand, we might pick up a few morsels of gossip at one of the less pretentious establishments along Harbor Road."

Slipping through a rear delivery door, we emerged into Harbor Road. Dense fog had settled along the street. Traffic inched ahead; pedestrians only feet away were shadowy wraiths.

We walked south slowly, navigating cross-streets with care. Above the muffled traffic sounds we could hear waves breaking on the rocky beach to our left.

About halfway down Harbor Road Leffing paused where shafts of light and considerable noise spilled over onto the pavement.

"Let's look in here, Brennan. The atmosphere seems to match our attire!"

The flickering neon name of the place was just visible: The Beach Bonanza.

We passed from banks of fog into clouds of smoke. It was the kind of tavern usually described as a dive—rough, argumentative customers draped on crowded bar stools; scattered tables; a burly bartender who probably acted as bouncer, and one bored busboy-waiter.

We sat over a pitcher of beer at a table toward the rear of the room. Nobody paid any attention to us.

Along with the smoke, snatches of conversation and bellows of laughter drifted our way. Although Leffing sat with a vacuous expression, I knew that he was listening intently.

We were both getting restless when two new arrivals took the adjoining table. Leffing slumped over his beer as if he were having trouble staying awake. Sighing, I refilled my glass.

For twenty minutes or more the conversation at the next table was desultory and trivial. At length one of the two brawny customers leaned toward the other with a conspiratorial leer.

"I heard the crazies were headin' for the hill tonight!"

The other nodded. "Those dumb cops better get their tails up there. If you ask me, that's where they'd find the mangler!"

Both Leffing and I were careful not to show that we had the faintest interest in these comments. We sat on, looking bored and sleepy, but actually on the alert for further information.

It was not forthcoming. The conversation trailed off. At length Leffing dropped a quarter on the table and stood up. We sauntered toward the door.

"What were they getting at?" I asked as we returned into the fog. "Crazies on North Hill?"

"I believe, Brennan, they were referring to *South* Hill, not North Hill. I suggest we drive up there."

"Where in blazes is South Hill?"

"South of Port Boulevard and the main business district. Uninhabited, too rock-strewn and steep for building. Still heavily wooded in spots. Apparently an ideal place for so-called crazies to cavort."

"Where did you learn all this?" I inquired with some irritation.

"I have not been idle, Brennan."

Although I was annoyed, as always, at his secretiveness, I did not press the matter. We hurried back up Harbor Road to The Ocean Arms's parking lot.

As we drove back south, the car lights barely penetrated the billowing blanket of fog.

I crept along as we approached the South Hill section. Almost by accident, I glimpsed a sign on my right: SOUTH HILL. PASS AT YOUR OWN RISK.

Even in daylight the rutted, overgrown road would have made driving difficult. In the fog it was a nightmare. When we finally arrived at a cul-de-sac, I sighed with relief.

"We can go no farther," I announced.

"We can by foot," Leffing corrected.

Luckily, I kept a small flashlight in the glove compartment. After five minutes of groping we discovered a narrow footpath leading upward.

The path, like the road, was rocky, pitted, overgrown with brush and small trees. In addition, the dense fog made it slippery.

Single file, Leffing leading with the light, we skidded and scratched our way up the treacherous trail. Leffing moved with care but several times managed to release a branch, which whipped across my face.

I was gasping for breath when we finally reached a boulder-littered plateau. Surprisingly, the fog was far thinner here. Floating wisps were everywhere, but the heavy, blinding cover was gone. I concluded that, at this height, the harbor winds had more effect.

We were halfway across the plateau when Leffing snapped off the light and pulled me behind the nearest large boulder.

"Up ahead!" he whispered.

Looking out cautiously, I saw shadowy shapes assembled around the perimeter of a small, cleared area. One of the group was chanting something which was only gibberish to me.

"An invocation to Satan," Leffing informed me. "I think in Chaldean."

Crouched uncomfortably behind the wet boulder, we witnessed an eerie and disturbing spectacle. Enough moonlight penetrated the fog patches to make most of the weird performance visible, even though details were obscured.

About a dozen persons slowly circled the edge of empty ground about ten yards in diameter. In the exact center lay a large flat round stone.

As we watched, the participants began to move more quickly and the Chaldean invocation was chanted by all. Within minutes the demonic entreaty turned shrill and imperious; movements of the gesticulating dancers became frenzied. Clothing was ripped off and flung aside.

Unexpectantly, one of the dancers broke from the circle, bounded onto the flat central stone, raised her arms above her head, and stared skyward. Discarding her last shred of clothing, she stood motionless in the broken misty moonlight while a roar of approval broke from the throats of her companions.

Abruptly, they stopped circling and faced the flat stone. One of them stepped forward with a container of some kind, lifted it above the head of the motionless girl, and poured out the contents.

Within seconds she was transformed into a gleaming red statue.

A shrill, half-hysterical screech broke from the ranks.

They started circling again, even more wildly this time. Tossing aside the container, the votary who had drenched the girl with its contents joined the delirious dancers. As if turned to granite, the girl stood, unmoving.

I glanced aside at Leffing. "That paint could seal up the pores, could even be fatal! What—"

"Not paint," Leffing interrupted. "Blood!"

The urgent chant of the galvanized circlers turned to a rising roar that must have been audible for miles. After about five minutes, however, it gradually began to subside and the dancers moved more slowly. Suddenly the naked, blood-covered girl sank to the stone and huddled silently.

"He didn't come," Leffing muttered.

I turned. "Who?"

"The Devil."

In spite of my skepticism, I felt an icy twinge corkscrew down my spine.

"We had better get out of here!" I whispered.

Leffing gripped my arm. "Wait!" he cautioned, pointing ahead.

The devil worshippers were getting ready to leave. The chant ceased. Someone threw a blanket across the shoulders of the gleaming girl huddled on the flat stone.

"They'll spot us!" I warned.

Leffing shook his head. "I think not."

Following his gaze, I saw the shadowy figures straggling off toward the far side of the rock-strewn plateau.

"Obviously another means of egress," Leffing observed.

We waited until the last of them disappeared in the half-darkness.

Leffing touched my arm. "Stay here."

Keeping in shadow as much as possible, he made his way gingerly toward the cleared area. He reappeared carrying a blood-smeared tin pail.

"Enough for an analysis," he said.

We returned to the car without incident, although both

of us nearly pitched headlong during the slippery descent down the path.

Leffing placed the pail on newspapers spread in the trunk and I inched back toward Harbor Road.

"Are we thinking the same thing?" I inquired as I drove north toward The Ocean Arms.

"What is that?"

"Why—that we've possibly solved the Greystone Bay murders! Those devil cultists may have killed to obtain human blood!"

"Possibly, Brennan. Turn left at Port Boulevard. I wish to leave the pail at police headquarters for a blood analysis."

It was going on midnight; the officer in charge at headquarters was not overjoyed on having a bloody pail handed across the counter.

He picked it up with reluctance, frowning. "We've got only a small lab here. Might have to send it to the hospital for tests. I'll see what the chief says in the morning."

"Tests should be undertaken as soon as possible, Officer."

The police attendant shoved the pail under the counter. "As soon as possible."

"I presume we'll have the test results within a week or two," Leffing remarked sarcastically as we left the building.

After quick showers we both dropped into bed back at The Ocean Arms. I had fallen into a deep, dreamless, and blissful sleep when the relentless ringing of a telephone tore me back to wakefulness.

Leffing had taken the call by the time my feet found the rug.

He was already pulling off his pajamas. "Dress quickly! That was Chief Honderman. Another victim has been found!"

"South on Harbor Road. About where Port Boulevard intersects," Leffing instructed as I drove out of the lot.

"Found near the highway?" I asked.

"No, no. On the harbor side of the road. Apparently attacked on the beach and dragged under the boardwalk."

I had no trouble finding the place. Police cruiser lights were flashing and in spite of the hour a small crowd had gathered.

Chief Honderman was waiting for us. Following him across the boardwalk, we descended steep wooden stairs to the rocky shore of Greystone Bay.

The victim's body lay sprawled grotesquely beneath the projecting edge of the boardwalk. Under the stark glare of the lights it presented a spectacle better kept from the queasy. The attack had been so savage, the head remained attached to the torso only by shreds. Where the throat should be, there was only a tangle of ripped flesh and shredded tendon—a dark aperture still spouting blood.

The face, rent repeatedly, was an unrecognizable red mask. Silvery-grey hair, so unruffled it resembled a toupee just attached, added a final macabre touch.

The corpse was dressed in a neat-fitting grey business suit. The black shoes looked new.

Having looked once, I looked away and had no desire to look again. Leffing, however, eagerly bent over the mutilated corpse, scanning it minutely and at length.

He finally straightened up and turned to Chief Honderman. "Identification?"

"Paul Chessel. Boston. We think he was taking a late vacation here. Probably staying in town. It appears as if he was drinking at one of the bars till closing time and then walked along the beach—maybe to sober up a bit. Bartender from The Beach Bonanza, strolling the shore to get a breath of fresh air before retiring, stumbled onto him."

Honderman shook his head. "Respectable businessman, I'd say. Not a nobody—like the others. Won't be easy keeping the sensation-seekers off!"

"Not easy at all, Chief," Leffing agreed, "Mr. Lorcaster notwithstanding!"

Honderman looked worried but did not reply.

I followed Leffing back up to the boardwalk just as ambulance attendants were sliding the ghastly remains into a body bag.

We returned to The Ocean Arms for a few hours sleep. Leffing was pacing the floor by the time I got out of the shower.

"Any news?" I asked.

He waved toward a morning paper lying on the table. "The local paper mentions nothing. Probably put to bed too early. And I have heard nothing further from Chief Honderman."

"What kind of monster are we dealing with?"

"I suspect we are dealing with a madman, Brennan. But a madman with an uncanny ability to cover his tracks and elude apprehension."

"Previously you mentioned something about—*teeth*."

"My inspection of last night's victim strengthens my conviction that *all* of the victims were killed by an individual who—caught up in his obsessive madness—attacks like a rabid wild animal!"

"A werewolf then?"

Leffing shrugged. "An overly melodramatic term and one frequently misused—but it will perhaps serve in this case—for want of a better one!"

Honderman called later in the morning but he had only scant information. Paul Chessel had registered for a room at the Harborlight Hotel six days before his death. He had spent several hours at a Harbor Road bar, The Seven Sirens, on the evening he was killed. The exact time of his departure was uncertain but was estimated to be shortly before midnight. Chessel, 47, an insurance investigator in Boston, was divorced, childless, had no arrest record.

While I remained at The Ocean Arms to monitor the telephone, Leffing spent a fruitless hour at The Seven Sirens in search of further information concerning Chessel.

None was forthcoming. He returned grumbling and frustrated.

We were about to leave for lunch when Chief Honderman telephoned again. Had we seen the headline in the early afternoon edition of *The Greystone Gazette*? Mr. Lorcaster was furious. He wanted Leffing to announce that in his opinion Paul Chessel had been knifed to death in a drunken brawl. Would Leffing agree?

Leffing would not, and hung up the phone. I hurried down to the lobby and bought a copy of *The Greystone Gazette*. The headline leaped at me: *Boston Man Savagely Murdered*.

The article mentioned the three previous victims and speculated that a bloodthirsty, probably insane, killer was prowling the Bay area.

Leffing read through the article and tossed it aside.

"I don't see how Lorcaster can downplay this one!" I remarked.

"Perhaps," Leffing replied wryly, "he'll purchase *The Greystone Gazette* and publish a retraction!"

Very shortly Honderman called again to ask why Leffing had left for analysis a dirty pail smeared with goat's blood. Leffing detailed the circumstances, assuring Honderman that he had not known the nature of the blood at the time he brought in the pail.

As we sat over a light supper in the hotel's dining room, my friend came to a decision.

"I fear there is no help for it, Brennan. You and I must act as bait!"

"How would we go about that?"

"We will dress as down-and-out drifters and haunt the bayside bars during late evening hours. Just enough pocket change to keep us sipping beer. I propose we enter taverns separately and pretend we are strangers to each other. We can work out further details as we go along. We will wait a day or two for possible developments, but I doubt there will be any of much significance."

The next morning Chief Honderman reported he had tracked down the group of "young devil dancers" we had observed on South Hill. "They're crazies all right, but they wouldn't kill anyone," he told Leffing. He seemed reluctant to divulge any details such as names, addresses, arrest records, etc. Leffing was understandably irked.

"Probably a number of the crazies are scions of some of the best families in Greystone Bay," he said. "Possibly Honderman's job hinges on their goodwill. Or there may be other reasons. Who knows, Brennan? It appears to be a secretive sort of town!"

"I have growing doubts about Honderman," I remarked.

"We must go along, Brennan. I am beginning to take a personal interest in this case. I would not want to abandon it."

Before the day was over, Miles Lorcaster telephoned. He wanted to see Leffing at once.

As we started up Sea Cove Drive, fog was drifting in across Harbor Road. In the settling mist the Victorian mansions appeared distant and dim, as if they were merely the ghosts of houses materialized from a time long past.

Kemble, looking more stooped, pallid, and melancholy than before, answered our ring.

Miles Lorcaster was pacing in his study when Kemble admitted us. Turning, he waved curtly toward chairs and sat down.

He came to the point at once. "Honderman tells me you are not being very cooperative."

Leffing registered surprise. "Indeed! In what manner, sir?"

"I wanted that insurance man's death to go down as the result of a routine drunken brawl. The papers are making it look like a page from *The Hound of the Baskervilles*!"

"The condition of Paul Chessel's throat did not indicate a routine drunken brawl."

Lorcaster scowled. "I disagree. A drunk with a knife is capable of any atrocity. The attacker probably just slashed in a frenzy, scarcely aware of what he was doing!"

Leffing nodded. "A frenzy—yes. But I doubt that the killer attacked with a knife."

Lorcaster bent forward over his desk. "What then?"

Leffing considered his reply. "Ponder your reference to *The Hound of the Baskervilles*."

Lorcaster flushed angrily. "I don't appreciate riddles, sir!"

"Riddles," replied Leffing, "are my business. And I intend to solve this one!"

Lorcaster appeared speechless with rage. When he found his voice, however, it was strangely subdued.

"Kemble, show these—gentlemen—out."

As we drove off through the mist, I shook my head. "I don't understand it at all, Leffing."

"What is that?"

"Well, why didn't he sack you? You obviously enraged him. Yet he calmed down and let us walk off without another word."

"Perhaps he didn't want another headline: Lorcaster Fires Private Detective. Or possibly he is a more complex person than he first appears to be."

After we arrived back at The Ocean Arms, I sat down to write a letter. Leffing departed after a few minutes, saying he intended to "take a stroll down Harbor Road." It was nearly dinnertime before he returned.

"On an impulse," he told me, "I stopped in at the local library. On Port Boulevard, just around the corner from Harbor Road. I managed to unearth a good deal of information on the early settlers of Greystone Bay. A remarkable lot, Brennan! Free-thinkers, opportunists, political protesters, and some plain undesirables."

"A motley cargo."

"Just so. And their ocean voyage was a prolonged nightmare: raging storms, food shortages, illness. There were many deaths, some from privation and exposure, a number mysterious and unexplained. The ship was even boarded by pirates, who were finally beaten off, but only after a fierce struggle during which a number of passengers and crew were killed."

"A most remarkable saga!"

"Remarkable indeed—but incomplete. There are gaps in the story which I can't explain. I had the impression that some manuscript pages and some printed matter as well must have been lost."

"That's not unusual," I said. "I think it's surprising that so much detail survived."

"Perhaps so," Leffing agreed. "In any case, I spent an interesting hour or two."

Over dinner we decided to wait no longer to put our previously agreed-on plan into operation. Returning to our rooms, we dug out our ragged drifters' clothes. After dark we left through the delivery door.

The bars along Harbor Road were relatively quiet early in the evening. We walked for some time before Leffing decided to look into The Seven Sirens. After waiting outside for a few minutes, I followed him. We sat apart, with no sign of recognition. We sipped beer, listened carefully to whatever conversation we could hear, observed the customers, and finally left separately after a half hour. This procedure was repeated in no less than seven bars during the course of the evening.

By midnight the bars were crowded and noisy but not disorderly. It was nearly one A.M., and they were starting to close, when Leffing and I conferred in an alley off Harbor Road.

"If the killer is prowling the taverns," Leffing whispered, "he would have spotted one of us by now. We'll go down to the shore and wander awhile. Keep well behind me, Brennan. You have your thirty-two in one of those patched pockets?''

''I have it—*sans* permit—but I'm not an expert shot and I'm sure vision will be limited along the beach. I don't like this, Leffing!''

''We must risk it. I will be alert and ready. Don't rivet all attention on me. Keep a close watch behind you!''

Crossing the walk, we went down steps to the beach. I waited while Leffing started along the rocky shore. As previously agreed, he walked along near the tideline while I trailed after him, keeping in shadow along the projecting edge of the boardwalk as much as possible. There was some moonlight but drifting clouds and patches of fog hampered visibility. On several occasions Leffing appeared to be vanishing into the harbor. At best he looked dim and wraithlike.

We walked the entire perimeter of the bay, up and back, before he decided to call it a night. For a time a group of celebrants had serenaded us from the boardwalk. Later one lone drunk had staggered down to the water's edge, retched a few times, and retreated toward Harbor Road. Otherwise we had the beach to ourselves.

I returned to The Ocean Arms exhausted and fell into bed. Leffing had little to say other than a ''Well, well, another time, Brennan.''

The following day passed uneventfully and that night our bar-hopping and beach-prowling was repeated with minor variations.

Over a late breakfast the next morning I made no effort to conceal my querulous mood.

''It's an exhausting and I think futile procedure, Leffing. Far from taking the bait, the killer may be miles away by now. The tabloid headlines will have made him wary. He is surely too cunning to kill again—at least in Greystone Bay.''

Leffing refilled his coffee cup. "You may be correct. But we have tried our little maneuver only twice. You are much too impatient!"

Of course I agreed—reluctantly—to prowl the bay shore again that evening. I left the hotel shortly after breakfast to do some routine shopping. When I returned, Leffing was pacing restlessly.

"Any news?" I inquired.

He stopped pacing and sat down. "I called Chief Honderman a half hour ago with that same question in mind," he told me. "He did not show up at his office this morning and he does not answer the telephone in his bachelor apartment."

"Seems strange," I commented.

"The officer in charge—a Lieutenant Markell—does not seem unduly alarmed. Apparently Honderman has been known to drop out of sight briefly in the past—without prior notice to anyone. The last time he was reprimanded by the board of police commissioners."

"Does Lieutenant Markell have any explanation?"

"Markell seems to suspect that from time to time Honderman personally engages in undercover work that requires the strictest secrecy. It is of course possible."

"He's probably taken a page from your own book, Leffing! Gone in disguise to ferret out the killer!"

Leffing managed a crooked smile. "It may be as simple as that, Brennan!"

The day dragged. Leffing remained restless and irritable. I was glad, this time, to put on tramps' clothes and begin our evening tour of the Harbor Road taverns.

When we started out, the evening was clear and warm. By ten o'clock, however, heavy, clinging fog began moving inland from the harbor. By midnight a nearly opaque wall of mist had settled over the entire Harbor Road area. Car lights were scarcely visible; passersby were phantoms sensed rather than seen.

"We'd better get back to The Ocean Arms while we can still find it!" I told Leffing as we left The Four Candles Cafe.

"Pshaw, Brennan!" he exclaimed. "Our beach patrol has not begun yet!" All his irritation and restlessness seemed to have disappeared. He was alert, excited.

I sighed and shrugged, my visions of a warm early bed at The Ocean Arms evaporating into the fog.

After groping our way down from the boardwalk, we started out along the rocky beach. I protested, meanwhile, that it would be impossible to keep each other in sight.

Leffing would have none of it. "We both have ears, Brennan, and strong voices. Follow along the water's edge. I will call when I decide to turn back."

Muttering to myself, I scrambled after him. On my right the waves plashed and whispered; underfoot wet rocks made walking treacherous. The fog, if possible, had thickened.

Once I stopped to listen but I could not hear Leffing's feet on the stones ahead.

"Must tread like a cat!" I grumbled.

I picked my way along, shivering as sea mist soaked through my worn sweater.

For some reason, perhaps the proverbial sixth sense, I stopped abruptly and listened. At first all I heard was the rhythmic breaking of surf, but as I went on listening, between the regular beat of waves I thought I detected another sound—a soft padding, to the left, somewhere in front of me. It was so faint I was half convinced that I had imagined it. But as I stood hesitating, I was aware of something rushing through the fog, only feet away.

A moment later I heard a startled cry from Leffing, then a thud.

Springing forward, I yanked the .32 from a trouser pocket.

"Freeze!" I commanded, thrusting the little automatic

forward and down. Even as I spoke, I wondered if I addressed anything human.

Although it was blurred and indistinct because of the layered mist, I doubt that I shall ever entirely forget the face that was turned to look at me. It was a countenance that combined the utmost in human depravity with the ultimate in animal ferocity—eyes burning with a savage obsession, lips lifted back from projecting teeth, the whole a twisted mask stamped with consuming evil.

I fired instinctively, without thinking, almost without aiming, and immediately regretted it. Leffing was trapped beneath the murderous thing. The bullet might find him instead of that nightmare shape.

A cry burst from the creature's throat—a hideous howl combining rage, pain, and frustration. It hesitated momentarily. In that instant Leffing somehow struggled to his feet. The monster veered sideways and lunged off into the mist.

"After it!" Leffing shouted.

We could hear the creature bounding over the rocks ahead as we raced after it up the beach.

Although we ran on recklessly, heedless of the danger if the pursued should suddenly turn, the thing steadily gained on us.

Leffing, a vague figure in the fog, swerved sharply to the left.

"Heading toward Harbor Road!" he shouted. "Faster!"

The boardwalk ends as Harbor Road continues northward. Here the shore merges into sandy bluffs extending well past North Hill. The road runs parallel to these bluffs. Farther on, the highway passes an extensive tract of undeveloped marshland, a desolate place taken over by tufts of swamp grass, tangled tree creepers and, according to rumor, several treacherous pools of quicksand.

As we approached the bluffs through a brief rift in the fog bank, we glimpsed our quarry rushing along, apparently seeking a way to the highway. Even as we watched, it made a tremendous bound, landing atop the nearest bluff, and disappeared from sight.

The bluff at that point was far too steep for both Leffing and myself. We were forced to run on for some yards until we found a less precipitous means of ascent.

Reaching the top, we ran toward the highway. Traffic was light; we quickly darted across Harbor Road.

"Hurry!" Leffing urged. "It will head for the marsh!"

We sprang off the road toward the marsh, now completely shrouded in harbor mist.

The rest was nightmare. We sank into pools up to our hips; we were lacerated by briar-laden vines clustered on invisible trees; we were slashed by swamp grass as sharp as upright razors. Once we heard something splashing through the watery waste ahead of us, but we were unable to gain on it, much less apprehend it.

At last Leffing gave up. He stopped on a small brush-covered knoll just ahead of me and I joined him.

Staring into the fog, he shook his head. "No use, Brennan. It has escaped."

"What now?"

"Back to the highway. Out of this lethal morass. We must get help. Form a search party."

It took twice as long to get out of the marsh as it had to get into it. We were soaked, scratched, and nearly exhausted.

When we reached Harbor Road, we tried to hitchhike, but no motorist would have any part of us. One look at our mud-smeared faces looming out of the mist was enough to frighten off anyone. We trudged wearily down the side of the highway until we located a telephone booth.

The switchboard operator at police headquarters connected Leffing to Lieutenant Markell's home.

After an animated conversation Leffing hung up.

He looked grim. "Lieutenant Markell refuses to help in organizing a search of the marsh. Says it would take him hours merely to round up enough men. He adds that in any case it would be suicidal to try combing the marsh at night in a blinding fog."

"In view of our attempt, I suspect he may be right," I said.

We tramped through the fog back to The Ocean Arms, showered, changed clothes, and sat down to discuss our next move.

"Did Lieutenant Markell say whether or not Chief Honderman has returned?" I asked.

"He has not returned."

Our eyes met and I wondered if we were both thinking the same thing.

Leffing frowned. "We must not jump to conclusions at this point."

I made no reply, even though conclusions were pretty well established in my own mind.

Lieutenant Markell knocked on our door early the next morning, but Leffing could furnish little additional information.

Markell, young, ruddy-faced, obviously impatient, was disappointed. "I've sent a team up to scour around the edges of the marsh, but the chances of finding anything seem slim."

"Slim," Leffing agreed. "But worth a try, Lieutenant."

Before noon Markell telephoned that his team had found nothing and that he was terminating the search. There was still no word from Chief Honderman.

We were about to start out for lunch when someone tapped on the door. Leffing swung it open to admit a nervous, almost gnomelike little man wearing an expression of permanent apology.

"I do hope I am not intruding, Mr. Leffing."

"Not at all, sir! Brennan, this is Mr. Weeden from the Greystone Public Library. Mr. Weeden is in charge of reference and research. He was most helpful the other day when I was investigating the settlement of the town. Mr. Weeden, my assistant, Mr. Brennan.''

We shook hands and Mr. Weeden sat down.

''I won't stay but a minute,'' he assured us. ''What I wanted to say was—well, I heard that Chief Honderman was missing. And I thought that I might mention to you that he stopped into the library the other day, that is, the day before he—dropped from sight.''

He leaned forward. ''The thing is—he rarely—almost never—visits the library.''

''Indeed,'' Leffing commented. ''Tell me, Mr. Weeden, what was Chief Honderman looking for.''

''That's just it. The same thing you were. Information on the settlement and early history of Greystone Bay!''

A familiar questing light burned in Leffing's eyes. ''Did you report this to the police?''

Weeden shrugged. ''I spoke to someone there—by telephone—and he said—sarcastically I'd say—that the department wasn't interested in Chief Honderman's reading habits, but that they might be interested if I could tell them where he was.''

''Typical bureaucratic response,'' Leffing observed.

After thanking Weeden with warmth, he ushered out the little man and began pacing the floor.

''I'm of two minds, Brennan, two minds.''

''You might let me in on *one* of them,'' I suggested.

Ignoring my remarks, he paced some more and paused. ''We had better pay another visit to Mr. Lorcaster. Technically, Honderman hired me but Lorcaster is police commissioner. Perhaps we had better clarify my status at this point.''

He had little to say as we proceeded up Sea Cove Drive toward Lorcaster's house. The heavy fog had drifted away but unmoving slate-colored clouds hung overhead. In grey light the trim lawns and well-tended gardens lost much of their charm. The Victorian mansions appeared cold and bleak.

Kemble, looking more fragile than before, admitted us.

Lorcaster was waiting in his study. He did not get up.

For a moment or two he sat without speaking. He seemed alert and aggressive, but tired and concerned as well. His face was scratched, as if he had shaved hastily, and he held one arm somewhat stiffly against his chest. It was obvious to me that Chief Honderman's disappearance was weighing heavily upon him.

Glancing down at his arm, he grimaced. "Damned arthritis! Comes every year, usually with these late summer fogs."

Frowning with effort, he moved the affected arm onto the desktop. "I hear you were set upon, Mr. Leffing, and of course I am concerned but, frankly, right now I am far more concerned about Honderman. Ugly rumors are floating around. I want them scotched. It is most unfortunate that you were attacked during his absence. The unwashed imbeciles put one and two together and invariably come up with four."

As if as an afterthought, he spoke again. "By the way, what was it you wanted?"

Leffing's gaze was level, his voice controlled. "What I wanted is not what I want now."

Lorcaster flung himself upright. "What do you mean by that, sir?"

Leffing remained seated; his voice was still calm. "It is pretty obvious to me that although your face is badly scratched, you shave with a safety razor. Also, you do not appear to have arthritis."

Rage swiftly distorted Lorcaster's patrician features. His eyes flamed with fury; his lips twisted back from gleaming teeth; his entire countenance altered—hideously—in an instant.

I sprang up, sure that he had gone suddenly mad.

As I stood, I was transfixed with horror—I realized that I had seen that same expression of mingled ferocity and monstrous obsession before.

Leffing arose. For some reason the fact that his voice remained conversational under the circumstances exasperated me.

"The game is up, Lorcaster! You may as well sit down and spare yourself useless effort."

Lorcaster—or what had been Lorcaster—shoved himself backward, toppling his chair, and sprang straight over the desk.

Leffing sidestepped at the last instant. Lorcaster's teeth snapped shut an inch or two from his throat. With appalling agility the wolf thing whirled, ready to try again.

By this time I had the .32 automatic in my hand, but the action was too fast for me to aim and fire.

As Lorcaster leaped toward him a second time, Leffing lifted his chair and swung it in one sweeping motion. Lorcaster collided with it in midair. The impact seemed to stun him momentarily. He staggered backward but quickly recovered, gathering himself into a half-crouch. The visible stamp of any human attributes drained from his face. His glaring eyes resembled those of a rabid animal; saliva dripped from his gaping mouth; a sustained, savage snarling rumbled in his throat. In spite of the circumstances, I reflected how incongruous such a creature looked clothed in a conservative business suit.

Glancing aside as I heard something at the end of the study, I saw Kemble enter like a ghost rising from the grave.

He stared at Lorcaster. "Oh, sir! No more! It will leave you soon! Just wait a bit!"

Lorcaster ignored him, watching us. He saw the gun in my hand, the heavy chair in Leffing's, and hesitated.

Before either of us could act again, he suddenly spun about and raced for the open study door.

Kemble screamed. "Not the tunnel, sir! It's too late, sir!"

Leffing ran toward the door. "After him, Brennan!"

As we rushed down the corridor, he called over his shoulder. "Which way is the tunnel, Kemble?"

The old servant's voice was shrill with hysteria. "The subcellar! Against the north wall!"

We pounded after the thing racing ahead of us, down the corridor, through anterooms into a huge dining room, into a kitchen, through a butler's pantry, down a dim flight of stairs to an even more shadowy cellar. Here we paused, gasping for breath.

"Look for a trapdoor," Leffing shouted. "Near the north wall."

Even with the aid of a small pocket light, minutes passed before we found the ring attached to the trap. Lorcaster had taken time to close it over his head as he dropped through.

Lifting the door, Leffing started down a metal ladder. I followed. At the end of twenty-odd rungs we found ourselves in a damp and narrow tunnel scarcely five feet in height. In places where dirt had fallen through, weak spots had been reinforced with propped timbers. In several places fieldstones had been employed to buttress the sides. The tunnel led only one way—northward.

We learned—later—that the tunnel had been dug in Colonial times to permit the early Lorcasters a means of escape in case of Indian attacks. The Victorian mansion had been built on the site of the original Lorcaster house.

I started along, gun in one hand, light in the other. "I don't like it, Leffing. If he turns on us, we're at a disadvantage."

He pressed behind me. "No help for it. Hurry!"

Bent over, breathing fetid air with difficulty, slipping on the damp ground, we moved along in a kind of frantic shuffle. I thought I heard the sound of feet receding far ahead.

The tunnel ran relatively straight but seemed interminable. I wondered what would happen if my pocket light failed.

It was beginning to flicker when I noticed faint light ahead. After making a right-angle turn and advancing a few more yards, we found ourselves in a burrowlike rocky cave. Light filtered in a few feet away. Pushing aside a dense, matted mass of briars, we found ourselves in full daylight. We were standing on the edge of the notorious marsh that lay adjacent to North Hill.

I was all for quitting the chase, but Leffing would not hear of it.

"Our luck should change! We have daylight instead of darkness and fog!"

He took the lead, bounding from tussock to tussock like a hound on the trail, stooping to scrutinize the pools, the ragged fringes of swampgrass, the stunted birch and alder trees. Here he found a broken branch, there a bent twig or a pool that looked muddied.

Luckily, the marsh was interspersed with a few small knolls, raised above the general level of the boggy terrain. When we reached one of these, we rested for a few moments. But only a few, and Leffing was off again.

At length my legs started to weaken. I began to breathe with some difficulty. "Got to stop!" I gasped.

Leffing turned. "We're almost up with him! A few more yards, Brennan!"

I shook my head.

He looked concerned. "Well—we'll stop a minute."

As we rested, the marsh appeared to darken. Glancing up, I saw that the cloud cover had increased. Lowering masses of occlusion threatened a momentary downpour.

We were about to start off again, when a fearsome howl sounded nearby.

Without waiting to see if I followed, Leffing leaped forward.

He was standing, staring off to one side, when I reached him.

Following the direction of his gaze, I at first noticed nothing. But as I looked more closely, I saw two glaring eyes set in a head that appeared to be floating on the top of a pool about fifteen yards away.

Understanding at once what had happened, I grasped Leffing's arm. ''He's caught in quicksand! We must try to save him!''

Leffing stood unmoving. ''Nothing we can do. No time. He'll be under in a minute at most.''

The desperate eyes saw us; the lips parted—to curse or plead. I will never know. Only the sound of a strangled scream reached our ears as the thing's mouth filled with swamp water and the head abruptly sank beneath the surface.

A few swirls briefly stirred the surface of the pool. When they subsided, Leffing tied his handkerchief to a nearby bush and turned away.

''I prefer even this devil's marsh to the tunnel, Brennan. Let us make our way out of here with care. Quicksand may be on all sides.''

Nearly forty minutes passed before we stumbled into Harbor Road. As before, we were wet, lacerated, and exhausted. This time we were lucky. A passing police car, driven by an officer who recognized us, whisked us to headquarters.

After listening to our account, Lieutenant Markell promised to head an investigative team within the hour. We were returned to The Ocean Arms Hotel.

Darkness had fallen and a driving rain was drumming against the window before Markell returned. He shed his raingear and sat down.

''A grim business,'' he began. ''We found the old servant, Kemble, dead in the kitchen. Heart attack or stroke, I guess. I suspect the old boy knew about Lorcaster's—hobby.''

I thought his hand shook a little as he accepted the glass of brandy that Leffing held out. "We found Chief Honderman—buried in the tunnel. We took strong lights in there and noticed disturbed earth about halfway along.''

He downed the brandy at a gulp. "A shallow, hasty grave. His throat had been torn to ribbons.''

He shook his head. "He must have gone there—why I don't know. Maybe to verify something. Lorcaster realized that he knew or suspected something and killed him.''

He arose wearily. "We'll try to recover Lorcaster's body tomorrow. Have to move some heavy equipment in there. Won't be an easy job.''

It took a week to recover Lorcaster's body. Meanwhile, however, police searching the mansion located a locked metal box containing manuscripts and printed pages missing from the collection in the Greystone Bay Library pertaining to the early settlement and history of the town.

It was readily apparent why some Lorcaster had contrived to have this material removed from the library.

The pages revealed that a Lorcaster had arrived on the *Sea Star*, the ship that brought the first settlers to the site of Greystone Bay. Apart from deaths attributed to storms, exposure, and fever, there had been several other strange and unexplained deaths that some of the crew and passengers had blamed on this first Lorcaster. Throats of these unfortunates had been mangled. The captain had decided that in despair these passengers had cut their own throats, but there were many who disagreed.

After the *Sea Star* finally struggled into harbor, Lorcaster had been shunned by the other passengers. He had prospered, however, built a sturdy house on North Hill, married, and bore a son. The son, in turn, had amassed a large fortune as merchant and trader. The dark legend concerning his father was almost forgotten when his own son revived it. Accused of slashing the throat of a young farmer and dragging his corpse into the marsh, the third Lorcaster had disappeared—only to return decades later with a grown family. These Lorcasters had built a new mansion on North Hill, but the legend concerning them persisted. It was said that every third Lorcaster, due to a hereditary taint in the blood, became a werewolf upon reaching maturity. The fits of obsessive madness persisted for a period of hours, or perhaps a full day. The victim of the curse then returned to normal life, probably fatigued, but altered little if any in appearance. The episodes of murderous, uncontrollable ferocity were unpredictable and irregular.

I put down the pages and looked up at Leffing. "If this is all true, why didn't the Lorcasters simply destroy the accounts instead of carefully preserving them in a metal box?"

"Who can say, Brennan? Obviously the Lorcasters were not normal people. Possibly they took some kind of perverse pride in their heritage!"

"Hard to accept," I objected. "But I think we know now what Chief Honderman was looking for at the Greystone Library. Probably he had heard hints of the legend, and after the recent killings, became suspicious of Miles Lorcaster."

Leffing nodded. "Exactly. And when he foolishly visited Lorcaster, probing for information, he was killed for his pains. Probably Lorcaster then decided he might as well make it appear that Honderman was the werewolf!"

"A few things still puzzle me," I admitted. "How did you know Lorcaster used a safety razor and what was the implication? Also, how did you know he didn't have arthritis?"

"Dear me, Brennan, you must be more observant. There was a safety razor in a case on the corner of Lorcaster's desk. The scratches on his face obviously came from something else—perhaps briars and thorns as he fled through the marsh! The arthritis was a calculated lucky shot. I had seen no previous indication of it and I knew that your thirty-two had struck him somewhere. When I mentioned the safety razor and arthritis, Lorcaster knew I had unmasked him!''

On the morning of our departure, Lieutenant Markell, named acting chief of the police department, came to shake our hands and say good-bye.

''Your, ah, fee will be forwarded a little later,'' he explained to Leffing. ''The usual paperwork. We are certainly grateful. Everyone in Greystone Bay is relieved the nightmare is over. Save for your efforts, it might be going on still!''

As we drove over the hills west of Greystone Bay toward the interstate highway, I stopped for a last look. An early autumn fog had crept in from the harbor, completely enveloping the city.

''I wonder what else it conceals,'' I murmured.

''Ah, who can say, Brennan? Probably much that is better left undisturbed!''

The Only
by
Al Sarrantonio

*When you meet Harbor Road, turn south. Now I can
almost hear your footsteps. Walk until the breakers on
your left seem about to wash up around you over the
boardwalk, and the shop lights become dimmer, more
secret. The shadows hug themselves here. Your footsteps
are tentative now, but you are close—when you pass under
a dull yellow streetlamp that hums, blinking out and then
flaring on again, on the verge of an extinction never
achieved, look up. There is a sign in a window, of three
letters, and inside and upstairs, as they told you, you will
find me. This is what you must do.*

I can hear you coming.

Bill was drunk when they met him at the bus terminal.
When Paul held out his hand, a lopsided smile of welcome
on his face, Bill only grinned widely and put a half-empty
pint of Jim Beam into his palm. "There's one or two more

of those somewhere,'' he said, patting at his drab green coat. He grinned again, an elfin thing from this small man, smaller-looking under the army crew cut that was beginning to fill out on his head.

''Bastard,'' the third member of their party, silent till now, said. He looked as if he were brooding, but the other two knew he wasn't.

''Bastard yourself,'' Bill said, and then he hugged the other, holding him out then at the shoulders. ''How are you, Jimmy?''

''Good enough.'' The thin, sour features turned wry. ''Better than you, you drunk bastard.''

''Hah! And more of that to come! I want to hit Harbor Road.''

Paul began, ''I thought we'd go back to my place for a while, have a couple of beers—''

''Beers, bullshit. I want to see the Bay, relive old times. Four friggin' years. . . .''

He looked down at his shoes, shiny black, trying to remember something, feeling around his memory.

''Four friggin' years. . . .''

''Come on,'' Paul said, taking him by the arm. ''We'll do it your way. I know just where to start.''

''Oh?'' Bill said, and then he smiled and held out his hand to take the pint of Jim Beam from his friend.

It was late and grey. It had been warm in the afternoon, the thermometer crawling up from the damp thirties to hover, exactly at midafternoon, near fifty. But now the mercury was falling again, and the sky was falling with it. It had been a damp October and now a damp November, and the weak try at Indian summer the weather had given the past couple of days looked now to be losing out to the inevitable cold. It would be chilly tonight, and there was already, out over the edge of the Bay, a hint of mistiness that would turn to thick fog by morning.

They walked east, toward the water. A movie marquee

said HALLOWEEN FRIGHT WEEK, but the *K* in *week* was already down and an attendant on a ladder was carefully removing the other letters one by one; the posters in the window now showed two lovers in a close-up 1940's-style embrace. They walked past a couple of bars, but even Bill didn't turn his head; this wasn't their section.

"The Sirens?" he asked. "To see Snooky again."

Jimmy nodded dourly, and Bill smiled.

A hard left onto Harbor Road, and there was the water to meet them. Their legs carried them on, but suddenly Bill stopped short, staring out at the Bay.

"What is it?" Paul asked.

"Nothing," Bill answered, staring into space. Again he seemed lost, searching for something. He shook his head. "It's just that I haven't seen that water in a long time, but it seems like I never left it."

The Seven Sirens looked barricaded against winter's advent. The green and white striped awning was rolled flat against the front, and the take-out window, open wide in the summer to serve clams and shrimp to the tourists who didn't know about the back room or were too shy or polite to barge in on the regulars, was pressed down tight and caulked. The porthole in the door was steamed; there was an untidy pile of late-season discards—paper cups and napkins—that swirled like a miniature leaf storm on the boardwalk out front.

Jimmy was pushing open the door when Bill held back. He was looking out over the water again.

"Okay if we stay outside?"

Paul looked at the two round picnic benches yet to be stored; the seats were up on the tables and the beach umbrellas—again, green and white striped—were missing from their holes. "Little cold to sit out, Bill." Then he added, "Sure."

He disappeared inside, returning with a tray of shrimp and paper cups of beer. "This stuff's on Snooky," he said. The other two had set up one of the tables, and Bill was once again smiling, holding the open bottle of liquor under Jimmy's nose.

"Come on, puritan. Just a sip." He turned to Paul, beaming. "Goofball still won't drink, will he?"

"Been trying to break him down for years."

Bill took one of the beers and drained half of it in a gulp. His back was to the Bay. The open bottle was in front of him, nearly empty. He was quiet for a few moments and then said, "I don't know why I came back."

"That's not what your letter said," Paul offered.

Bill shrugged. "All that stuff about being with your pals, the guys you grew up with, the places you know . . ." He shrugged again, then grinned. "I was drunk when I wrote that."

"That wasn't hard to figure out," Paul said.

"You misspelled *pals* four times," Jimmy said, straight-faced. "Spelled it with an *I*."

"That's what you guys are," Bill said, and suddenly he stood up, looking down at them. "My pils." He sat down again. "Hey Paul, you still teaching at the old school?"

Paul nodded.

"Why *did* you come back?" Jimmy said, and now there wasn't a hint of anything but seriousness on his face.

Bill was staring down at his hands, working his fingers over the knuckles. For a moment they thought he wasn't going to say anything. He reached for the bottle, then let his hand fall back on the other one again. "I truly don't know."

He looked up at them, and now there was a kind of pleading in his eyes. There was something he wanted them to tell him, some word or phrase to make him say what he wanted to say. Suddenly he blurted out, "Do you know what a *shit* I feel like coming back here? *Do you?* I was the big mouth, the one who always said that this wasn't the place to be, that there was a big world out there, that I

was . . .'' His hands were fists and he knocked them one
against the other. ''. . . That I was going to grab the world
by the balls.'' He laughed. ''That's what I said: *grab the
world by the balls*. You know what I did?'' He laughed
again, a snort. ''I grabbed myself by the balls.''

''Hey, Bill,'' Paul began.

''No, let me. You knew this would happen. The two of
you knew that if I really did come back I'd go on like
this.''

''We knew you'd come back,'' Jimmy said quietly.

''That's a really fucked-up thing to say.''

Abruptly the hands unclenched, resting on the picnic
table. There was a small plate of shrimp in front of him
untouched, and as if his hands now saw what his eyes
didn't register, his hands moved the plate away from him.

He went on, his voice lowered. ''Do you know that two
weeks ago, when my hitch was up, I had every intention
of signing back up? I'd never even thought of doing
otherwise. They were paying for computer school, I was
up for a promotion in rank in a few months—shit, I was
even getting along with the hard-ass sergeant I wrote you
about. Things were going great with Julie too.''

''You wrote about her,'' Paul said. ''Said she was
okay.''

Anger crept into Bill's voice. ''Did I write that I wanted
to marry her? That was up the line too. And then—'' He
made as if he were holding a pen, poised above the table,
frozen. ''And then I had that paper in front of me, and
suddenly I didn't want to sign it anymore, I wanted to
come back to Greystone Bay. More than anything else in
the world, I wanted to come back here.''

''You remember your early letters? They were full of
homesickness,'' Paul said.

''Come on, that was three years ago! I told you later on
I washed this place out of me. What the hell is there for me
here except you guys. After my old man died and the bank

took the house—shit, there's nothing here at all.'' Once again anger came. ''Do you know what my long-range plans were? Another hitch, then boom, out of the army with all that computer training behind me. I was going to go to Boston, get a job with one of those big computer places on Route 128, be set for life. And with Julie. And then suddenly, none of it means anything anymore. I had a fight with her just before I got on the bus, and ended up telling her to go to hell. We'd never even had a serious argument before.''

''You can never go home again,'' Jimmy quoted laconically.

''Thomas Wolfe my ass. I'm here, aren't I?''

The anger had drained out of him, leaking away to the water behind him, and now he saw the bourbon bottle in front of him and he finished it with one swallow. Another sip of beer and suddenly he smiled, washing everything else from his face. ''So I'm here, I came home, and, well, I guess it's all right.'' The smile trailed a bit and his eyes wandered. ''I guess it's all right. . . .''

It was getting dark. Out in the harbor, where bay met and kissed ocean, a lonely foghorn sounded once, then again. Nearer, a buoy slapped itself, the mild lash of a rope on hollow metal. The air thickened, became moist, and already the few fall stars twinkled desperately, trying to shine through the heavy night coming.

They rose, and moved on. As Bill pushed his chair back he saw Snooky regarding him inscrutably through the small front window; the old bar owner nodded once in salute, and Bill waved back. There was more drink in him than he thought. He stood and found the world turning for him momentarily; then it steadied and Paul and Jimmy were there beside him. There was a heaviness in the pocket of his coat and he felt down to find the smooth glass of an unopened pint of bourbon. He left it there, tightening the collar of his coat around his neck.

They turned south, passing Port Boulevard once again, where the bright lights of the shops and stores were beginning to turn to the dimmer ones of closing time. Bill felt oddly warm and peaceful. He remembered a time when he had stolen a newspaper from one of the stands next to Woolworth's, because his old man liked the *Tribune* so much and wasn't buying it because the factory had had a layoff and they were keeping every nickel until they found out how permanent it would be. He'd walked two blocks, fast, with the paper tucked so tight under his arm it hurt, and then when he finally slowed down he looked down to see that he had taken *The New York Times* by mistake. He'd sneaked the paper back to the newsstand, not so much out of guilt as that if he had brought the *Times* home his old man would know he'd stolen it and whip him till his pants bled.

They passed the Boulevard, leaving the lights behind. Again the buoy slapped itself, and suddenly Bill crossed the boardwalk, facing the Bay; he put his arms on the railing and looked down the steep embankment before turning to his two friends. They saw he had a newly opened bottle of bourbon in his hand.

"Had enough?" Jimmy asked.

Bill answered, "Never. I want to toast you two guys now." He held the bottle out straight over the railing. His head swam but his arm was steady as the rocks below. "To the two biggest bastards I know."

He offered Paul the bottle, and, after Paul swallowed, he was astonished to see Jimmy take it also, a discreet sip passing into his mouth.

"Mother of God," Bill said, his eyes growing wide, clutching at his chest. "The world is surely ending when Jimmy Hoffman takes a drink."

Jimmy shrugged sourly and handed the bottle back.

"Do you know," Bill said, pausing to lighten the bottle himself, "what I thought of the other day? I thought of the time the three of us went looking for that old man in the chair. Remember? There was that story we heard, I can't remember any of it, but there was something about an old man who sat in a chair all the time.''

He looked at his friends; Paul was staring out at the water, Jimmy moving a hand along the railing, lips puckered, the taste of alcohol still in his mouth.

''Come on,'' Bill continued, ''don't you remember? It was one of the biggest things we ever did. *We* found the guy in the chair. We must have been in third, no, fourth grade. Mrs. Johnson was our teacher. She still at the school, Paul? You ever see her?''

''She's Vice Principal,'' Paul said flatly.

''You see? I remember it was fourth grade because we had Mrs. Johnson for our teacher and because that was the year we all fooled Benny Lakeland into asking his old man for a box of rubbers for Christmas. You remember that? The poor dumb bastard didn't know what a box of rubbers was.''

Jimmy was smiling, and suddenly Paul broke into a laugh. ''I remember that.''

''Don't you remember the other thing? The guy in the chair?''

''Do you?'' Jimmy asked, oddly.

''Sure I do!'' He stopped, racking his memory. ''Somebody told us all about this guy who did nothing but sit in a chair in a little room somewhere in Greystone Bay, and the three of us went looking for him, and we found him.''

''And?''

''And nothing! That's all there is. What's the big deal? The point was, *we* found the guy and nobody else did.'' He pulled the bottle up to his mouth and kept it there a long time. ''Jeez, you guys are bastards all right.''

''I remember,'' Paul said, almost in a whisper.

''There, you see!'' Bill's eyes brightened.

Paul took the bottle from him and they all looked out

over the Bay. There wasn't much to see now, but they had
never needed eyes here anyway. The ears and the nose did
all the work, with the salt in the air and the good dampness
that was always there, especially in the summer, and the
squawk of gulls and the tiny splash they made when they
dived to snare a shiner from just below the surface of the
water. The foghorn wept again, out somewhere in the
loneliness, and now, close by, they heard that tiny splashing sound and then the triumphant sound as a gull reared
blackly up away from them, its prize in its mouth.

"This *is* a beautiful place," Bill said quietly.

The others nodded, and then Paul used the bottle before
Bill took it back.

The night closed in on them, and they walked on.
South, still, along the boardwalk that creaked in places
like the steps in a haunted house. "You remember the time
we went to that haunted house near South Hill?" Bill
began, but then he said, "Forget it." He was awash in
alcohol, and the red and white neon lights stabbed at his
eyes painfully, making him shield them. Everything was
too bright, surrounded by too much darkness. He heard
Paul and Jimmy walking beside him, but had to reach out
his hands to clutch their coats to make sure they were
really there. He wanted to throw up, but instead, took the
bottle to his mouth again, as a baby might take a nipple.

"Where are we?" he said, not sure if the words had
made it to his lips, but he nodded when Jimmy answered,
"Harbor Road still, down near the end."

"Ah," he said, once more wanting to throw up and then
suddenly, from far away, he heard a vomiting sound but
was surprised to find that it wasn't himself but Jimmy who
was bent double.

"Never could hold your liquor," Bill said, slurring out
a laugh. "One drink in his whole friggin' life and he barfs
up. Here, have another." He held the bottle under Jim-

my's nose but Jimmy pushed it gently away, rising up slowly.

"Where are we now?" Bill asked, and then he stared at the front of the building they stood before.

"This is it. Goddammit, this is it!" There was drunken victory in his voice. He turned to his two companions, who only stared at the front glass window, a small square cutout with a neon-scripted Bud sign that was not lit.

"This is where the guy in the chair was!"

Suddenly he heaved over, throwing the acidy contents of his stomach onto the small stoop in front of the bar. He stood, cleaning his mouth with his sleeve, and then found that the hand within the sleeve still held a bottle with a half-inch of bourbon in it. His stomach protested loudly, but he took it down anyway, closing his eyes momentarily before focusing them again on the building before him. He dropped the empty bottle and it spun once on the sidewalk before settling, label down, next to the stoop.

The liquor, all-encompassing as it was, had now deposited him in a place that was crystal-clear. He saw the door, the brass handle on the door—

"We're going in."

His leg lifted, and he was up on the stoop. Without looking, he knew that Paul and Jimmy were with him. He could feel their bodies beside him, their wordless rapport.

"You don't remember anything?" Paul asked; his voice was low and Bill couldn't locate Paul's face to go with the voice.

"Dammit, this is the place!" he said in answer.

His hand was on the door—old, notched wood, a lock that had been replaced more than once; he pressed his hand, his body, against it.

The door opened inward easily. A push of tobacco smoke, thick as dust, greeted him, along with the stronger smells of any old bar: urinals long uncleaned, their towel machines empty, soap dish empty, a run of gurgling water in the brown-bleached sink, and a protesting squeal followed by nothing when the hot tap is turned; and beer, sour, run into every corner, dried but never gone, spills on the floor, green tiles rubbed nearly black with cigarette filters and the detritus from a thousand heavy shoes. There was a jukebox flat against one wall, in the shadows, its lights out save one faint amber bulb that pulsed like a retreating heartbeat. Pegs set into the warping paneled walls, dark as the floor, stained, another leak of water running silently from one ceiling corner to meet an ancient pool on the ground that never grew and never receded. The bar was not long but filled, smudged wood polished by coatsleeves, tarnished footstools with torn red leatherette seats. A bowling machine off in another corner showed no lights at all, a rug of dust covering its alley, the plug draped across the top.

The seats were filled with old men who turned as they entered; it was as if a nest of old birds had been disturbed, swiveling their hooded eyes to see what sort of animal approached. The bartender looked like one of them, perhaps elected to lift his aging body from his barstool, worn topcoat and all, and serve his fellow passengers. There was a glass in his hand, clouded, and he paused only a moment as they entered before turning his back on them to refill it from a bottle under the smoky mirror in back of the bar. His eyes turned up to the mirror, watching them there.

Someone at the bar snorted; swallowed phlegm.

"North Hill boys," someone grunted in dismissal, and the old men turned back to the bar, but all the eyes in the mirror, between the whiskey bottles, stayed on them.

"Dammit, this is it," Bill said too loudly. The world pendulumed up away from him, came to a standstill, pendulumed back the other way. He wanted to sit down. Once again his eyes were hurt, and the world was divided into glowing blobs of light and surrounding darkness.

"We sneaked in and went right over there," he got out,

pointing crookedly to an indistinct dark corner next to the jukebox.

"Follow me," he said, stumbling toward the dark corner.

His feet would not work properly, but suddenly he was there, falling onto the jukebox, his face bumping flush with the scratched dusty glass. "NIGHT AND DAY"—A-4 he saw, and then, mercifully, there were hands under his arms and he was pulled away. He expected to be taken to where damp sea air would greet him, but instead, there was a shuffling and his feet were on steps leading upward. He had never been so drunk. His boots scraped leadenly but then he remembered how to use them and he lifted one, then the other. He felt like a marionette, his feet flailing out and up in an approximation of climbing and yet smoothly supported by the arms that held him.

"Up?" he said, slurring his word horribly so that it sounded like the cry of a baby. He tried hopelessly to right his head and bring his eyes to focus, and then abruptly he could see for a moment. There was a steep upsloping bank of steps ending in a wall. The wall got closer and then turned, and he looked up to see another series of steps ending at a huge—

"Paul? Jimmy?" A trapdoor dropped open in his mind, and he remembered it. He remembered where he had been. He heard giggling and he turned to see Paul beside him, his nine-year-old face stifling a laugh; Jimmy was on the other side and now Paul reached out, poking a finger into Jimmy's ribs and Jimmy threw his hands over his mouth, his eyes wide, trying not to cry out, and then turning to tell Paul in a severe whisper to shut up. They heard a creaking sound from below and the three of them stopped dead, leaning back against the wall and peering down into the shadows.

"You think someone saw us?" Paul whispered.

"Nah," Bill said, "not those old men. They're lost in their beer."

Jimmy nodded, and they waited, still as mice, for another sound from below that didn't come.

"You really believe that crud about 'the man in the chair'?" Paul snorted in a low voice.

"You were there, you heard," Bill shot back, glancing up at what lay before them. "And pipe down."

"I think you put your big foot in your mouth," Paul persisted. He too was looking at the top of the stairway, but his tone remained derisive. "A bunch of bull—'one man, and one only, from all the men in Greystone Bay, must always sit alone.' " He waggled his hands before him, his voice mocking in a whisper the spooky sing-song of a tale-teller around a campfire. " 'So was the pact made, and so it continues—the safety of Greystone Bay for the life of one only.' " He opened his mouth and eyes wide, feigning fright, then broke into stifled giggles.

Beside him, Jimmy smiled grimly. "Didn't have to say you could find him, Bill. Everybody knows that story. I say there's nothing to it."

"I said I'd find him and I meant it. Let's go," Bill said, and they turned once more upward.

"Looks like the door from *Twilight Zone*," Paul said, but Jimmy hushed him as another creaking sound came. "That was you, idiot," Bill said, and he put his foot where Jimmy's had just been, producing another low crack of old worn wood.

The door was huge to them—four panels, two on the top smaller like squinting eyes. The knob was cut crystal, tarnished, like the ones in Bill's grandmother's summer house; he wondered if he would be able to turn it since he had so much trouble with those others—but then that had been because he was only three and he couldn't open any doors without difficulty.

"I hear somebody inside," Paul hissed, and they halted until Paul poked the two of them in the ribs, making them smother shouts. "Thought I did," Paul laughed.

"Come on," Bill said.

His hand was on the knob. It was just like those others, a thousand cut facets like imperfect prisms. It was slightly oval, fitting into the palm of his hand like a smooth Bay rock, a good one for skimming. He turned to smile at Paul and Jimmy, one step below him.

"Go ahead," Paul said, grinning stupidly, and Jimmy stared at him unblinking.

He turned the glass knob.

The door swung inward, as if pulled back by weights and pulleys. For a moment he saw nothing in the room but grey-yellow light and dust: a small hexagonal skylight choked with dirt, plastered walls with great rivers and tributaries of cracks, flaking holes, dark wood molding at the ceiling sagging out of its nail holes, pieces of it gone here and there, the floor covered with a sheen of undisturbed dust—and then he saw a chair with an old man in it.

"Holy shit," Bill said, and he reached for Jimmy and Paul but they weren't there. He heard their yells, their feet clattering down the stairway to the bar below.

The man in the chair opened his eyes once, a flutter of ancient eyelids like a lizard's, and it was over. *After me, only you*, Bill heard, though he didn't see the old man's lips move.

Bill blinked; time moved.

"Jimmy? Paul?" he called out. He stood over the threshold, the smell of mustiness in his nostrils, the glaring dead light from the six-sided skylight throwing the color of mustard at him. The room was empty. The arms were gone from under his; again, as before, he heard the sound of steps moving down the stairway behind him. He looked down, saw his army boots, and he felt his fatigue coat buttoned high around his neck. The room spun, came still; he saw off in one solitary corner the empty chair, highbacked, seat worn smooth—

"*Jimmy! Paul!*" he cried, knowing that his voice carried empty down the turning stairs, buried deep before it reached the floor below.

"Jimmy . . ."

He walked, and the chair held up its arms to him, and he embraced it. . . .

So that is what was. So long past, so many sour shines of moon and sun through my little window above. My eyes never open anymore . . .

But you are here now. I hear you. On the stoop, hesitation at the door, and then you push it open. The smell of beer and smoke. No one looks up as you sneak past—how many of you are there—two? Four? It doesn't matter. Only one will enter. To the back, past the jukebox, up the steps. A hesitation, another.

Come closer.

The Disintegration of Alan
by
Melissa Mia Hall

I can pinpoint almost the very second it began, the disintegration of Alan. It was the morning of October one; I had just glanced at the digital clock. Seven A.M., five or four minutes past. A Wednesday. In Greystone Bay. His right hand. He was reaching for the sugar at the breakfast table and as I watched his familiar hand pass through a diagonal shaft of sunlight, I saw his thumb fragment into nothingness. For a moment I thought it was due to my nearsighted eyes. I blinked groggily, coffee cup halfway to my lips.

"Alan?"

He thought I was beginning the old antisugar routine.

I swallowed heavily and set the cup down, staring at the space where his thumb had been. The index finger next to it looked like it would follow the thumb any moment, the fingertip shortening to the first joint. I exhaled slowly, resting my eyes on the crumpled newspaper beside my chair. I adjusted my glasses and returned my gaze to Alan.

He watched me curiously. The wrist of the disintegrating arm rested by his plate.

"Anything wrong, sweetie pie?"

"It's just—"

"Don't worry, if it bothers you that much, I won't take any sugar."

"Alan—"

"Now, Gabrielle, don't be a nuisance—"

Biting my lip, I continued to stare.

"What's with you?"

"I don't know," I said truthfully. I picked up my coffee and turned my head toward the window over the sink. "Go ahead, put some sugar in your coffee."

"I don't want to," he said.

"I said, go ahead."

"And I said I don't want to!"

"Why not?" I looked at him again. The disintegration had progressed. I wondered why it had begun at such an unlikely spot and not at his feet or his head. Then I realized the insanity of such reflections. Heat rose in my cheeks.

Alan's left hand reached toward the sugar bowl.

My heart sank. "Alan, why are you using your left hand?"

He shrugged his broad shoulders and the solidity of his chest only emphasized the absurdity of what I saw occurring before me. "Why not?"

"You're right-handed," I said.

Beads of perspiration broke out along his forehead. He scratched his mustache nervously and then tugged at his white collar—all with his left hand.

"Alan, what has happened to your right hand—your arm?"

His handsome, well-ordered face crumpled into confu-

sion. "Nothing's wrong. I don't know what you mean.
You're always finding something wrong with me. I don't
know—I'm sick—sick to death." He pushed back his
chair and stood up. "Call the office and tell them I'm not
coming into work today." He glared at me, but the force
of his chaotic anger had already dissipated. He looked
constipated.

"Alan, really—"

"Shut up. I mean it." His mouth turned down at the
ends and quivered. "I want to be alone." With that, he
went to the doorway.

"Alan—please tell me what's going on."

"Nothing; it's the flu or something," he said, a touch of
the shriek in his tone.

"Your arm—"

"What about my arm? There's nothing wrong about my
arm!" He lifted the affected appendage and waved it
around. It was grotesque.

I gasped. "Alan, can't you see—it's disappearing!"

"It is not!" he said before stomping down the hallway.

I sat in my chair and considered the situation. It was
ridiculous, horrifying, and repulsive. Funny, too—well, a
little. I hit my spoon against the tabletop. A sharp pain
needled my temples.

The clock rang out. Time to leave for work. I had to call
the *Gazette* and tell them Alan wasn't coming in. It didn't
take long. I had to call in too. No way I could go to work
either. I dialed the number. My secretary answered, her
Brooklyn accent bright and sure over the line. I told her
that I wouldn't be in and all the other things I was supposed to. I hung up the phone again and took off my
shoes.

Down the hall, past the bedroom, to the studio I went.
The drawing board was just as I had left it. I sat before a
half-drawn pencil sketch of Alan. I had tried—

I looked at it a long time. Finally I covered the sketch

and played on a new piece of paper, blending lines and shapes without meaning. It was midmorning before I got up and stretched my legs. They'd almost fallen asleep. I had to go see about Alan.

He didn't call out to my query when I knocked on the door. I pushed it open slowly. Our room was paneled in dark wood and had never been very light. That morning was no exception. My eyes had to adjust to the dimness before I could see what was left of him, sitting in the striped armchair by the window. He looked at me and shrugged. His head, shoulders, and a portion of his torso were all that remained.

I wanted to vomit but did not. I held my hands to my mouth. What could I say?

He gazed at me vacantly, as if he could see me, but did not know me or the reason why I was there. He might have been thinking. Of other things. As I watched him I could detect recognition struggling in his eyes.

His mouth opened. "I'm sick. Please leave me alone for a while. I'll be okay if you'll just leave me alone."

He was afraid.

I was sweating. I took off my jacket and pushed back my hair. Then I went to him and tried to touch him. He jerked backward.

"Alan—please—"

"Gabrielle, why?"

I reached out again, trembling. My hands slid through. It's not always easy to face a reality like that.

He had been real. We had made love; we had taken baths together; we had hiked in the Vermont mountains. He liked Gatorade and tennis. I hated tennis. He liked beer. We saved beer cans. There was a huge bag of them out in the garage. The color orange was his favorite. He preferred Kleenex to Puffs. He didn't like the same kind of music I did and resented me singing along with the radio when we were in the car together. He always wore his hair

parted on the right side. He liked watching the boats in the
harbor. I liked sailing them.

There was nothing I could do. Soon he would be gone
entirely. I thought of the police. Could such a thing be
explained? "My husband disintegrated this morning and I
thought you'd like to know." A giggle mushroomed from
the madness and spilled out. I couldn't help it. Poor Alan.
He twitched at that giggle.

"I'm sorry, Alan."

I would tell the police he just left me. Men do that
sometimes. Nothing you can do to stop them—I don't
think.

I straightened up, folded my arms. I regarded him with a
sudden clarity. I was a camera remembering rolls of film
that had passed through my chamber. Images, yes, yes—
flash forward and flash back.

"Alan, is there anything I can do?"

"Well—" His head swiveled back and forth. He was
trying to think of something.

I stared at the space where his bottom had been. I had
not seen that disappear. It was unfortunate. Manic laughter
pushed in my throat, wanting out. I clamped my lips and
waited. I would be generous, kind.

"Yes, Alan?"

Childlike, shrill, he said something I couldn't quite
understand.

"What?"

"I said, I guess I'm going away."

To just fade away, like that?

"Must it be like this—" Perhaps his image would firm
up again—strong Alan, stalwart reporter. My stomach
churned or maybe it growled. I hadn't eaten much breakfast and it was noon or after.

His mouth worked like a fish out of water. He'd always
been rather clumsy.

"I don't want you to think I don't care about you, Gab."

I flinched. I hated him to call me Gab.

"Aw, Gabby, I really don't know why this has to happen. I thought we had a swell marriage and I've had a neat life, with the paper and all. But you know—I never really had control. This isn't that much a surprise."

His big blue eyes were mistlike. Sunlight glowed through his hair.

There was nothing I could do. I tried to kiss him. It was like kissing air. I couldn't even smell the after-shave he used to put on every morning.

The futility of life descended upon me. But I had to be brave.

"Wish it would get over with," he said. His voice was whistle-thin.

"Do you have anything else to say? Any—last words?" I gasped back the sobs.

"It's not my fault."

Childish of him. Always that petulant tilt to his lips— that too vivid, colorful face. What color? He was pale.

"Didn't you love me?" I asked, blushing at my boldness. It was now or never.

He looked at me like he didn't understand.

I left the bedroom. I thought I could hear him crying.

The studio was my sanctuary. I went to the drawing board and sat down. I looked out at Blind Point, at the ocean beyond. I pulled out the portrait of Alan and studied it intently to see if I could save it. Frowning, I took my favorite artgum eraser and finished erasing it.

I have always been a competent artist and I know a failure when I see one.

In a Guest House
by
Steve Rasnic Tem

Sometimes Brian thought he heard voices. They began
in the worst heat of summer, and he thought they came
from the marshland, or maybe the forest. *Christ, I must be
dying*. But he was never sure if they were really voices, or
just the white noise made more articulate by the pressures
he was feeling.

He'd hear them when he was doing the bills, and there
was never enough money in the account to cover all the
checks that *had* to go into those envelopes. Greystone
Shingle was doing well, but he was only a junior salesman. There'd be a soft murmur that distorted the voice on
the TV his kids were watching in the next room.

He'd hear them when he was trying to get to sleep, but
couldn't sleep for worry about those bills, and for all the
things the family needed but couldn't afford, for all the
things he could not do with his life for worry over the bills.

Under the fan blade whirring, growling, and whining because they couldn't afford an air conditioner.

Sometimes he thought he might be hearing the tourists, drunk in one of the harbor bars. They filled the town in summer, but seldom ventured out of the Harbor Road area. Brian never understood the attraction—if he had the money for vacations, this was the last place he'd go. The intensive restoration of the harbor homes and businesses made them look too new, too bright, despite the fact that they were so old underneath. Unreal, like large dollhouses. Not something you'd want to live in, unless you were doll-like yourself. And of course many of the old ladies living in those homes *did* seem like dolls to Brian. Small, with synthetic hair.

Or maybe it was the fishermen he was hearing, unloading their daily catch in the docks. He thought it odd they'd work so long after dark, but then, competition with the large fleets made it tough for them. They probably had to work harder. Still, it was strange seeing one of the old boats slipping into a dock at night, a bulky shadow drifting over dark water. You wondered where the boat might have been, what kind of men would work at those hours, what kind of fish could be caught at night.

But voices couldn't possibly carry that far.

Sometimes the voices would bark in his ear, tearing him out of a hard-won sleep. He'd sit up in bed staring out the window into the heated dark, trying to rub the pain of their sharp speech out of his temples, wondering if the dogs had jumped the fence again and were about to earn him another fifty-dollar fine.

He slept uneasily in the house they could not afford, but required. Too far up on North Hill to afford, and yet not far enough to really feel a part of the neighborhood. They'd lived in the harbor when they were first married, before the kids and before restoration had overpriced the apartments there. With the first child they moved into one of the cheaper developments out on the western road, where they always felt unsettled, not a part of the Bay at all. With his first healthy raise Elizabeth insisted that they take this house. All she could see was the largeness of the house, the prestigious North Hill location. What she didn't see was the small yard, the fact that it was downhill from some of the largest homes. Some rich man had once housed his servants here, and the older residents of the Hill would know that. The large house payments made them dangerously vulnerable to any financial setback, and all to buy their continued status as interlopers.

He wondered if the house would ever be theirs completely. But more than that, he wondered if he would ever feel at home here.

Brian would have done anything to escape those voices. Perhaps that was why he wasn't too surprised to find himself in a stranger's bed one morning, in a stranger's house. When he first awakened there, he thought he was back in the apartment they'd had before the kids came, above the tobacco shop, overlooking the Bay. The bedroom walls were just that close, and comforting.

But that apartment had gone to someone else, a long time ago. He had awakened in some stranger's home.

The sunlight filled the window here, heating the bed and burning out the tension in his chest. Their new house had a tree by the bedroom window; he'd quite forgotten what it was like to wake up in sunlight.

The sunlight filled the room, making the yellow wallpaper glow, putting a glaze on the old-fashioned water pitcher and bowl on the washstand, bringing out the crescent-shaped highlights on the tall mahogany bureau and the four cherrywood posts rising out of the corners of his bed. The shadows in the dimpled ivory ceiling filled with it. The pastel paintings of orchards and haystacks and children playing in front of a bloodred barn came to life with it.

Someone had hung his tan corduroy sport coat neatly on the back of an ornate, high-back chair. His brown trousers were folded on the seat. He rolled his head a bit and could see the toes of his shoes peeking out from under the side of the bed, brightly polished.

He always called this his "salesman uniform." They were what he wore when he visited out-of-town clients.

He closed his eyes and thought about that, trying to force alertness into his system. His boss had sent him out of town to call on some roofing contractors. That must have been what happened. He'd asked for some extra work—they always needed the money—and there was that new line of shingle material that had to be introduced.

But then he remembered that his boss had said no, said it was the wrong time of year for that. And he couldn't remember packing. He couldn't remember saying goodbye and driving here.

He opened his eyes. He glanced down at his chest, felt the soft material of his pajamas. The new ones Elizabeth had bought him only a short time ago. He just hadn't gotten around to wearing them before. He looked around the room, but was reluctant to lift his head completely off the pillow. He couldn't figure out what had happened to his shirt, or to the suitcase carrying his change of clothes.

He twisted his head back toward the window. The sun appeared to be high in the sky, the shadows of the tall trees late afternoon shadows. He could see a part of the yard, bright green with a sprinkler feeding that green. A child's red wagon. Bright yellow flowers bordering a flagstone path that led away to an immense barn in the distance. A line of trees beyond that. And deep blue. He had awakened in a stranger's home after a long afternoon nap.

A slight breeze rustled the pink-tinted curtains. It carried a scent of green, but Brian could distinguish it no further.

He could heard the voices of children calling from the fields beyond. A woman read softly to another child, somewhere below his window. He could hear the child asking questions, knew they were questions from the lilt of the sentences, but he could not make out individual words.

He sat up in bed until dizziness passed, then gained his feet. The ivory ceiling seemed far away. He drew nearer the window but still could not see the children. But he did see more of the yard: a wooden wheelbarrow in need of paint, a collie sleeping under it. He heard someone, male or female, calling dinner.

He wondered how he got here. He tried to think about a car, but the image wouldn't come. He wondered about what he must have been doing before he fell asleep. Perhaps listening to a woman singing a young child to bed. He wondered about how he had closed his eyes—slowly with fatigue, heavily with alcohol, or quickly with determination.

He wondered if it had been raining at the time, or if a wind had been coming up.

Someone had called Brian from downstairs.

He opened his eyes uneasily; he had fallen asleep again. He wondered if it had been such a long trip, to make him so tired. Boston, New York, maybe Bangor. Someplace in the country, outside one of those cities. He used to dream about places like this. He used to gaze out of his living room window, over the scattered lights along Port Boulevard, to heavily wooded South Hill, where there were no lights, where it was always dark. Too steep for building, everyone said. South Hill was so high he couldn't see over it, even when he walked to the top of North Hill. He used to wonder what was beyond that rise, and beyond the forest. Maybe fields with restful houses like this one. Places where a guest would fit so comfortably.

But someone had called him down to dinner, and he had to be properly dressed. He stood and walked over to the tall bureau. He knew shirts were often kept in the top drawer of such pieces. But when he opened the drawer he could not bear to reach his hand inside.

He saw four freshly starched shirts, bleached blazingly white, folded stiffly, rigid in blue paper wrappers. Fresh from some local laundry. He didn't think they were his shirts—if they were, they had been seriously transformed by the laundry. He dared not touch them.

He didn't know why. Maybe it was the fineness of the material, and the unbidden thought that the cloth seemed like a kind of skin arranged in neat, antiseptic folds. Or maybe it was the stiffness of the shirts, the edges and angles so sharp he wondered if they might cut, might slice through layers of flesh.

He was afraid the shirts had death inside, all folded neatly away, creased and wrapped in blue paper.

Somewhere a meal had been prepared, a meal so quiet and perfect it was like a party. Brian knew they expected him; a place had been set. Dinner would not be the same without him. Children were dressed in their best, sitting quietly with expectant faces because a stranger was coming to dinner. They were hungry, famished after a long day at play, but could not eat until their guest had arrived.

Brian opened the second drawer, which held two or three much friendlier polo shirts, each striped in a different color and bearing an arcane symbol on the one breast pocket. He slipped one on hurriedly, pulled on pants and shoes, and opened the bedroom door.

He could tell at once that the house was an old Victorian, trimmed with ornate woodwork. The lamps were old, the electricity new. Numerous doors led off a narrow central hall. He assumed that he must be staying on the second floor. Here and there the ceiling tilted at a sharp angle. He wondered if there was one of those old barnlike attics overhead.

He could see the tops of the heavy staircase rails at the end of the hall, so he made his own way there. He could hear the metallic sounds of cutlery being applied to a table somewhere below, so he quickened his pace. His gallop down the stairs cleared his head and made him wonder when was the last time he had eaten. His stomach growled; he tightened it in embarrassment.

The dining room was to his left at the bottom of the stairs. A broad round table. A half-dozen people dressed variously in suits and workclothes seated around it, postures erect, waiting, three small children staring up at him wide-eyed. Several cats wandered the room, periodically making their way through the maze of legs.

A large bald man began to smile. The effort appeared to blush his face scarlet, swelling his cheeks. "We thought we were going to have to start without you," he said in a friendly tone. "Glad you could make it."

Brian made himself walk into the room, suddenly shy. He wasn't sure if he had ever met any of these people before. Maybe they had all come in late the night before, after his own arrival, whenever that was. "Sorry," he mumbled, and took his place at the one empty seat.

No one said anything for a few moments, then the bald man passed serving plates around, nodding vigorously, as if it were the most wonderful thing in the world to be doing. Brian took a little bit of each dish, muttering thank-yous, and doubting he could eat anything. Suddenly his appetite was gone. Occasionally someone would add something to his plate when he wasn't looking, so he found himself eating just to keep the food from overflowing onto the dainty lace tablecloth.

"We'll fatten you up," the bald man said with a wink, and Brian thought he could feel nerves tugging on the skin covering his abdomen. He turned his head slightly left and right, confirming his suspicion that the children were still staring at him. He wondered how long he had been here. His wife might be worried. He'd call her but he didn't think they'd have a phone. He was almost sure they didn't have a phone.

Sometimes he would gaze at another guest, and they'd raise an eyebrow or make some ambiguous gesture with a raised fork and Brian would stare down at his plate again. He could hear people working in the kitchen and he'd wonder if they were servants, or members of the family that owned the house. He'd look at each diner around the table and doubted they belonged here, except for perhaps the children. He wasn't sure about the bald man. Maybe he was a local who stayed here frequently, which made him like a member of the family. Maybe he was the family retainer, entitled to speak for all of them.

Just when he was looking for an excuse to leave the table, Brian saw a pale hand wrap around a door on the other side of the room. Two dark eyes peered round, the forehead sloped so steeply Brian couldn't see the hairline. Two dark lips like crusts of bread opened and closed, seeming to nibble on the paint along the edge of the door. Then the lips, the eyes, the hands were gone. Brian stood up abruptly.

"Delicious meal," he said, then paused awkwardly. "Thank you." He turned and headed up the stairs.

Brian sat on the edge of his bed, listening to the sounds of the house: pipes banging, footsteps, the occasional murmur of voices like small winds trapped in the walls. Although he was reluctant to go down the steps again and visit with the other guests—for he'd finally decided this must be a guesthouse, or a boarding house, a place where traveling salesmen spent a night or two—he knew he liked it here, would always like it here.

He'd found his suitcase in the closet, and carefully searched it, as well as the room, for any papers regarding the purpose of his visit here. There were none; he'd apparently planned to stay. He supposed there was a way to find out—the bald man might know. In any case, the lack of documentation gave him an excuse to stay as long as he liked.

Elizabeth might be worried, but she also knew that these trips sometimes took longer than planned. At least she wouldn't be panic-stricken. He wondered how she was doing with the bank account, with writing the checks. He'd probably have an enormous paperwork mess to clear up when he got home. She always wanted to put off paying the credit cards, or the loan accounts, or the utilities, in order to buy something for the house or the kids. She just couldn't understand why that filled him with such anxiety. He could see the bills accumulate—he was the one who dumped them into the bill basket each month. And the payments due seemed to increase geometrically once you got behind. Brian never completely understood the almost-mystical mathematics of it, but that's the way it was. He was surprised they hadn't had to declare bankruptcy at least once. Half the year they spent trying to catch up from the other half; they were never ahead.

He used to spend hours each night worrying about the money—adding it up, rearranging it, trying to make it fit into the seemingly countless hands and pockets that demanded it, that demanded it from *him*. He was always trying to think of other ways to make more money, and he discovered early on that he was quite poor at that. In fact, he seemed poor at most things involving money. He couldn't save it; he couldn't even spend it wisely. And bill collectors terrified him. They had a way of making him feel worthless, insignificant. They implicated his common sense and his honesty. Every phrase seemed to veil a threat.

If he had the money, he'd buy them all off. He'd pay the bills and pass out the insults. Elizabeth could do what she wanted then; nothing would bother him.

He was tired of thinking about it. Elizabeth didn't realize. It would kill him. He couldn't imagine it not killing him in some way or other.

He didn't have to worry about the bills here. In some way, his company was paying for this. He wouldn't be here if it weren't. And there was nothing he could do about his family's bills while he was out here, which must be a long way from home. Elizabeth would have to take care of things. Let her put off making the payments, then she'd have to talk to the collectors. She'd find out soon enough what it was like.

He heard footsteps outside the room. Shadows stopped for a time in the thin crack of light beneath his door. Someone was whispering in the hall.

The sunset through his window was a beautiful, exotic bruise. Brian had never seen one quite like it before.

He imagined the guest house to be pretty self-sufficient. Grow your own food, rent out the rooms. No collectors to pay. People like these always made their payments on time. They didn't like to owe.

After dark Brian went downstairs and out to the front porch. He sat by himself on a large, handmade swing that might have held five or more. All the other guests must have retired to their rooms, or to some television or reading room or other he didn't know about yet. At some point he would ask the bald man about that.

With no street lights it was almost black outside. He could barely make out the outlines of the barn, but nothing else beyond the front yard.

Suddenly the swing was rocking, and the bald man was sitting down beside him. Brian didn't see where he had come from.

"Nice night." The man sighed. "Enjoying your stay with us?" Brian couldn't see the bald man's eyes, just his jowls and large, florid lips.

"I am, very much. Nothing much to worry about here, is there?"

"Oh, no." The bald man chuckled. "We don't worry much at all, about *anything*, in this house." He patted Brian's arm and Brian felt himself draw away. "No need for you to worry your pretty head about anything either."

Brian didn't know what more to say at first; he felt his cheeks go hot. He moved his head back and forth slightly, still trying to see the bald man's eyes. Then after several minutes he remembered what it was he wanted to know. "By the way, did I mention how long I was staying here?"

"No, you just said as long as it took, didn't you? I could be mistaken, I suppose. Nothing to worry about if you didn't. We'll let you stay as long as it takes, even if it takes forever." He laughed, but Brian wasn't sure why.

Something rustled out by the trees. A tall, thin shape. Pale hands were flapping in the moonlight.

Again the next day Brian couldn't bring himself to try the shirts packaged so neatly in the top drawer of his bureau. Instead, he took another polo shirt, but felt seriously underdressed. A guest should dress nicely, he thought.

He spent most of the day on the porch, watching the children play around the barn. Once he helped the six-year-old untangle a kite.

Nothing to worry about here.

These children sang more than any others he had ever encountered. They watched him as if he were something different, something more than a stranger.

Sometimes he'd awaken abruptly from a nap, his thoughts disjointed. It was the silence that frightened him. But there was nothing to worry about here. Sometimes the breeze seemed unusually cold. Perhaps he'd arrived here by train. He saw no cars, and he thought those were iron rails glistening out in the fields under the midafternoon sun.

Brian felt inconspicuous here on the porch. Maybe that was the most wonderful thing of all. No one could see or hear him here, in the guest house. Voices faded into the dark.

Brian tried to imagine a new guest arriving at night. All the guests seemed to arrive at night. For there were always new faces around the table in the mornings. By train, having to walk across several yards of grassy fields to reach the house. Dark windows and stark outline against the expansive sky. The front door opening to welcome them. A dark hat gesturing respectfully from the entranceway.

Dinners were interrupted more and more frequently by glimpses of pale, bloodless hands and faces, whisperings in the kitchen and pantry, closets, the dark corners of the house. The bald man tried to keep Brian in a festive mood, always talking about getting up chess and bridge games, activities in which, he claimed, Brian's participation was essential to the well-being of all.

Cats walked through the dining room one at a time, whispering to unseen presences standing behind the many doors of the guest house.

Brian saw a desperate white hand drawn out of hiding, sliding out from a doorway and squirming on the floor, trying to steal a piece of discarded meat from a calico kitten's mouth. They tusseled awhile and the cat won, the hand withdrawing slowly in defeat.

It was like looking up from your meal and spying the dead, beckoning you from distant rooms. Brian found it difficult to swallow.

But there was nothing to worry him here. All bills had been paid in full.

Brian had fallen into sleeping most of his days. He ceased to wonder about his family.

He'd eaten little on his plate. He was too busy trying to catch another glimpse of those who did not eat in the dining room with the other guests. The ones who scavenged. When he looked around the table he discovered that all the faces were unfamiliar. He'd been in the guest house the longest, with the exception of the bald man.

A tap on the shoulder. The bald man stood over him.

"You can't eat here tonight, I'm afraid," the bald man said.

"My name is Brian. Brian."

"But you can't eat here, you see. The guest house is full now, and there are more people coming." The bald man's voice was gentle, but Brian could see the definiteness in the man, the assumption of unquestioned authority.

"You never call me by my name. You never did," Brian said.

"I'm sorry. I'm truly sorry." The bald man's eyes held tears. Brian wondered if they were sincere. "You have to leave our table now."

"Nothing to worry yourself about," Brian said. And stood.

They'd given Brian the shirts to wear with his freshly pressed trousers. He wore a new one today, but then, they seemed to be new every day. Crisp and sharp.

The collar sliced a piece out of his neck. Blood encircled the starched collar like a necklace. When Brian buttoned the cuffs the stiff material tore into his wrists, managing extensive damage when he walked and swung his arms. By the end of each day he was sore and bloody, but he felt fashionable, a well-dressed guest with no need of money.

Now he motioned from the pantry. Or from the closet near the stair. He robbed the cats of their small portions of food. The guests at the dining table tried to ignore him, but some were less successful than others. Some quickly lost their appetites and did not survive.

At night he would stand in the shadows, watching new guests arrive, making their way slowly toward the dark house in the field, its windows full of night, the dark hat removed from a bald head beckoning from the open door.

Welcome, he thought. *You'll need no money here. Worrying is just a waste of time.*

Power
by
Kathryn Ptacek

The door to the Trailways bus slammed shut, the driver checked his left for traffic, then the bus roared away from the curb, spewing a choking cloud of dust and exhaust. She slung her duffel bag over one shoulder and stared down Port Boulevard.

Ten years ago . . . a decade since she'd left Greystone Bay, and the main street, the town—nothing—appeared to have changed too much. It was just as grey, just as dull as ever. The late afternoon light painted the two-storied wood and stone buildings with a faint golden wash, giving them an almost magical quality. Almost. Because, she thought, there was nothing magical, nothing special about the town. It was just the place where she'd been born, had grown up, had endured until old enough to escape.

And yet . . .

She shrugged, feeling the reassuring weight of the bag's strap, then walked away from the bus stop outside the

VFW hall. Overhead grey and white gulls wheeled in lazy
circles and screamed, at times dipping toward the telephone wires that gleamed dully in the diffused sunlight.

She didn't know why she was here. She shouldn't have
come back. Not now; not after so long. But she'd had the
dreams, which triggered the terrible memories, and by the
end of last week she'd known she would return to Greystone
Bay.

She passed some stores now empty and boarded up, but
most of the businesses in the downtown section were
thriving, and hadn't changed much from what she could
remember. At the corner of Atwood and Mayfield she
stopped outside Krueller's Drugstore, its front windows
plastered with hand-lettered posters proclaiming cut-rate
prices and bargains galore. As she studied the displays she
hooked a strand of hair behind one ear. Once it had fallen,
straight and midnight dark, to her waist. Once. Never
again would it be that long.

She pushed the glass door open. The store smelled of
perfumes and astringent and chocolate, and as she glanced
toward the back, she felt the years shimmering away. Ten
years ago there'd been a small luncheonette in the back.
Actually it had been two booths, and a small counter at
which four could perch on the spindly stools there. Tuna
sandwiches and cheese sandwiches, milkshakes, and five
different flavors of pop were the only items on the menu,
but that had been enough. In those days it had been
popular with her crowd.

She pulled her lips back into a grimacelike smile. Her
crowd. Who was she fooling? She'd never had a crowd.
Not then, not now. Nevertheless they'd all come here after
school and had sat around, six or more high school students crammed into each booth, and they'd gossiped and
eaten their grilled cheese sandwiches and drank their cherry
Cokes and chocolate Cokes. She'd sat there on one of the

bar stools, with them and yet not, and watched, not speaking unless someone else spoke to her.

Now the luncheonette was gone, replaced by an expanded medical supply section, and a single video game machine which hummed and beeped to itself. She looked around, aware that the druggist seemed puzzled and was looking toward the door. She left without buying anything.

A block later she reached the old high school. She glanced once at the ugly stone building, its few windows grey in the light, and shuddered.

She couldn't go there, couldn't see it yet.

She continued walking, aware of the empty streets. Not many residents were out today. Even though the season was fairly early yet, the weather had turned raw, and a damp mist was settling over the town, blown in from the east across the Bay. She shivered, even though she wore a down jacket, and she massaged her left hand. It ached again, the dull throbbing spreading up her arm; it always hurt in the cold, no matter what she did, and she thrust it deep within her pocket now, hoping the pain would ease. She was heading eastward toward Harbor Road, which followed the curve of the Bay, but she knew the Bay, too, could wait. Tonight wasn't the time. She cut southward through the residential streets, and with each step came the memories she'd thought long buried.

The one time she'd been invited to a dance.

The time Ken Adams had cornered her out back of Krueller's and kissed her, and how she'd fought his unwelcome embrace.

The others . . . standing around and grinning; her raking Ken's face with her nails; his screams, and his ugly tone when he said he'd get even.

The kids in grade school calling her an injun. She kept patiently correcting them, kept telling them she was Indian, not an Injun, and more properly a Seneca, although she knew many different tribes blended within her veins.

Honest Injun, they had said, their eyes wide with mock
innocence, then swept away giggling.

Grandmother said it wouldn't be easy, being the only
Indian in school, and she'd been right. Most of the kids
didn't mind; a few were hostile, like their parents, because
she and her family were different, and so she'd progressed
through her grades knowing the names of her classmates,
but not knowing them.

In high school she'd gone from a shy gawky girl with
overbig eyes to a shy slender young woman. She knew she
was pretty. Her mirror told her that. Her grandmother told
her that. The looks in the eyes of the boys at school told
her that, and she was afraid. Afraid because she didn't
know what to do about it. Afraid of the looks of the boys,
especially Ken and the Adams cousins, the three boys she
liked most in school.

She looked up, and saw she was already at South Hill.
Beyond lay the forest where her grandmother lived, where
she had grown up. A wave of fog, white against the
greyness of the day, rolled toward the trees, tendrils slipping out to embrace the boles. Dampness plastered her
bangs across her forehead; she rubbed her cheek and found
it wet too, but whether it was from fog or tears, she
couldn't tell. She followed the overgrown path through the
dense woods, threading past the gnarled maples and oaks
and ashes, their long drooping limbs bare of leaves already. The fallen leaves crunched underfoot, and once she
heard the rustle of a squirrel in the bushes, whose long
thorns curved around bright red berries.

Few sounds drifted from the outside; she couldn't even
hear the whistles of the tugs in the Bay. Even the fog did
not enter; and as daylight faded and the woods grew darker,
she quickened her pace. At times the trees bent so close to
the path that she could hardly squeeze through them, and
once a branch reached down, scratching her along the
cheek. Impatiently she pushed it away. Once she thought

she saw something red out of the corner of her eye, but when she whirled around, she saw nothing. The way was much longer than she remembered, more lonely too, but finally she stood in the clearing, not more than a dozen yards distant from the log cabin built by her grandfather, dead now some twenty years. She saw no smoke coiling from the stone chimney, and a chill slipped down her spine. She thrust her hands more deeply into her pockets.

The cabin looked so deserted. Where was her grandmother?

Once on the porch made of wide planks, she knocked on the door, and when no one answered, she pushed it open. Inside, the large single room was precisely as she remembered. The handmade quilts neatly piled on the top of the bed; the cast iron Dutch oven and kettle on hooks above the old wood-burning stove; the rows of maple cabinets along each wall; the table and set of chairs in the center; the pictures she'd painted as a promising art student framed and hanging in prominent places. Off to one side was the bathroom, no larger than a closet.

She called out, but no one answered.

Even the smell was the same: camphor from the stored blankets, and pine from the logs stacked in the wood box by the fieldstone fireplace, and the delicate scent of herbs grown and dried by the old woman. At the rear of the cabin, next to a diamond-shaped window that looked out onto the garden in the back, a ladder led up to the loft. She climbed it quickly and looked around.

This narrow space with its slanting roof was where she had slept, done her homework, drawn the pictures, dreamed her dreams. Her box of watercolors sat on the table, the brushes still strewn as she'd left them; a chunk of charcoal sat, smudged, on a piece of cream-colored vellum paper. Her bed was neatly made, waiting. The deep box of toys, the bookshelves over the bed, the small closet by the ladder. The rug she and her grandmother had braided one long winter's evening as they talked about their once large family, now reduced to the two women.

She ran her fingers along the handmade bookshelves, felt the layers of gritty dust, glanced at the yellowed paperbacks there. She looked out the back window. The garden was overgrown with weeds, with the forest's wildness encroaching upon it, and strangely, still no sign of her grandmother.

She dropped the duffel alongside the bed, not bothering to unpack. She was tired from traveling, tired from the weight of the memories. So tired.

By the time she stretched across the bed and closed her eyes, it was after six, and not long after that she was sound asleep.

Her dreams that night were of red-splashed clouds.

In the morning she woke early with an image of her grandmother in her mind, and knew why she had not found her at the cabin. The old woman no longer lived. Sadness and regret filled her, for she hadn't seen her in ten years, hadn't written to her; now she never would.

Her grandmother was one of the reasons she'd returned, and now she wondered if she should stay. Yes, she still had some things to take care of. Wearily she closed her eyes and tried to go back to sleep, but couldn't, and after a while rose, changed into a fresh pair of jeans and a shirt, and went outside. With nothing else to do, she went back into town, and as she walked down the streets, she felt the presence of even more memories, memories that threatened to overcome her.

Edward Tanner. He'd taken her out, just once. His father, the town's most prominent doctor, had just presented him with a car, a blue and cream Thunderbird, for his birthday. Edward had dropped by her last class of the day, asked if she wanted to go out with him, and surprised, but secretly pleased, she'd nodded, and she had followed him away from the school. They'd gone to a seafood restaurant along Harbor Road, and the window by their table had framed the waterfront. The harbor, where her father, and his father before him, had fished for a meagre living, but she didn't tell Edward that.

Instead, she listened to him talk about his car, and his father, and his father's career, and how he was going to be a famous and rich doctor too. Afterward, they'd gone driving, and he'd pulled off onto a remote road in the woods, and he had shifted, suddenly pushing her up against the car door. One hand had gone down the neck of her blouse, the other up her skirt. She had kicked him in the chest, managed to open the door, and had run through the woods back to her grandmother's cabin, back to the old woman who sat waiting for her.

The next day her classmates had giggled and pointed as she went by, and she knew what Edward had told them. She was easy. Fast. And all the boys wanted to make her after that. She'd almost dropped out of school, but her grandmother had asked her to stay in, and because of the old woman, she had.

She shivered, then stepped across the street to the office of the *Gazette* and asked to see obituaries for the past ten years. They were on microfiche, and so the chore went more quickly than she expected. The record of Sarah Little's death was brief, a few sentences about the old woman who had died only the week before.

Just a week ago. She had been so close to seeing her grandmother. So close.

Afterward, she walked toward the hospital. Stone painted a fresh white every year, the hospital was small, privately funded, and the volunteers all wore pink, and bright smiles, yet nothing could disguise the stench of sickness and death.

Sarah Little had been in the ward on the third floor, the

ward where they put old people who didn't have much money. She took the elevator at the end of the lobby, walked down the linoleum floor, passed rooms in which people moaned or called out feebly, and when she reached the west wing she paused. She looked into the ward.

She thought she could see what it must have been like that week before. The tiny woman in the bed, the bottles hung like glass fruit on the lifetree, dripping their clear liquid into her veins. Plastic tubing running from her nose, the jagged rise and fall of the narrow chest. This frail creature with the silver hair and pale wrinkled skin was—had been—her grandmother. Prominent blue veins, fingers gnarled. The woman moaned, her tissue-thin eyelids fluttered, and she opened them, her dark eyes barely focusing.

"Time," she thought she heard the old woman whisper. "Time for you. It is—"

"Excuse me," boomed a cheerful male voice.

Startled, the scene before her dissolved and she whirled, then took a step backward as she looked up into a familiar face, a face aged ten years, but still unmistakable.

He was just as handsome, just as arrogant-looking. Edward Tanner.

And he recognized her.

"You!"

"Yes," she said evenly.

"What—?"

"My grandmother."

"Of course. I should have known." He paused, played with the pen in his hands, flipping it end over end in his fingers. Her fingers could no longer close around the barrel of a pen or pencil.

"You're a doctor now."

"Yes, just like my father."

"Yes, just like your father." Her tone was faintly mocking. She looked him straight in the eye, and after a few seconds he grew red, dropped his gaze. "What was wrong with her?"

He was the efficient doctor now, talking to a family member about a lost patient. "A severe case of pneumonia, compounded by various viruses. She was old, and didn't have the strength and resistance to fight illness off the way she used to. I prescribed bedrest, a large dose of Tetracycline, but she was so stubborn."

"She wouldn't listen."

"Right. She really should have recovered," Tanner protested. "Pneumonia just isn't that serious anymore." His father had never liked losing a patient either. For the Tanners it was more a matter of pride than concern for the loss of a life.

"I'm sure you did what you thought was best," she said, moving even farther away from him.

He licked his lips. "We tried to contact you, but she didn't have your address."

She said nothing, and as he stood there, looking at her, she knew what he thought. He was remembering that evening too. And the other one.

He looked as if he wanted to speak further to her, but she had nothing more to say. Without another word she walked away.

Outside, away from the odors of disinfectant and urine and rubbing alcohol, she breathed deeply. She had been shaken to see him; but he had been more shaken. She smiled. That was good.

Sarah had known she would come back; had waited as long as she could, but it had been too late. She knew now what she had to do. Sarah would have wanted her to return to the cabin, to take . . . to take what was rightfully hers. Her inheritance. She shuddered as a long grey cloud passed over the sun, blocking out the dim warmth of the day, and she rubbed her throbbing hand.

She had no choice. She had to go back. She had to do it.

For ten years she had wandered. After she left Greystone Bay, she'd gone to New York to work as a waitress in a dingy restaurant in the Village, where they served tofu soup and bean-sprout sandwiches and everyone was very chic, very dear. She hadn't lasted long. From there she took a job as a clerk in a small insurance office, but she couldn't type, not anymore. She tried a few courses at a university, dropped out after a semester. Hitchhiked up to Boston to work in a bookstore, found she didn't like the hours, wound her way slowly down the coast to Florida. She stayed there for a while, changing jobs every few months, and finally she went out to California.

Someone had told her that Hollywood directors were looking for Indians, particularly Indian women, for the movies. She refused the casting couch, though, and so went back to waiting tables in a small town outside Los Angeles. She went to Las Vegas then, and, finally, had started back east a few years ago, moving from city to town when she got bored; a week before she had reached New York, and there it had begun.

The problem was, she knew, she lacked ambition. Had since she'd left town. Before that she'd had more than her share of ambition and dreams and—

No more.

Now she lay on her bed in the cabin and listened to the wind soughing through the branches of the pines outside. Something scratched along the roof. A branch, she told herself. No more. At times she thought she could hear her grandmother's voice calling to her, whispering her name, and she smiled. She was close to the old woman, close as she had not been in the past ten years.

She closed her eyes, and she could see Benjie Adams, Ken's cousin. A big hulking kid, who played football and enjoyed smashing into others because he could knock them down harder and more often than they could him. His longish thatch-colored hair never looked combed, and his grin was lopsided, his face pleasant, though hardly handsome, and somehow he was endearing.

He'd been there too. Oh yes. He'd been the one who held her—

No.

No, no, no.

Inside she felt hot rage coil, felt it twist through her guts again as it had off and on for so long. Tears of anger burned her eyelids, and she dashed her right hand across her eyes.

Weeping was for children, for lost girls, for the past. Not the present.

The wind rose, moaning, and she thought she could hear other voices on it, voices that encouraged her and angered with her, and she wasn't scared. Wasn't her grandmother always right? Nothing could harm her here, not in the cabin. Away from the cabin, yes; but not here, for here she was protected.

She smiled and sat up in the darkness, looping her arms around her knees. Tomorrow she would begin looking for the others.

Outside, in the storm-cloud-laden sky, the moon was not yet full.

Her dreams that night were of grass kissed with crimson dew.

What she had to do was . . . powerful. In a way she wasn't sure she understood yet. She shivered as the wind swept across the sidewalk, scattering dried leaves before her.

Power.

The word hung in her mind. Her grandmother had been powerful. Wasn't that what the townsfolk whispered? She'd

never seen the old woman do anything that could be
described that way. What Sarah had done was . . . right
. . . natural . . . and when she'd been a young girl she'd
learned the ways too, never knowing, never suspecting
that someday she might have to—

No.

She was waiting outside the hospital, across the street,
when Tanner emerged that afternoon. He saw her at once,
and bent his head down, as if shielding his face from the
wind. He walked rapidly to the parking lot and to his car,
a new white Cadillac. She did not follow, and was gone by
the time he drove out of the lot. She continued walking,
and when she looked up to see where her feet had led, she
wasn't surprised. She went inside, out of the cold, damp
weather.

Ken Adams owned a family-style restaurant overlooking
the harbor and Bay. Evidently Tanner had phoned him the
night before because Adams wasn't surprised when she
walked in. Across the room he tried to smile, but couldn't
twist his flaccid lips enough. She smiled and found a booth
along one wall, slid into it, and opened the menu. She
knew he was watching her.

Finally, she closed the menu. Instead of sending one of
the red-and-gold-attired waitresses to her table, Adams
came over. It was Saturday night, a night when many of
the middle-class families in Greystone Bay traditionally
dined out, and soon the restaurant, The Golden Oyster,
would be filling up with mothers and fathers and their
screaming progeny. She had come early enough, though,
so that she might miss all of that, might miss glimpsing
another familiar face. She wanted to see only three.

"What do you want?"

"I'll have the New England clam chowder," she replied, knowing that wasn't what he meant. "And the
oysters on the half shell."

"They're expensive."

"I have the money." She gazed up at him coolly. Her nails hadn't left any scars. His hair was cut shorter than she recalled, and he had a few silver hairs curled at his temples. The grey did not lend him dignity; instead it aged him so that he looked some ten years older than he really was. His waist had thickened too, and he kept licking his lips as he watched her. "My order," she reminded him gently.

"Yes."

Abruptly he left the dining room and she waited. She wanted to toy with the fork or spoon, but she didn't want him to see how nervous she was. She'd found two of them so far; had let them know she'd returned. Now, for the third one.

The chowder smelled good, but she ate little, and only pushed the oysters around on the plate. As she did so, she knew that he continued to watch her. When she finished her meal, he walked over, and without waiting to be invited, he sat.

"What do you want?" he repeated.

She smiled and pressed the white napkin daintily to her lips. Her lipstick left a smear like blood.

"How is Benjie these days?" she asked, leaning back in the booth. She saw that he was sweating. Good.

"H-he doesn't live here any longer," Adams said. "He moved away."

"That's not what the telephone directory said."

"It's out of date."

"I called his house. His wife answered. She sounds very nice. Very middle class."

Adams paled. "What did you say to her?"

"I said I was sorry but that I thought I must have the wrong number."

"Look, can't we forget what happened? It's been ten years. Over ten years, for Christ's sake." He watched as she reached for her water glass. Her left hand could scarcely close around it. His eyes were fixed on the ragged scar that ran between the thumb and forefinger and wound across the back of the hand, puckering the tender skin there.

"I have a long memory. Tradition, you know."

"I have a wife, a family, a good business. What do you want from me?" His voice dropped and he leaned forward confidentially. He smelled like sour sweat, and she wrinkled her nose. "Look, if it's a matter of money, I've got some put by. I was gonna use it on a summer cabin, but I can give it to you."

"Money," she said, rising, and setting the napkin alongside the plate, "can't buy what you took away." She smiled. "Check, please."

She paid, left, and did not look back.

She walked along the wharf. It was seedier than she remembered. Too, she was looking at it from an adult's perspective, and she'd found that nothing from the past looked as wonderful as it had when she was so young. Few ships were berthed there now because over the years the fishing fleet had decreased, and so the harbor had turned to another business: that of luring tourists to its quaint waterfront.

Mist rose around her legs, swirling as she cut through it, and she breathed deeply of the damp, briny air. She was aware of a tingling within her, an anticipation, almost, of what was to come, and she realized she hadn't felt so good in a long, long time.

Out on the water were docked the four sailing ships that had come across the Atlantic in the seventeenth century. All were remarkably well preserved, and one even contained a tiny nautical museum. She passed them, hearing the gentle lapping of the water on their ancient hulls. Her father had taken her on board one once. She didn't remember much about it, except that everything had been smaller than she'd expected.

Once past the harbor she stopped and gazed up into the night sky as the clouds parted for a moment. The moon was almost full.

Her dreams that night were of red eyes weeping.

On Sunday morning she went to church, and as she sat in the front pew waiting for the service to begin, she knew that Benjie Adams wouldn't leave town. He couldn't.

At that moment the minister entered, and when he turned around to face the congregation, he paled. He reached out to the railing with one hand, as though he feared he would faint.

She smiled.

He looked away, and opened his prayer book and began reading, but beneath his voice she heard the tremble, and from time to time he stared at her. When he went to make the general church announcements, he said he had none for that Sunday, a statement that brought a sound of surprise from the churchgoers. She smiled, knowing he was rushing through the service.

Afterward, as she stood in line to shake hands with the minister and praise him on his sermon, she listened to the comments around her. Most of the congregation had noticed their pastor's distress, and they wondered what the source could be. He was such a nice man, wasn't he, dear? Whatever could be the matter?

When she was once more face to face with Benjamin Adams, she gave him her hand, hers cool against the fevered palm of his, and he cried out. She left the vestibule, went down the sidewalk paved with flagstones, and crossed the street. At the end of the block she turned and saw that he was still watching.

At lunchtime she went down to the harbor and sat in The Golden Oyster and read the church bulletin and studied Ken Adams. He was just as nervous as he'd been the previous night, and when he came over to her, she rose and left the restaurant.

Power, her grandmother had once said, was in everyone. In one way or another. We all have our special power, and it's particularly strong in women, Sarah claimed. Especially in women of their family. Sarah's talent had been for healing, and through the long years many of the townspeople had drifted out to the cabin, seeking one or more of Sarah Little's herbal concoctions. Power for burns, for sterility, impotency, broken bones, for wasting illnesses and hacking coughs. All who had been seen by Sarah had been cured.

And though she hadn't given it much thought when she was younger, she'd presumed hers had been in creating; now she wasn't sure.

She shrugged and headed down the street toward the hospital. A white Cadillac sped past her, and she raised a hand in greeting. It was Edward Tanner, and he turned his face away. She wandered through the streets, so replete with memories, so few of them good, and slowly began tracing the terrible route where it had begun so long ago. Went to Krueller's back lot and stared at where they'd first found her. She had escaped that time. Walked past the school, past the library, where she had always felt safe, then she began heading toward the woods surrounding the cabin. There it had begun; there it would end.

She wondered where the three men were, what they were doing, what they were thinking. No doubt they were meeting with one another, trying to decide what to do about her. All the better. She wanted them to worry about her, wanted them to lay awake at night thinking of her. She paused at a public phone and called Benjamin Adams's house. When he answered, she didn't speak.

"Hello?" he repeated. "Who is this."

She didn't say anything, but simply hung up. She had heard the strain in his voice.

The afternoon sun faded quickly, leaving behind a twilight strangely tinged with red; it dimmed even as she
passed through the trees, and darkness enveloped her. The
dark was sable, and she heard voices once more. She
stopped and looked around, felt the wisps of cobwebs
caressing her skin. She smiled in the darkness. She stretched
out her arms, flexed her fingers, and even her damaged
hand hurt less than usual.

A few minutes later she reached the cabin. She circled
it, wandering through the remnants of the garden, remembering the summer days when she had helped Sarah with
her herbs and squash and tomatoes, and she smiled. That
was a good memory, one of a few.

Inside, she went through the room and the loft, feeling
its emptiness as she never had before, and she touched
each object, as if she would gain some part of Sarah
through the action.

Yes, her grandmother had been right: She knew what to
do now.

She did not doubt they would come, and so she waited
patiently.

And when the full moon rose above the trees, she went
out onto the dark porch and watched as they came to stand
on the fringes of the clearing.

Ten years before they were waiting for her that night
behind Krueller's Drugstore. She had to get something for
her classes the next day, a pen, she didn't remember what
now; and when she rounded the corner on her way home,
Ken Adams leaped forward and grabbed her long hair,
twisting it cruelly in his strong hands. She could smell the
alcohol on his breath.

"You little bitch, I'm going to give you something," he
said.

He forced her to the ground, and pressed his mouth
against hers, bruising her lips. She spit on him, and he

backhanded her. The others stood around, laughing, enjoying their buddy's fun.

She wrenched herself away from him, some of her hair tearing out of her scalp, bringing tears to her eyes.

"Look at me," he said, "I done scalped me an injun." She leaped at him then, raked her nails across his face, almost snagging one of his eyes. He shouted that he would get even.

She ran away. She fled through the outskirts of town to the woods. Her woods. Her comforting woods. Her harsh breath was torn from her by the distance and the wind that whirled around her, and she never even heard the sounds of her pursuers.

They caught her just outside the clearing. Benjie tackled her, then hit her on the jaw, momentarily stunning her. They stuffed one of her socks in her mouth to keep her from screaming. Each boy took some article of her clothing off, and when she was naked, they dropped their pants, and took a turn on top of her, the other two holding her down for the third.

They raped her soul. And when they were done, the three came at her again. She wept, little girl that she was then, wept hot tears that stung the cuts and bruises on her face, tears of anger and humiliation. She was sixteen; they were seventeen. They laughed loudly, grown bold from an evening of drinking, and boasted about their prowess, and each thrust tore her up inside. She tried to struggle and got cuffed more than once, and toward the end when they were beginning to tire, Edward Tanner, who would one day be a surgeon, suggested they cut her up a little, just to teach her a lesson.

It was when he pulled out his Boy Scout knife and flicked it open that she wrenched a hand free, and hand and knife met, and the sharp blade sliced through the skin and muscle and nerve and tendon. Blood spurted onto the boys, and, frightened, they leaped to their feet. They pulled their pants up and ran away, leaving her on the ground, and never once looked back.

Sometime later it began raining, not a heavy fall, just enough to wash some of the blood from her face. She continued lying there, not able to move, her thighs bruised, her knees pressed unnaturally outward into the soft ground. She felt the blood trickling from her mutilated hand, her left hand, the hand she drew with, and she knew she had to do something. She pulled the sock out of her mouth and flung it away, rolled over onto her side, and groaned from the pain that shot up from her groin to her face. She wrapped her other sock around her hand, found her jeans and blouse and underwear and pulled them on with difficulty. She never found her shoes.

She crept quietly into the cabin, not wanting to disturb her grandmother, although the old woman generally slept heavily. She washed her hand in the bathroom sink and watched the blood swirl downward into the drain. She cried from the pain in her fingers, from the pain of knowing she would never be able to paint or draw again. She poured antiseptic on the deep cut that circled her palm as well, wincing as it stung. When she was done bandaging her hand, she stared at herself in the dimly lit mirror. Ugly bruises discolored the skin around her eyes, her cheekbones, and she had a long scrape along her jawline. Her entire face was swollen. From the stiffness and pain in her body she knew it matched her face.

She did not think about what had happened. She kept her mind a blank, and took her clothes off and shredded them, then threw the rags away. She dressed in clean jeans and shirt, and took down a small suitcase in which she packed what clothes would fit, a hairbrush, and a few other items; then she went back to the cabinet by the stove and took out the kitchen scissors, and once more in the bathroom, she held her hair up by the handful and began hacking. When she was finished, she washed the basin and swept the floor clean of hair clippings, picked up her suitcase, and left the cabin.

She had not come back until a few days ago.

The wind whistled through the treetops, stirring the branches so that they clicked like dry bones. Somewhere in the woods beyond the cabin an owl hooted once. And the full moon bathed the clearing in a pale light. The air smelled of damp leaves and another odor, one that was almost musky, a scent that wasn't pleasant. Their fear and upset, she thought, savoring it.

She left the porch, and the three men stepped forward. In the moonlight she could see their features, their expressions.

"I thought you were . . ." Ken Adams began, then glanced at his cousin. "Were dead."

She smiled.

"We didn't hear from you," Benjie Adams said, "and so when you didn't come back to school the next day . . . Your grandmother never said what happened. I mean." He stopped, his face red.

"We didn't mean to hurt you," Tanner said, speaking for the first time. "For God's sake, you've got to know that by now." She looked him directly in the eye. She did not know that, nor did she think he meant it. Not now, certainly not then.

"It's been ten years," Ken Adams said. "C'mon, let's forget it. These things happen. Especially when you're young and you've been drinking, and when the girl is . . . well, quite pretty."

She rubbed her hand, and his eyes slid away.

There was silence among them for a few moments, then: "You can't prove anything," Tanner said.

"No," she replied softly.

He continued. "There's no proof after all this time.

None at all. We're all three married, respectable citizens now, fathers even.''

"I could never have children," she said.

"What the hell is that supposed to mean?" Ken Adams demanded.

She stood without moving. "It means that you tore me up so badly that night that I couldn't have children after that. Not that it really mattered, I suppose."

Tanner laughed shortly. "You don't have my sympathy, believe me. You could have had your hand looked at by someone. My dad could have fixed it up like new. If you'd just gone to him."

"Look, if you're after money, we're not going to pay it."

"You're very bold, Ken, but then you always were in the company of your friends."

He took a step toward her, his fists balled. Overhead a branch cracked and fell to the ground, missing his head by inches. He leaped back and stared at her, his face gone white.

Something rustled in the underbrush, and Benjie Adams whirled around. "What was that?" He touched the cross he wore.

"Don't let her get to you. She's just trying to spook us."

"Sure, Ed."

She took a step forward and the Adams cousins glanced at each other. The wind stirred the fallen leaves.

"Come back for more, eh?" Tanner chuckled. "You should have seen your face at the hospital."

"You should have seen *yours*."

"So, c'mon. We know you wanted us out here. Don't you have demands or something?"

"No, Ed. I have no demands. I haven't come back for money or blackmail. That doesn't interest me."

"What does?"

"You three, and how you're to pay for what happened to me."

They laughed together. "Pay? I thought you weren't interested in money. You know, we aren't going to feel guilty. Hell, that happened such a long time ago," Tanner said. "No one can prove it."

"No one can disprove it, but some of us still bear the scars."

The wind quickened, and the dead leaves leaped upward, swirling around the men, and once more Benjie fingered his cross. A cloud, long and wraith-thin, passed over the face of the moon, darkening the clearing, and the leaves gusted up into their faces. Tanner thrust them away with his arms and began advancing on her. She stood her ground. A long vine, its leaves red, whipped out of the brush and wound around his ankle. He bent to untangle himself from it.

"Funny. Very funny." His voice was tight.

"I think we should leave."

"Shut up, Benjie. I told you we have to deal with her. We can't have her coming back."

"C'mon, Ed. She can't hurt us now, not after so long."

"I told you. I want to take care of unfinished business. We should never have left her that night, at least not alive."

"Ed," Ken Adams said, "for God's sake, take a look at the clearing."

Piles of leaves ringed them now like the low walls of a natural fortress, and onto the piles had been flung dried brambles, twigs, and splintered wood from the trees. The wind rose to a roar through the trees around them, snapping branches back and forth like wooden whips, but none of the leaves in the clearing were disturbed. There, everything was still, unnaturally so.

"It's a trick," Tanner said. "Just like what her grandmother used to do. Nothing more."

"I don't know, Ed. I don't like it."

Overhead, blue lightning jagged through the sky, and thunder rumbled, ominously near. The musky odor grew stronger.

"Settle down, Benjie. This won't take long." Moonlight gleamed on a sharp hunter's knife that had appeared in his hands.

"You were always partial to knives," she said, her voice faintly amused.

"A gun could be heard," he said reasonably, "and traced more easily as well."

"Jesus, Ed."

"I just thought we were going to scare her a little. Not . . ." The minister couldn't say it.

She smiled as Tanner walked toward her. She knew what to do now, had known since this afternoon. If her grandmother was a healer, then what could she be? She knew that for every yin, a yang exists. For every positive, a negative. That which is true, that which is false. Good and evil. Sarah healed; she did not.

Tanner stood only a few yards from her; behind him came the Adamses, although more hesitantly, but growing bolder by the moment.

"You won't touch me ever again," she said, her voice cold.

Tanner laughed, and around them the wind screamed. They began circling her, calling to her, the comments growing cruder as they crept closer and closer. Suddenly the piles of leaves and branches burst into red flames.

"What?" Benjie Adams whirled.

"Don't look!" Tanner yelled, and he rushed her. As the three men grabbed at her with their rough hands, an electric shock flared through their fingers up into their wrists and arms. They stumbled backward, nursing their hands. At that moment Tanner cried out. His clothes were beginning to smolder—from the inside out. He threw himself on the ground and rolled in crazed circles.

"Jesus!"

The cousins backed away as they stared in horror at the smoke seeping from Tanner's mouth. Suddenly a tiny flame flickered between his lips.

"Jesus, Jesus," Tanner cried, "I'm burning up. I'm on fire. Help me! Get the flames out!"

The Adamses looked at each other. There were no flames to put out.

Lightning crackled and struck one of the trees, leaving an odor of ozone in the air and sparks which ignited the dried leaves. Suddenly the cousins writhed. Their blood began heating. Tanner shrieked, an inhuman sound, and burst into flames. Benjie and Ken threw themselves onto the ground and rolled back and forth, as if trying to put out the fire that had not yet burst from their bodies.

Her lips moved, and their clothes and hair ignited in a shower of sparks. Around them flames from the burning leaves shot a dozen yards into the sky. She watched silently, impassively, as the men shrieked and howled, their cries inaudible over the roaring wind and the sizzling of the flames.

Tanner, still rolling, still screaming, couldn't dampen the flames, and his cries grew more and more agonized. The other two, whimpering piteously, collided in an explosion of fire. They called to her, their hands, the skin and muscle burned away, raised in supplication, but she looked away into the woods and saw the red eyes glowing. Gradually the terrible cries stilled, and when it was finally silent, she looked back and saw three piles of smoldering ashes.

Overhead the clouds grew together; lightning slashed through the clouds, and the first fat raindrops began falling. Raindrops hit the ashes with a sizzling sound, and she watched as the ashes grew wet. The wind stirred and blew them away from the clearing and into the woods until nothing remained of the three men. Then she brushed the soot from her hands and face, went inside the cabin, closed the door and did not look out again.

In the morning the cabin was empty.

Chroniclers

REGINALD BRETNOR lives and works in Oregon, has a worse postal system than New Jersey, and has had his fine-edged stories appear in such diverse markets as *Esquire*, *Ellery Queen*, and *Twilight Zone*.

ROBERT E. VARDEMAN lives in Albuquerque, drives a car that talks back when you do bad things to it, and is the author of over forty novels, including the Cenotaph Road series and, with Geo. W. Proctor, the Swords of Raemllyn series.

DOUGLAS E. WINTER is a Washington, D.C., attorney who spends his real time as a critic, interviewer, and writer. His latest books include *The Art of Darkness*, and an as yet untitled collection of interviews with writers of dark fantasy.

GALAD ELFLANDSSON lives in Ottawa, Canada, and while most of his deceptively gentle stories have been in the dark- or heroic-fantasy fields, he is currently working on a hard-boiled detective novel.

NINA KIRIKI HOFFMAN lives on the West Coast and has been, among other things, a cook, a janitor, and an extra in a Burt Reynolds film. Her stories have appeared in *Universe, Clarion Awards, Shadows*, and many of the major SF and fantasy magazines.

ALAN RYAN has been a theater publicist, teacher, and salesman at Macy's. No longer caring about a weekly paycheck, he is now a writer, editor, and reviewer. His latest novel is *Cast a Cold Eye*.

ROBERT R. McCAMMON is a soft-spoken young man who lives in Birmingham, Alabama, and is the author of the best-selling *Mystery Walk* and his latest, *Usher's Passing*.

CHELSEA QUINN YARBRO is a northern California writer who is best known for her works of historical horror, including the St. Germain series of novels and stories. Her latest novel is *A Mortal Glamor*, and her latest passion is a colt named Magic.

ROBERT BLOCH lives in California, where he continues to produce the best in terror and suspense. His latest novel is *Night of the Ripper*.

JOSEPH PAYNE BRENNAN is unquestionably one of the masters of the genre, both in fiction and in poetry. He lives in New Haven, Connecticut, where he works on a typewriter older than most states.

AL SARRANTONIO is a former Doubleday editor turned crazed writer and keeper of his children. He lives in New

York State, and his first novel, *Worms*, has just been published.

MELISSA MIA HALL is a poet, photographer, and short story writer from Fort Worth. Her work has appeared in most major markets, including *Twilight Zone* and *Shadows*, and she has just completed her first novel.

STEVE RASNIC TEM survives in snow-bound Denver with his wife, Melanie, and is a poet, novelist, and short story writer. His work has appeared in virtually every major anthology and magazine in the genre.

KATHRYN PTACEK is a New Mexico native who now lives in New Jersey, collecting gila monster memorabilia. Her novels include *Shadoweyes* and the best-selling *Blood Autumn*.

BESTSELLING BOOKS FROM TOR

MORE BESTSELLERS FROM TOR